Praise for the first edition of *Cognate*:

"...a ripping good space yarn that keeps the reader engaged with each new twist of the plot..."
~Lambda Book Report

"Filled with action, emotions, and adventure, Brojim's novel will thrill any fan of the various *Star Trek* or *Star Wars* shows. Even if you're not exactly a Trekkie, you'll more than likely enjoy this book that is medical mystery, rescue a damsel in distress, finding oneself and more. The story will have you turning the pages non-stop until you reach the end. It truly is difficult to put this book down, even for a moment. With all the potential left here, clearly a sequel is in order."
~The Virginia GayZette

Cognate

Cleo Dare

Quest Books

Port Arthur, Texas

ISBN 1-935053-25-6
978-1-935053-25-5

Previously published as "Cognate by R.C. Brojim"
Second Edition revised and re-edited

First Printing 2009

9 8 7 6 5 4 3 2 1

Cover design by Donna Pawlowski

Published by:

Regal Crest Enterprises, LLC
4700 Hwy 365, Suite A, PMB 210
Port Arthur, Texas 7764

Find us on the World Wide Web at
http://www.regalcrest.biz

Printed in the United States of America

Acknowledgments

I would like to thank Cathly LeNoir for taking a chance on me and on this book. There is no question in my mind that Cathy is the most generous and considerate, and yet also, the *boldest* publisher in this industry. Thanks also to Verda Foster for doing such a professional job of editing; Angel Grewe for playing both reader and copyeditor; and Donna Pawlowski for her marvelous cover art and design.

For Herb, wherever you ride among the stars

Chapter
One

THE DEAFENING HARANGUE of the klaxon pounded through the haze of noxious yellow smoke cloaking the bridge of the *U.C.S.S. Boadicea*. Captain Danielle Artemis Forrest, rooted to the aft deck, strained to glimpse the flash of billowing gold sleeve that was all she could make out of Ma'at, as the Nhavan rolled in battle with a giant reptilian creature.

The captain fought to push herself through the uproar of hand-to-hand combat waging on the bridge. The choking haze shifted deceptively before her eyes. As she moved, her legs grew heavier as though the gravity of a thousand Earths dragged her down.

Ma'at cried out, "Dani, help me!"

Tears of despair leapt to Dani's eyes, blinding her. She would never reach Ma'at in time. Then the murk cleared. The lizard creature staggered up from the deck, its face a grinning mask. Beneath its feet, like a broken toy, lay the still body of Ma'at, the wo/man's blood spreading in a pool, making incarnadine the purple sash circling the intersexual's waist.

"Captain Forrest to the bridge, please."

Dani jerked upright in her bunk, drenched in sour-smelling sweat. A long shuddering moment passed before the specter of Ma'at's torn body faded from the screen of her inner vision. She made an effort to re-orient herself. What she had exaggerated into a cry of unspeakable anguish by Ma'at was only the measured tones of her first officer signaling her over the intercom.

"Captain Forrest to the bridge—"

Dani punched the intercom button. "What is it, Ma'at?"

"Just a courtesy call, Captain. You're late for your duty shift."

"Damn." Dani forced her legs out of bed. Holy planets, but she was stiff. She massaged her calves with brisk kneading motions. Tired after only a few moments of exertion, she cradled her head in her hands and worried that she was sick. She hadn't slept solidly in a week. She'd thrown unappealing breakfasts back down the recycling chute the previous three mornings. This morning she hadn't had the guts, literally, to even venture into the mess.

She knew she wasn't pregnant. She knew because she hadn't slept with a man since her final year at the Academy when she was still trying to prove she was heterosexual so she wouldn't be commissioned to serve in the Minority Fleet.

At first, she hadn't been. She had proudly, if furtively, begun her career as a command ensign aboard the dreadnought, *Christie May*. She'd gone on fooling her superiors for a few years, rising with speed to the rank of Lieutenant. Fooling them, that is, until Castle came into her life.

Castle, with her long willowy limbs, her skin the color of apricots, her eyes translucent gems of aquamarine. To touch Castle had been to melt into clouds and hear celestial choirs singing hymns. Castle was irresistible, luscious...and not sufficiently discreet.

Dani tried to shake off the memory, but now the events flipped past her inner eye like an archaic album of analog snapshots, forcing her to view each miserable scene. She wondered why any of it still mattered and why, every so often, she felt compelled to torture herself with remembering.

When the scandal broke, Castle left the service in disgust, never looking back, never saying goodbye, never telling Dani what their affair meant to her. To Dani, it was love of the deep and painful kind, the kind she could not talk about. The kind she knew she would never find again.

Dani weathered the waves of gossip and, because she was a good officer, was shuffled quietly off to her first post in the Minority Fleet, the *S.S. John Kettle*. Once aboard, she was promoted to Lieutenant Commander without any of the usual attendant fanfare: an ironic acknowledgment of her military ability, shrouded by the shameful punishment meted out to her for her societal non-normativity.

She hated the 'Frying Pan' as everyone called the claustrophobic scout class ship, hated herself, hated her gay shipmates and hated Explora Command for handicapping her career. For the first two years, the only sound that could penetrate the wall of outraged pride she had built around herself was the 'tsk-tsking' of her straight colleagues in the service.

But the years passed and, whether through sheer anger or sheer ability — and she was not, even now, sure which it had been — she was promoted again and assigned to the *U.C.S.S. Boadicea*, a genuine starship, albeit a Minority Fleet one. When its charismatic and beloved captain, Gary Steele, died six years later, she was appointed his able successor.

It had been a rigorous five years since but she stuck with it; stuck with it through the High Command homophobia, the institutionalized misogyny, the close calls, the deaths of friends.

She'd long since made peace with her sexuality and even indulged it on occasion on shore leave, careful to ensure no one deeply touched her heart. What she had never made peace with was the military structure that condemned her, and others like her, to a dimmer future than that countenanced by her heterosexual counterparts in Explora Command.

Dani pushed herself off the bunk, stripped off the smelly sleeping tunic, and stepped into the pulse shower. The water beat her neck and she wondered again at the unaccustomed soreness in her muscles. She stepped out of the shower, toweled her body dry and slipped into, and sealed closed, her spandex body suit, striped green and gold for command.

With the agility of years of practice, she french-braided her damp brunette hair. Her fingers didn't fly as they usually did. She looked in the mirror and decided that, except for the olive-dark circles under her hazel eyes, she was passable.

Ma'at would notice her exhaustion but then Ma'at noticed everything. Dani experimentally flexed her shoulders. Playing *dankin* against the genetically-stronger Ma'at three times a week kept her fit, even though she tended naturally toward the chunkier side of trim.

She just wished exercising could chase away her blues and ease her irritability. Goddess, but she hadn't been so irritable since those first lonely months aboard the Frying Pan. In the past week alone, she'd taken two innocent jokes personally and unfairly reprimanded their perpetrators. Strangely, the undercurrent of irrationality she felt had not passed away but grown stronger. She was even looking forward to the long-promised shore leave scheduled for *Boadicea*, which wasn't like her.

Dani eyed herself more critically in the mirror. She checked for fine wrinkles at the corners of her eyes and searched for strands of grey hair among the brunette, but didn't find any. If her sheer irritability was a sign of oncoming menopause, she was being spared the telltale physical signs. Besides, she had only just turned forty-two. Maybe Sly would recommend hormone therapy.

Captain Forrest stepped from her cabin, with an anxious frown creasing her brow.

Chapter
Two

"ON SCREEN, LIEUTENANT Deva."

The helmsman of the *I. S. A. Heaven's Bow* tapped a button on his console. "On screen, sir."

Captain Bajana Ki edged forward in her hexagonal command chair and searched the star-cluttered panorama, which had blossomed at the touch of the helmsman's fingers. High in one corner, a silvery dot moved out of synch with the other more placid stars.

"Analysis?" The captain swiveled to face the science console. Luluai, the first officer, answered. "A vessel of some kind, Captain."

"Can we get a bearing?"

"It is on a course, mark—" There was a significant pause as the young Sirensi re-scanned the reading.

"—directly for us, sir."

On the bridge of the Khrar *Star Spawn*, a Ggr'ek-class Predator, Commander Kholg also demanded information.

"What is it?" he snarled at Korga, his second in command.

"A ship approaching, Commander."

"What kind of ship?"

Korga, more delicate of voice and feature than the usual heavy-boned Khrar, focused intently on her console screen. "Disk-shaped hull, single warp nacelle, rich metalwork on the hull. An unusual bas-relief design. It's a—"

"—a Coalition ship, you fool." Her laudatory description irritated Kholg. It was well known on all worlds that the Empire could not be bested in ship design...or anything else.

"But not a cruiser. It's too small."

Kholg yanked down his view scope with a grunt and took a good look at the approaching vessel. "Scout class. We could take it out in a second." His low growl was laced with blood lust.

"Commander, we should not—"

Kholg spun in his command chair, his eyes dangerously narrowed. "We should not what?"

"The ship is not approaching from Coalition territory, Commander, but from unexplored space."

"What do we care where it comes from?" Kholg licked at his lips and raked his fingers through the coarse straggly hairs of his chin. "It's in our space now."

Korga's almond-shaped eyes went wide at his remark, enhancing their alluring vulnerability. At the sight of them, he felt his blood lust eclipsed by animal lust. Her odd sensual beauty was the sole reason he tolerated her impudence. There had been a suggestion that her slight features were the result of mixed bloodlines but Kholg had ruthlessly stifled that unworthy implication. And its perpetrator.

"Enough talk, Korga! Prepare to fire on my signal."

"Commander!"

Every muscle of Kholg's face and body tensed. This was too much, even from Korga. Was she making her challenge?

He began a slow rise from his command chair, every battle-tried sense alert. But his alarm was unnecessary. In a gesture of fealty, Korga brought her fist to her cheek in salute.

"Glory to our ancestors." she intoned.

Kholg smiled, a pleased secret smile, and faced forward again. Perhaps tonight, after the victory, there would be a small party in his quarters.

A very small party.

"COMMUNICATIONS! PROGRESS REPORT."

"I've tried everything, Captain. They're not answering." The communications officer's delicate olive-skinned fingers traversed the array of buttons crowding her board.

Lieutenant Deva broke in, excitement palpable in his voice. "Vessel still coming at us, Captain."

The captain turned to Luluai. "Science station, status report."

"If the vessel maintains its current course and speed it will impact with us at 09:36 hours or," Luluai calculated, "in approximately 83.22 seconds."

Captain Ki rammed a button on the command seat and the bridge pulsated with the hypnotic beat of purple light and the wail of the ship's siren.

"Shields up! Battle alert!" There was a sharp tensing of spines all around the bridge. "Helm, prepare to take us to sublight on my signal."

"Interesting," Lieutenant Luluai eyed Captain Ki with appreciation. "When we drop from warp, they will pass right through us as though—"

"—we were no longer there. Yes."

But it was not to be that easy. The other vessel stole the advantage of surprise by dropping to sublight almost as quickly and firing a salvo that slammed the starship hard, rocking it violently to port.

By sheer force of will, Hasitam Deva kept his seat and presence of mind. As the bat-winged shape skimmed overhead with only meters to spare, he discharged a savage volley into its vulnerable underbelly.

The viewscreen went blindingly white, the force of the explosion hurling the scout-class size ship backward in space. But not far enough to miss a falling rain of metal from the sundered Predator. Jagged mountain-size shards bounced against the ship's shields then ricocheted eerily away into the frictionless void of space.

Crewmen knocked from their posts rose from the bridge deck, mesmerized by the scene filling the viewscreen. The white heat of destruction shaded to a burning red afterglow, which noiselessly faded, swallowed by the black primacy of space.

A poignant image of brilliant orange poppies burst into Bajana's mind. Like the wrecked ship, she had seen their showy petals blackened and twisted into lifeless hunks by a single night of frost.

As for this ship, her own precious ship, what might happen to it in this unknown vastness? The helmsman shattered the captain's reverie and the crew's awe-struck silence with a pair of fists banged down with exuberance on the console.

"We got him, Captain! We got him!"

"Hasitam, what have you done?" The tone of Bajana Ki's voice expressed her horror. Hasitam felt the captain's eyes boring into his back. The crew had frozen awkwardly in place, like children playing a game of Statue. He pivoted to meet the captain's gaze. Her chocolate eyes, normally bright and friendly, were black with anger. A sheen of sweat broke on Hasitam's brow.

"I gave no order to fire." Captain Ki's voice thundered in the strangled silence. The force of her own pronouncement shook her. She felt a shiver of uncertainty. She had never upbraided a Shivani officer before. As a Brahuinna...*Stop!* she commanded herself. Brahuinna or not, she was captain of the ship and she had to know why Hasitam had fired.

"What do you have to say for yourself?"

"It was a perfect shot, sir."

The bridge crew sucked in its collective breath. Hasitam's answer was more than daring. It was heretical. Tense seconds ticked past before the captain spoke again.

"Granted, Mr. Deva," she said. "But as a result of your expertise, other beings are dead. Doesn't that shame you? You are a Shivani."

Hasitam repressed a shudder. He was all too aware of his people's doctrine of non-killing. But ever since the social maelstrom generated on Nirvannini by the Brahuinna Question, he had leaned toward the arguments of the New Progressives. They held that non-killing, or *amsa*, didn't work and it was time for the Shivani to develop their own philosophy.

He had signed on the *Heaven's Bow* to escape societal strictures, not be bound by them. He wanted to fulfill his lust for life and death. To experience such a moment as he had just experienced. To feel again that surge of adrenaline.

"Hasitam, answer!"

"Captain, we were under attack!"

"Mr. Deva, we are engaged on an exploratory mission. Our weapons system is intended for last resort defense—"

"It was—"

"And only upon my order."

"—defense, sir."

"It was out-and-out destruction!" Captain Ki's voice rose to an angry shout.

"But—"

"Confined to quarters, Mr. Deva," she snapped. "While I review the matter."

"As you command, Captain." A barely visible tremble shook Hasitam's trim frame. He saluted her by raising both of his right hands to his forehead.

"Dismissed," she ordered curtly.

Around him, Hasitam sensed the disgust of his fellow officers. Without a look at any of them, he stalked across the floor of the bridge to the exit spiral.

The moment the spiral's doors securely closed, Bajana lapsed into her command chair. The bridge crew, eyes judiciously averted, made an appearance of returning to their tasks. She knew it was a show put on for her benefit. They all—Shivani, Sirensi, and Brahuinna alike—could only feel shaken after such a scene. Not simply because of *amsa* either.

They were babes in space, pioneers of a fledgling space program in an untried ship. They were strangers to each other, an uneasy amalgam of three different humanoid races, led by an unseasoned commander.

They had only an ancient document of a previous adventurer's space journeys as guidance for their mission. And this was one of those moments when Bajana knew in her heart of hearts that that document, *The Glorious Interstellar Journeys of Indrashtra*, revered as it might be, was not enough. None of them, not even Sukha Jabala—the Shivani mastermind of this journey into the unknown—could anticipate what would befall them in space.

She rotated her chair to face the science station. "Luluai. Damage report."

The Sirensi first officer complied with a cursory glance at her screen. "Minor damage to the electronic circuits in the engineering section, sir, when Chief Engineer Jabala was thrown against them. Engineering reports that repairs are underway."

The captain sprang to her feet. "Sukha? Is he hurt?"

"Sickbay reports both right arms broken, simple fractures. First degree electrical burns on his back and right arms from the circuitry he frizzled."

"Luluai, notify the infirmary I'm on my way. You have the helm."

"Of course, Captain."

Heart thumping, Bajana dashed from the bridge. When she reached the cupboard-sized alcove designated as the *Heaven's Bow's* infirmary, she saw that Sukha Jabala was in good hands, if webbed ones. Looking crisp in their turquoise tunics, embroidered with encircling waves of cobalt blue, Doctors, Torilli and Tilorri hummed over him while splinting both of his right arms.

Bajana was fortunate to sign on the elderly Sirensi sisters for this mission into the unknown. Sirensi, an amphibious race that reproduced parthenogenetically on Nirvannini's neighboring planet of Elysiansus, were not aficionados of space travel.

These twins, their golden hair gone grey and cut short for the journey, had signed on because, as they laughingly told her, they had lived a full life on Elysiansus and were ready for 'real' adventure. Sirensi doctors were renowned musicians, knowledgeable herbalists and master physiotherapists. Their healing chants were considered as good as the medicines and technical medical advances of Nirvannini.

Even so, there had been more than a few snide remarks when Bajana announced to the I.S.A. stockholders that her medical staff consisted entirely of two Sirensi physicians. She had ridden out the criticism and now, watching the women work, was glad she had. Even if, at this moment, she wondered if the mission itself was not a mistake.

"You're upset," Sukha said.

"And you're hurt," she countered. His white tunic had been cut away from his chest by the doctors and she could see the burns blistering his broken right arms. A few braided strands of his waist-length silver-streaked hair had straggled out of his topknot and his blue skin looked paler than usual. Sukha shrugged at her remark, shifting his arms in the process.

"Don't move," the doctors sang together. Sukha subsided and smiled with reassurance at Bajana, whose face was strained with worry.

"Bajana, what happened on the bridge?"

"Oh, gods," Bajana moaned. She dropped into a chair. Her eyes were dark with distress and her rust and gold tunic, which usually sparkled, complementing her flowing chestnut hair and dusky-golden skin, drooped dully from her shoulders.

"It can't be that bad," he said, careful not to move his arms and annoy the doctors again. "Tell me about it."

Sukha had chosen Bajana, as opposed to himself, to captain the *Heaven's Bow* because he believed that on a journey to find the Brahuinna homeworld, a Brahuinna should be in command. And who could be more qualified than his own daughter?

As a Shivani and scion of one of the households of Nirvannini's ruling families, Sukha's relationship to Bajana was more than unusual. It was unheard of. But Sukha had not been deterred by the elitist disdain of his milieu when, twenty-six years earlier, the opportunity to adopt an abandoned Brahuinna baby was made known to him.

From her infancy, he had read to Bajana from the *Glorious Interstellar Journeys of Indrashtra*. He had chanced upon that moldering document in the monastery of Tal in Rajaska Province when on a youthful 'truth visit'.

Making a lifelong study of Indrashtra's tale, Sukha had uncovered a truth that had been cloaked in secrecy for thousands of years: the Brahuinna people were not indigenous to Nirvannini. They had returned ten millennia before with Indrashtra from a planet called 'Many-Splendored', bearing knowledge, arts and materials theretofore unknown.

When Sukha published *The Journeys*, the Shivani ruling class was incensed to learn the Shivani religion had been originated and imported by the Brahuinna, a cultural group scorned on Nirvannini and long treated as second-class citizens. Proof of Indrashtra's — and Sukha's — assertions was demanded by restive Shivani and disadvantaged Brahuinna alike.

Facing mounting public pressure to resolve the issue of Brahuinna origins, and sick to death of Sukha's impassioned pleas, Nirvannini's government agreed to subsidize the private stockholding company Sukha had founded to pursue his goal of sailing forth to seek the Brahuinna homeworld. In the Shivani Year 62433, Jabala Enterprises was rechristened the Inter-Solar Alliance, a quasi-government institution.

In 62433, spaceflight was a localized activity, consisting of business and cargo transits to Elysiansus and pleasure trips to her five moons. Building and equipping spacecraft for longer journeys had not been attempted since Indrashtra's day. Nevertheless, a mere three years of hard work, financial and engineering setbacks, government hand-wringing, and innumerable tests later, Sukha's masterwork, the *Heaven's Bow*, emerged from her hangar into glittering daylight and, in time, into starlight.

"Bajana," he urged again, "tell me."

"I have failed." She bit her lip and he saw tears pooling at the corners of her eyes.

"It's impossible to fail," he answered gently. "You can only learn from your mistakes."

Over the last year, he had intentionally reduced his role to let Bajana flex her new command muscles. Little by little, he had stepped to the side, redefining his role as Technical Advisor, while encouraging her to take up the reins of the *Heaven's Bow*.

"This was a big mistake."

"What?"

"Choosing Hasitam as helm." Her voice was full of self-recrimination. "I could have chosen Sikkhasta — "

"Too overbearing. We agreed he would have questioned your authority at every turn."

" — Or Durna."

"You didn't like Durna. He was too slow-witted."

"Well, Hasitam is not like Durna. He is quick-witted; in this case, far too quick-witted."

Even though they had discussed every crew member in detail, he left the final decisions in her hands. In space, they would have to be as tightly knit as a family whose membership could not be rejected at whim. They would be trapped inescapably together, in one tiny vessel, on an immensely long journey. Discipline had to be crisp, lines of command clear and Bajana completely comfortable with her leadership.

"What has Hasitam done, Bajana?" Sukha's limpid blue eyes, usually full of laughter, were serious and watchful. Bajana leaned her head against her palms, not daring to look at him. She mumbled something he couldn't quite hear.

"What?"

"We destroyed another ship."

"Didn't you know?" interjected the sisters in melodic harmony.

"I was temporarily knocked out." He returned his gaze to Bajana.

"We — "

"Are you telling me that after we were hit, Hasitam — "

" — fired. I guess it was a lucky hit. Nevertheless, I never gave the order to fire."

"And the other ship was utterly destroyed?"

"Utterly." Bajana's voice was glum. There was a brief silence before Sukha spoke again.

"There's nothing we can do about it."

"Father!" Bajana jumped up from her chair and began pacing the cramped space. "We destroyed other beings! It was you who taught me the philosophy of non-killing from my very infancy. Don't you care?"

"I care, Bajana," Sukha said. "But there is still nothing we can do about it now."

"Aiee," Bajana yowled, throwing herself back down into her chair and slamming her fist against her teeth. The tears had begun to flow. Sukha touched her on the shoulder.

"Now you know why we have always held to the philosophy of *amsa*. Once something or someone has been killed, there is nothing more anyone can do about it. There is no correction or recompense. You are left only with grief or remorse."

"I don't know what to do."

"There is nothing you can do, Daughter."

"Can I be sorry?"

"Your sorrow will not help the dead. Or, I daresay, their living families. But you can learn, as I told you earlier."

"I didn't give the order."

"Blame is not a good habit in a commander. You must take full responsibility, Bajana, as I must for creating this mission."

"Why you?" Bajana asked through tears.

"I failed to seriously consider, even though the ship is equipped for it because Indrashtra's was, that we would meet other beings and find ourselves engaged in battle with them."

"Surely the mission itself can't be a mistake?" Her question came out somewhere between a shriek and a sob. Bajana had spent her entire life preparing for this mission. It was her dream as much as it was Sukha's ambition. Nearly every waking moment had been devoted to it in some way or another. She couldn't imagine it not existing.

"Bajana," Sukha stood up from the bed, the Sirensi sisters trailing after him trying to keep his arms in a field of green light. "Remember that we are new in space. You have learned something of vital importance today. Do not forget it."

"I must be in better command."

"You are doing well. Rigidity will no more result in better command decisions than slipshodness. Do not make that error, Daughter."

"What should I do about Hasitam?"

"We have no other helmsman and we are too far from Nirvannini to turn back now. I do not need to tell you to be just or fair because you always are, but I would suggest you be careful in whatever method you use to temper his trigger-finger."

"Perhaps the reprimand alone?" Bajana suggested.

"Perhaps," Sukha agreed.

"But Sukha, don't you think it odd that he had no difficulty killing or even remorse afterward? With all our training in *amsa*?"

"He may have fallen prey to the heated rhetoric of the New Progressives, Bajana. They are openly advocating killing."

Chapter
Three

Dani viewed the bridge from the womb-like safety of the kinelift. All appeared quiet. There were no unidentified entities or enemy vessels loping across the screen. Nor were there any odd masses of light-shifting debris as there had been during the ion storm. Dani was convinced it was the worst *Boadicea* had ever weathered. Not just the crew, but the ship herself needed a hefty dose of R & R.

Ma'at, of course, had been as happy as a pig in slop during the ion storm. Dani guessed her Nhavan first officer would take objection to such a crude remark by a Nebraska farm girl like herself, if the Nhavan wo/man even knew what a pig was, which Dani doubted. Ma'at came from a desert planet and belonged to a mostly-vegetarian race of humanoids. Pigs, Dani suspected, would have gone largely unnoticed in such a society.

Dani accepted the fact that from Ma'at's point of view, the storm was an unparalleled opportunity for scientific research. She, however, was glad it was over. Dani stepped from the kinelift. The bridge crew worked at their stations with their usual unruffled competence. Only Ma'at glanced up at her entry.

The traditional dress of the intersexual Nhavans, a loose and v-necked gold tunic, lay in semi-transparent folds against hir alabaster skin, delineating hir high compact breasts. A broad royal purple sash ringed hir waist and hir tight black leggings and calf-high boots accentuated the small male organ at hir crotch. Like the rest of hir race, Ma'at possessed the organs of both sexes and could, by choice, establish romantic relationships with any other Nhavan as well as with either sex of human.

Dani could usually assess the state of affairs from the character of Ma'at's expression. Today, the intersexual's silver-blue eyes looked just a little more than normally serious beneath her long page-boy cap of raven black hair. That did not bode well. Dani slid with a sigh into her command chair. Ma'at moved to her side and waited politely, hands clasped behind hir long straight back.

"Alright, Ma'at," Dani said, "what kind of bad news are you planning to drop into my lap?"

"Into your lap, Captain?" The Nhavan, given to displays of cutting wit, pretended ignorance of the human colloquialism. "I assure you, I have no intention of allowing anything to collide with you while seated. In fact, I have always made every effort to prevent such eventualities."

"Ma'at," Dani said, the pretense at joviality already worn thin, "just spit it out."

"Very well, Captain. We have received a transmission from Explora Command: Top priority."

Dani grimaced. It was probably another in a series of the less-than-savory projects that got doled out to the Minority Fleet. Explora Command may have finally bettered the past by letting gays, bisexuals, transgenders and intersexuals serve openly in the military; but segregation, as history could easily have foretold, had led to all of the usual, and endlessly chafing, equality issues.

Explora Command's rigid stance on heterosexist normativity had gone so far as to force the physically and mentally superior Nhavans — those few who wanted to serve anyway — to limit themselves to the Coalition's Minority Fleet. It was xenophobia and homophobia at their worst and everyone knew it.

"Alright, Ma'at. Let's hear it."

Ma'at gave Lieutenant Patricia Mouneera a commanding nod. The handsome Latina punched at her board. There was a micro-slowed garble of noise, which sounded like dignified hiccupping, and a snow-hazed image of an older man's face, heavily-jowled and lined with wrinkles, flickered on, then off, the bridge viewscreen.

"What's the matter?"

"I don't know, Captain." Mouneera flicked another switch. The image reappeared, the outlines of the man's face fusing indistinctly with the background.

"Why's it so fuzzy, Ma'at?"

"We've been having difficulty ever since the ion storm, Captain. Some onboard equipment seems to have been affected, but even I," Ma'at said without a taint of egotism, "have not been able to recalibrate everything."

"Damn Niko!"

"It would make a difference if Ms. Parathi were aboard, Captain. But it seems to be a question more of fine-tuning than of major damage."

"Very good, Ma'at. But I want everything double-checked when we get to Spaceportal sixteen."

"Will do, Captain."

Dani knew Ma'at would use all of hir leave time to go over the *Boadicea* with a fine-toothed comb, Niko or no Niko. Dani was still annoyed with Chief Engineer Niko Parathi and the best helmsman in the fleet, Muhammed Sabi, for going ashore at Sentry Outpost 8, getting blind drunk and daring each other to get tattooed.

There was nothing wrong with a tattoo. Navy men and women

had been sporting them for centuries and it was an acceptable tradition. But standards of hygiene at whatever den of depravity they had chosen for this ritual had not been of the highest. In consequence, they had contracted hepatitis.

Dani had had no choice but to leave them at Spaceportal seven on extended sick leave. Niko had begged not to be separated from the ship but Dani knew if she let her stay aboard, the woman would have worked herself to death tending to every little detail of the ship's health instead of her own. Probably even going overboard to prove she wasn't sick instead of staying in bed and recovering.

Sly Jenks, the ship's doctor, had backed Dani completely. "You'll never get her to rest while she's aboard, Dani. Or Sabi for that matter. Not to mention it's a contagious disease and they're a danger to the rest of the crew. We're lucky no one else contracted it."

So with regret, Dani sent two of her best crew via the de-materializer, called the de-matter by the crew, to the infirmary on Spaceportal seven, with a promise to return for them when they were certified fit for duty. But she found herself missing them several times a day. Like now, when she was facing a fuzzed transmission that even Ma'at, with hir extensive electronic expertise, couldn't fix.

"I think I've cleared it now and can pick up the vocal," Mouneera said, still fussing with her communications board. The image stabilized at last.

"Oh, sister of mercy," Dani muttered under her breath.

"Captain?"

"Nothing, Ma'at." But Dani was none too pleased. The figure was Admiral Gordon Jameson, and Jameson and Forrest were not on the best of terms. Jameson's gay son had been killed in the line of duty as a command Ensign aboard the *Boadicea* two years earlier.

Ensign Jameson died bravely but Dani knew Admiral Jameson blamed her personally. Blamed her not only for his death but, in some twisted way, for his sexuality. Dani knew her teaching command scenarios for that single summer at the Academy had not made Ensign Jameson 'come out'. His 'coming out' had been the same painful process it was for everyone...but, she thought despairingly, try and convince the homophobic Admiral of that.

The Admiral's voice was finally coming through. "Dani Forrest. Well, well."

Dani stiffened with distaste but nodded a polite acknowledgment, "Admiral." The brief 'un'pleasantries over, she braced herself for the bad news.

"We have a pack of Khrars calling for Coalition blood, Forrest. But since we have you and your intrepid, if queer, crew out there in the skies we have nothing to fear, right?"

Dani twitched at the not-so-subtle ridicule. Ma'at crossed hir arms over hir chest. Having grown up in a culture where what one did mattered more than what gender/orientation category one belonged to—because every Nhavan belonged to all gender/ orientation categories—Ma'at found the entire issue of gender/ orientation discrimination incomprehensible.

Just like Dani, s/he knew why Admiral Jameson was angry at Dani, s/he just didn't understand it. It was hardly the captain's fault that the young Jameson had been killed. Dani was even less responsible for the young man's sexual orientation.

Still, despite the illogic of it, s/he knew from personal experience that most gender-normal heterosexual humans thought hir gender perverted, many of hir gay shipmates barely tolerated it, and only a handful, like Dani, accepted it without qualm. Ma'at suspected too that the few human intersexuals in Minority Fleet endured far worse discrimination and harassment than s/he did. Hir gender, after all, was not a result of chromosonal or hormonal variations like that of human intersexuals. Hir intersexuality was normative for hir race.

"Cat's got your tongue today, I see, *Captain*." Jameson sneered the last word.

"Please proceed with your business, Admiral." Dani's voice was unnaturally low.

"Love to, Forrest. The Khrar ambassador claims the Coalition vaporized one of their prize Predators. Of course, it might have just disappeared or it's on a secret spy mission. The ambassador claims it's not."

"He says that as an act of diplomatic restraint on the part of the Khrar Empire, they will hold off commencing an interstellar war for ten days to give the Coalition an opportunity to prove its innocence. Your orders are to conduct the investigation."

"Admiral," Dani voiced tightly, "I realize we are near the Free Sector. But *Boadicea* is scheduled for shore leave and repairs. We can't—"

"Gee, Captain, I'm sorry about that. You just seemed like the obvious choice." There was an implied threat, a sort of pleasure in the Admiral's voice at sending the *Boadicea* into danger that belied the innocence of the words themselves.

"Admiral, I demand—"

"You're not in a position to demand anything." The Admiral's voice held the coldness of steel. "Although I must say you do look rather beaten down for such a hotshot commander. First Queer Woman Commander and all that. Have you been overdoing it at Leather Nights over there?"

Something in Dani snapped. She jerked out of her command chair, jaw locked and clenched hands extended. If she'd been in the same room with Jameson, she'd have been squeezing him around the throat by now. Ma'at stepped smoothly forward.

"Admiral," Ma'at pointed out, "even hotshot commanders, as you put it, require periodic rest and rejuvenation, as do their ships. A recent ion storm damaged a high percentage of our equipment. The crew has not had leave for nearly a year."

"I'm sorry, Commander Ma'at." Jameson answered, keeping his eye on Dani "It was not my decision alone that you should handle this mission."

Dani doubted that.

"At worst," the Admiral continued, "you'll encounter a few Khrars. Naturally, Explora Command would prefer that you negotiate instead of fight. Now, if you have no further questions, Jameson out."

"Visual off!" Dani shouted hoarsely to Mouneera. The screen went dark. Dani paced wildly in front of her command chair, her hands chopping at the empty air.

"A few Khrars! Negotiate instead of fight! That man never met a Khrar in his life!"

"The details of the mission, Captain, are enumerated in a coded memo," Ma'at said.

"Of which you have already apprised yourself."

"Of course, Captain. We are to put off our visit to Spaceportal sixteen and proceed directly to the Free Sector."

Dani stopped pacing and resettled herself in her seat. "Alright, Ma'at. What are we looking for? A solitary rogue ship? A fleet? A natural phenomenon?"

"Our mission has been described as an investigation, Captain."

"Thank you, Ma'at, for the clarification." Dani's voice was heavy with sarcasm.

"You're welcome, Captain," Ma'at intoned blandly. S/he was relieved to see Dani focusing on the mission. The Captain's erratic behavior of late had caused ripples of rumor among the crew and so far Ma'at hadn't been able to ascertain a cause for it.

S/he had noticed no obvious changes in Dani's normal human routines of activity, eating, rest and recreation. Since as Captain, Dani could not consort with crew members, it would be practically impossible for her to carry on an *affair d'couer* with anyone aboard, even if she was so inclined. Which meant love—or its loss—was probably not the cause of her irritability.

"Very well, then. Mr. DeVargas, change course for the Free Sector."

"Aye, Captain. Implementing."

"On the other hand, Captain," Ma'at said in measured tones, "I have never seen such flimsily-disguised malice in a superior officer.

It went distressingly beyond the usual homophobia."

"You thought it was excessive too?" Dani asked, leaning back in her chair and stretching her aching legs out in front of her. She wondered when the day would come that Explora Command would act on what they already knew: lesbians, gays, bisexuals, transgenders and intersexuals were no different from anyone else. The day when the policy of separate and unequal would be exposed for the sham it was. "You didn't think I was just overreacting?"

"It would have been difficult not to react, Captain. However," Ma'at said, "as improperly as the Admiral may have voiced it, you do look tired, Dani."

The irritation Dani suppressed in front of the Admiral fanned back to life. "Ma'at—"

"Dani," Ma'at said, "there have been incidents—"

"Incidents!" Dani exploded. She wanted to shout, '*Et tu, Brute?*'. Instead, she said, "What are you suggesting, Ma'at? That I'm unfit to command?" Heat rose under the tight spandex of her body suit and she leaned aggressively forward.

"No, Captain. Merely that a visit to Doctor Jenks might be in order."

"Jenks!"

"You are behind in your physicals with the doctor, Captain. This would be a good time to complete any necessary exams—"

"Exams! Goddess, Ma'at! You're beginning to fuss over me as much as he does!"

"Captain," Ma'at said quietly, "I can insist."

"You wouldn't dare," Dani said, feeling her pent-up tension ease. Baiting Ma'at could relax her like few other pastimes. She trusted her first officer implicitly. They shared a close easy friendship, an emotional bonding between like-minds and like-souls. In that, as in so many other things, Dani had to acknowledge her indebtedness to her gifted first officer.

The very lack of sexual tension between them—even though Ma'at's sensual magnetism inexplicably turned up regularly in Dani's dreams—made their relationship one of the few places Dani could go to blow off steam from the pressures of command.

"I might." Ma'at stood calmly, hands clasped behind hir back, perfectly at ease and, Dani knew, ultimately immovable. She had lost the battle but it didn't mean she couldn't get one last thrust in.

"Ma'at," she teased, "I've never known you to act coy. Is this the beginning of a new chapter in our friendship?"

"As one of your own Earth proverbs declares, Dani, there is a first time for everything."

Dani raised a shocked eyebrow. "You don't say."

Ma'at grinned.

"Alright, you win. I'll go." Dani raised herself from her chair, startled by the effort standing required. Her calves ached as much as when she'd awakened. Ma'at was right; she did need to check in with Sly. She made her way to the kinelift feeling lightheaded. Her *tete-a-tete* with the Admiral had taken more out of her than she realized.

"Dani?" Ma'at gripped her by the elbow, steadying her.

"Just lightheaded for a moment there, Ma'at. I'm alright."

Ma'at frowned, releasing Dani's elbow. S/he observed Dani's progress up the stairs and across the aft deck. The commander's walk seemed normal enough.

"Dani," Ma'at said, "there is something further."

Dani turned."Yes?"

"How did you know the news I had for you would be—as you termed it—bad?"

Dani smiled. "I guess you've never heard that other little Earth proverb 'no news is good news'?"

"Hmm," Ma'at tilted hir head, concentrating hir full attention on the phrase. "Even according to the rules of human logic, the equation 'no news is good news' would mean good news does not exist."

"Ma'at—"

"Dani?"

"Let's discuss it later over pinochle, shall we?"

"As you wish, Captain." Ma'at moved smoothly across the deck to appropriate Dani's command seat. The kinelift doors closed on hir first command to Ensign DeVargas to handle the science station.

Dani leaned against the interior wall of the kinelift and closed her eyes in exhaustion. In the privacy of the kinelift, she could give in to the growing sensation of weakness dragging down her limbs.

What was wrong with her? The anxiety she had locked in her stomach at Ma'at's insinuation that there had been 'incidents' rose into her chest. She was loath to remember it but the most appalling such incident had involved Ensign Caitlin Eireann, a very straight, very fresh-from-the-Academy, Language and Cultural Attache who was aboard *Boadicea* as a transfer en route to Spaceportal sixteen.

Eireann used any excuse she could contrive to gain access to the bridge. Dani had even gone so far as to wonder if a male bridge crew member had caught the young heterosexual woman's eye. If one had, she assumed their lack of interest should have, by now, deterred the youthful cultural attache. There were no bisexual men on the bridge for this tour, just gay ones.

Two days earlier, on Eireann's third visit to the bridge during the same duty shift, Dani had simply lost control. She interrupted an inconsequential conversation between Eireann and Lieutenant Mouneera about Verpan dialects."Ensign!"

"Captain!" the young woman squawked in return, nearly

saluting in her surprise.

"The next time you come to the bridge, it had better be for a damn good reason!"

"Sir?" Hurt confusion flashed across Eireann's freckled face. Mouneera's jaw dropped in astonishment.

"You heard me, Ensign."

Near tears, Eireann dumbly repeated, "Sir?"

Only then did Dani realize how out-of-her-depth the young redhead was. Dani watched as Mouneera's dark eyes narrowed to take on a—you-will-pay-for-this—cast Dani had seen only a few times before. Dani's face flushed crimson and out of the corner of her eye, she saw Ma'at's eyebrows rise. But it was too late for apologies.

"Dismissed," Dani said and faced forward. She heard Mouneera snort in protest and knew the Latina's nostrils were flaring with indignation. Dani's anger at herself kept her from watching but she knew as surely as if she had eyes in the back of her head that Mouneera was doing a bang-up job of smoothing over her poor judgement.

She had been even more uneasy of what Ma'at would say after Eireann was escorted off the bridge, but her first officer had not directed a glance, much less a word, in Dani's direction. The only salve to her ego was that Eireann would quickly forget her in the excitement of her new duties on Spaceportal sixteen and Dani would not be reminded of an incident that caused her face to flush every time she thought of it.

Almost as if she were relieving the humiliation of the incident, sweat broke out above Dani's lip and a muscle shiver ran down the back of her legs. She pressed her full weight against the wall of the kinelift and felt nausea twist her stomach.

It was a good thing she was on her way to the infirmary. Sly could tell her what was wrong. Sly had better tell her what was wrong.

She had the odd perception of feeling her thoughts unraveling like plummeting skeins of yarn. Hypnotized by the self-induced image, she watched the skeins spiral downward, making elaborate twists and turns, differentiating into thousands of brightly-hued strands. She struggled valiantly to follow them all but it was too difficult.

Sleep. That's what she wanted. She wanted to sleep. Sleep forever.

Chapter
Four

DANI AWOKE WITH a start to Doctor Sylvestre Jenks' friendly black face looking down at her. She raised herself on one elbow and Sly pushed her back down on the bed.

"It's overwork, Dani," he said, without apology. "I'm recommending complete bed rest for at least two days."

"Sly —"

"Now, Dani. It isn't like we aren't on our way to the nearest Spaceportal for shore leave anyway. Let the youngsters manage the ride. You rest up." He patted her companionably on the shoulder and pulled up a chair, his face full of smiles for one of his best friends.

"Besides," he said, "you and I can have a blast on a Spaceportal for once if you're rested up before we get there. I can't wait to hit the gay bars. It's been way too long." Sly's dark brown eyes shone with anticipation. Dani knew that the gregarious, affable and very good-looking Sly, even approaching middle age as he was, never had the slightest difficulty picking up young gorgeous men of all races while on shore leave.

Dani hated to burst his fantasy-fraught bubble but she didn't see that she had a choice. "Sly," Dani made another effort to sit up, "there isn't going to be any shore leave."

"Now wait just a damn minute, Dani." Sly stood up. He was taller than her and still quite trim and muscular. "We need that shore leave. In fact," he yanked Dani's elbows forward and Dani fell flat on her back in the bed again, "as Chief Surgeon, I demand it."

Dani's mouth fell open in surprise. Sly had never used that trick on her before. He must have been serious about the bed rest. Dani folded her hands over her stomach and resigned herself to laying flat. Sly was still talking. Once he got started, it was hard to stop him. She had never been able to decide if his tendency to fully, and emotionally, express his views was part of his charm or detracted from it.

"Listen to me, Dani. The whole damn crew is about as edgy as a bunch of performance-starved drag queens and it isn't as if we haven't had plenty of shows lately. Look at yourself, for example."

"I'm acting like a performance-starved drag queen?"

"No. But you're exhausted and you're edgy as all get out. I've heard that you've been skirting the edge of bitchy."

"Bitchy? Someone actually said I was being bitchy?"

"Let's just say, that at the moment, you're hardly fit to tie your shoelaces, let alone command a starship."

Dani grunted her disbelief. She detected the self-satisfied twinkle in Sly's eye that meant he knew he had her over a medical barrel. As Chief Surgeon, Doctor Jenks was one of only two people aboard who was authorized to declare Dani unfit for duty. Ma'at, as First Officer, was the other.

And Dani knew her old Academy partner-in-crime well enough to know he would resort to that ultimate power if he had to. But at the moment, she assumed Sly — as Ma'at had predicted — was merely tickled pink to have her under his wing so he could run the latest medical tests she had been sneaking out of with one excuse or another for months.

Of course, Dani didn't have to make it easy.

"Shoelaces? No one's worn shoelaces for 300 years, Sly."

"My granddaddy wore 'em when he was a boy back in Oklahoma. He never did get used to the velcro that replaced them."

Dani grinned. She was always delighted to hear a new one of Sly's Okie tales.

"Perhaps, Doctor Jenks, it's a family trait."

They both looked up to see Ma'at lounging in the doorway. As usual, Sly couldn't help rising to the bait.

"What trait is that, Ma'at?"

"A tendency to wax nostalgic over the past."

"Well," Sly said, "at least in my past, there are things worth waxing nostalgic about."

"And undoubtedly, some not so worthwhile." Ma'at's delivery was absolutely deadpan.

Dani thought she detected little wisps of smoke curling up from Sly's ears.

"Ma'at, you are so —"

"People," Dani said before they could entrench themselves. Their favorite sport of mutual needling seemed a little more caustic than usual. Dani knew Sly secretly enjoyed these verbal sword fights and stored up inflammatory remarks to shower on Ma'at's head. But today the doctor seemed genuinely aggravated.

The idea that she might not be the only one feeling irritable made Dani even more edgy. As a result, her voice was harsher than she intended when she asked after Ma'at's mission in the infirmary. Her tone was not lost on Ma'at, who drew hirself up stiffly and folded hir arms across hir chest. Dani mentally kicked herself.

"I considered it important, Captain, to check on your condition. You did, after all, collapse in the kinelift."

Ma'at did not elaborate that Dani had been found in an

unconscious slump by Ensign Eireann, who had been on her way, yet again, to the bridge. Unfamiliar with shipboard procedure, Eireann had pressed the wrong button on the kinelift intercom and announced to the ship at large that Captain Forrest was dead and could someone please help!

Ma'at, making use of all the speed afforded by hir well-controlled Nhavan panic, was the first to arrive on the scene. S/he found Eireann weeping hysterically over Dani's supine form. She had returned the woman to her senses with a solid slap across the face but had done hir best to approximate the blow for a human and not what would be required to bring a Nhavan out of a similar state.

At the same time, s/he grasped Dani's wrist and searched for a pulse, which s/he found. To prevent ship wide histrionics, s/he broadcast to the ship at large that the captain was alive and the situation under control. Then s/he rang the infirmary and demanded a medic team.

"Already on their way, Ma'at. What's going on up there?" Sly demanded.

"She collapsed in the kinelift. She was en route to the infirmary at my request."

"Vital signs?"

"Unconscious but breathing. Pulse fast and thready. She has seemed over-tired of late."

"Very good, Ma'at. We'll give her a complete going over down here on our end."

"Excellent. Thank you."

ON THE BRIDGE of the *Heaven's Bow*, First Officer Luluai moved back to her science station to check and double-check readings on the composition of a sample of stellar dust, which had been collected on a driftmission by *The Chariot*, the *Heaven's Bow's* workbee.

Luluai was a perfectionist. From childhood, she had been obsessed with being the best at everything. Such an approach to life gave her an exceptional fund of technical knowledge for her age. In their first month aboard, she was reprimanded by Bajana to loosen up and take regular breaks from her duties.

"I can't have you going space-mad," Bajana had joked at the time, but the joke was followed by a prescription to get in the *Heaven's Bow's* dinky egg-shaped swimming pool at least once a day and play. Squeezing the pool onto the ship had been complicated and expensive but Sukha and Bajana insisted on its inclusion in the design.

Originally, it was intended for use by the Sirensi complement of the crew. Even though well adapted to land, Sirensi needed to periodically renew their contact with water to maintain good mental health. But over the past months, the pool had turned into everyone's favorite place to unwind and socialize.

Luluai was a Sirensi. She had the webbed hands and feet and the neck gills, as well as the more ordinary humanoid features of a nose and mouth for breathing. But she was different. Instead of the golden hair, sky blue eyes, and silvery-iridescent skin that all her cousins, aunts, and grandmothers had, her hair was a light brunette, her eyes a golden-hazel, and her skin a dusky golden brown. Admittedly, the shade was much lighter than the olive, red brown, and chocolate brown skin tones of the Brahuinna, but it was a uniform color nonetheless.

She hated her color and she hated the reason for it. She was the first of her race to have a father. A Brahuinna father. Thinking of it always made her face hot with shame. She was a half-breed; not that anyone on Elysiansus had ever teased her about it. In fact, everyone had always treated her with the utmost kindness. But it didn't mitigate her inner belief that they were being kind out of pity.

It hurt that she would never be a simple happy Sirensi, playing on the jeweled harp or ornamenting a wall with a mosaic or splashing in the sea without a contradicting thought. In space she hoped to forget that she would never be an effortless synchronized one of the perfect singing whole which was Elysiansus.

"Hey, Luluai," a familiar voice blew near her ear, dragging her from her self-punishing thoughts, "why so glum?"

Luluai quivered with distaste. It was Nachiketas Buono, the navigator. "Time to play," he said, "the captain's not here." Nachi had lively hazel-brown eyes set in a mischievous face. A dark mustache and eyebrows contrasted with his olive skin. Jet black hair curled freely to his shoulders. In another minute he would try to slip his hands around her waist and she would shudder.

"Go away, Nachi," she said, "I'm trying to work." She modeled one of Captain Ki's stances, feet apart and fists authoritatively on her hips.

"Aw, c'mon," he took possession of her chair and spun around in it, "let's do something fun."

"I mean it, Nachi; leave me alone."

"You're even prettier when you're mad."

Luluai felt like throwing something at him even as a small part of her warmed to Nachi's flattery. "I'm not pretty," she said, "so quit saying it."

His voice grew soft. "You're beautiful to me."

"Just leave me alone." She dropped her fists and turned her back to him.

"Luluai," he entreated as he had done a dozen times before, "how's it going to hurt you to have dinner with me some night in the mess? With all the other crew around?"

"You know I can't. I've already said 'no' a zillion times."

"Look, I don't care that you're a —"

"Don't say it!" she screeched, crossing her arms tightly and feeling tears start in her eyes.

Luluai wiped her eyes and plunked down into her seat. It was still warm with the heat of Nachi's body. When she was old enough to understand it, her mother explained the strange phenomenon of male-female sex. It repulsed her, seeming so much less perfect than the Sirensi way of going within oneself and choosing to bear a child. Her mother had laughed off her fears. "It's a lovely, delightful thing," she said.

Her mother was, to put it mildly, a maverick. When Luluai was a teenager, her mother moved off-world with Luluai's father, leaving Luluai to the care of her aunts and grandmothers. Luluai thought it was the most merciful thing her mother could have done for her.

Luluai had paid her mother a courtesy visit on Nirvannini before heading into space on the *Heaven's Bow*. She believed nothing her mother could say would shock her, and it hadn't. What had shocked her was that for the first time she found herself liking her father.

Luluai sneaked a glance at Nachi, who was leaning casually back in his navigator's chair. He wore a forest green tunic and black belt, which flattered his natural coloring. Her tunic was of a rich cream, belted with a narrow strip of tan. Although all crew, male and female, wore the same uniform of a tunic, tapered leggings, belt, and sandals, Captain Ki had let each crewperson choose his or her own colors and personal decoration.

Rank was not denoted on the uniform and everyone aboard, except Captain Ki, was a Lieutenant. She and Sukha had decided that in such a small crew — just thirty people — rank was likely to prove more divisive than helpful. Sukha held no rank. He was like the Founding Mothers of her own people: he was held in such reverence he didn't need any official designation.

Nachi shifted forward, reading something on his console, and then started to turn in Luluai's direction. She quickly bent her attention back to her screen so he wouldn't see that she'd been watching him.

"Captain," Nachi's voice was mockingly respectful, "according to my readout, we should be approaching a small planet. A planetoid, I guess you could say."

"I'm only acting as the captain, Nachi. You shouldn't call me 'Captain'." She drew her brows together trying to make it clear she was annoyed when, inwardly, she felt flattered again.

She punched access commands on her science console and studied her screen. Nachi was right. They would be passing quite close to a very, very small planet that Indrashtra, on his return journey, had labeled as having a breathable atmosphere.

It was time to call Captain Ki back to the bridge. She might just want to send a team down to study the planetoid. Which meant Luluai might get to lead it.

"COLLAPSED?" DANI WAS incredulous. She sat up in the bed and this time Sly didn't force her back down. "In the kinelift?"

Sly frowned, his medical instincts aroused by the captain's apparent lack of recollection. "You don't remember? Nothing at all?"

Dani stared down at the crisp white sheet covering her strong compact body. She shook her head. Sly and Ma'at exchanged looks. "Doctor?" Ma'at said, trying to hide hir concern.

Sly looked in exasperation from Ma'at to Dani and back again. "The fact of the matter is there's nothing wrong with her. Not that I've found anyway. No virus or bacteria. Her organs are in good condition. Muscles and nerves appear healthy. Frankly," he crossed his arms over his chest, daring them to disagree, "I think it's overwork."

"Sly—"

"The whole crew is exhausted, Dani. Everyone's nerves are frayed. That ion storm we weathered called on the crew's full capacities and I think everyone, except perhaps Ma'at here, was stressed beyond their limits."

"We've been through ion storms before," Dani said. "This is the best crew in Minority Fleet."

"I know. But even they have limits. And you—" Sly shot a worrisome glance at Ma'at and then plunged on, "—the truth is, Dani, you're not as young as you used to be. You just don't bounce back as fast from these stresses anymore."

"Believe it or not, Sly, I've taken that into account too. I know I'm getting older. I'm forty-bloody-two. But this doesn't feel like age. It feels like an illness."

"Dani," Sly said in his most professional voice, "I haven't found anything wrong. If I had, I sure as hell wouldn't be hiding it from you."

Dani looked to her first officer. "Would he?"

"I can think of no reason for him to do so, Captain. You are, after all, in full command of your faculties and Doctor Jenks has always held the best interests of this ship and its crew at his heart."

"But is it possible?"

"Mathematically, Dani, anything is possible."

"What we all need," Sly threw his hands up in a huff, "is a vacation! Including Ma'at." He glared at the Nhavan.

"Believe me, Sly, if it were up to me, I wouldn't be gallivanting off on another wild goose chase in search of goddess knows what, that may, or may not, have blown some bunch of Khrars to smithereens." Dani swung herself out of bed. "What are the odds, anyway, of finding the responsible ship, or even a host of ships — which may or may not exist — in the vastness of the Free Sector, with ten days to do it in?"

Her question was purely rhetorical but Ma'at answered it anyway. "About 16 percent. That's just a guess, of course."

Sly rolled his eyes. Undeterred, Ma'at continued. "As the size of the destroying force and the time and location of the encounter with the Khrar ship is unknown, that number can serve only as an approximation."

"Not very good odds, Ma'at."

"No, Dani, they're not."

"Encounter, Ma'at?" Sly was stimulated to battle again. "You call wholesale destruction — even of Khrars — an encounter?"

"Technically, encounter is the proper term. How the parties acted once they met does not in any way affect my usage of the word —"

"Oh, hooie," Sly said. Dani closed her eyes and started counting to ten.

" — which only refers to the actual —"

But Dani got only as far as four. "Ma'at! Sly! Take the day off from each other! That's an order, for chrissake."

They fell silent and stared at her. With a glare for each of them in turn, Dani pushed herself off the bed and hunched miserably across the room to the door.

Sly started after her. "Dani, where the hell do you think you're going?"

"Back to the bridge. I have a duty shift to finish."

Sly latched a hand onto Dani's shoulder to stop her. "Over my dead body." Dani turned and viciously knocked Sly's arm away.

They froze, both horrified. Ma'at's eyebrows rose into hir dark hairline. When Dani finally spoke, her voice was weighted with defeat.

"Ma'at, Sly, what's the matter with me?"

"Dani, you're tired," Sly reiterated.

"I haven't been this out of control since I was on the 'Frying Pan' making the life of the ensigns pure hell. Am I losing my command ability, Sly?"

"No. It's just plain old garden variety exhaustion. Nothing

several good nights' sleep won't cure. Let's get you to your cabin so you can get started on them."

"That's another thing, Sly. I've been having nightmares."

Sly looked startled, but responded confidently.

"We'll run a complete psychological on you tomorrow, Dani. For now, my prescription is a shared glass of the best Wiffilan brandy and something on top of it to assure a night of dreamless sleep. C'mon."

Sylvestre Adam Jenks knew he had just given a bravado performance of humoring the patient, but inwardly, he was worried. He glanced back at Ma'at, whom he could have sworn, despite the intersexual's pretense at calm, looked worried, too.

ENSIGN CAITLIN EIREANN sat alone at a table in the farthest corner of the officer's mess, picking drearily at the congealing pasta she had punched up for dinner from the automated shipcook. Although a full duty shift had elapsed since that humiliating moment in the kinelift, the slap Commander Ma'at had imparted still rang in her ears.

Coupled with the equally mortifying episode on the bridge with the captain, she figured she'd better not raise her head for the rest of the voyage to Spaceportal sixteen. No one had dared comment on either incident to her face, but how thoroughly they were enjoying her discomfiture behind her back, she didn't know.

Caitlin felt a twinge of nausea, set down her fork and pushed her plate away. She fished a chewable vitamin from the breast pocket of her civilian khaki jumpsuit and munched abstractedly on it. Why was she screwing up so badly? As irrational as it was, she wanted to blame Captain Forrest.

Whenever she was around the captain, good judgement seemed to fly out of her head. And she knew she wasn't gay or even latently gay. Like everyone else, she'd had to take a battery of tests at the Academy to ferret out such tendencies. And even if there was still some old-fashioned nonsense floating around about homosexuality being a choice, she knew it wasn't. You were either born to it or you weren't.

She knew her hysteria in the kinelift had been heightened by the fact that she had been on her way to the bridge to apologize to the captain for causing the original scene. Her plan was to beg forgiveness and then keep out of her way, and everyone else's for that matter, until she was off *Boadicea*.

Caitlin was thinking so hard, she didn't notice anyone approaching until she heard a voice over her head. "Is this seat taken?"

Her head jerked up. It was Commander Ma'at, the Nhavan intersexual, towering on the other side of the table waiting for her to answer. All her instincts told her to run but she was glued to the chair with fear. She wasn't queasy anymore. Her stomach had solidified into a hard mass of undigested pasta.

"Eh, no. Sir. Commander. Sir." Breathless, she sucked in air.

"Thank you." Ma'at drew out a chair and sat down. S/he unfolded hir napkin and dug, without a word, into a green salad sprinkled with toasted soybeans. Caitlin's thumping heart began to slow. The measured action of Commander Ma'at's careful eating was calming. She watched hir lift fork to mouth in unwilling fascination.

If Ma'at minded being stared at like a zoo exhibit, by the normally spunky freckle-faced redhead while making hir steady way through hir meal, s/he gave no indication of such to the ensign. S/he was, in fact, studying her. Even if she was going to be aboard for only a short time — and that time had just been lengthened by the *Boadicea's* change of assignment — Ma'at decided s/he needed to form a better understanding of Eireann. The young ensign had managed, in short order, to disrupt not only the captain's normal equanimity but that of the entire ship.

Nothing in Eireann's personnel profile, which Ma'at had taken care to review, indicated any personality disorder or mental illness. She had never been prone to dramatics through her years at the Academy, even under the most exacerbating conditions; conditions that were designed to bring exactly such hidden traits to a cadet's — and the cadet's trainers' — awareness.

In fact, her records were filled with evidence to the contrary. Her teachers considered her a lively, charming student with a strong bent of curiosity, who had engaged passionately, but not theatrically, in her studies. She had been popular with classmates of both human sexes and always ready to lend a hand.

As first officer, it was Ma'at's duty to report Eireann's behavior, if s/he determined it to be at all abnormal, to the medical department. S/he didn't know yet if it was. At the moment, though, s/he thought the young woman's actions unusual for a human. Ma'at had been around humans long enough — nearly twenty-five years now — to know it was a human trait to cover up for moments of embarrassment or fear by speaking, preferably about something unrelated, like the weather or the latest game scores.

Yet Ensign Eireann had not spoken since s/he sat down. That in itself constituted some provocation, since her emotional reaction to the blow Ma'at had administered could not have mellowed by now. Ma'at also didn't know how anxious or phobic Eireann's response to hir intersexuality might be or how isolated she might feel as the only straight person on a gay ship, which would have been a reverse from her everyday civilian and even academy experience. All considered, a substantial amount of uncertainty and stress for the young woman to handle.

Ma'at finished eating, laid down hir fork and watched Eireann's peculiarly glassed-over eyes follow it to its resting place on the tray. S/he pushed the tray aside and observed the ensign's eyes follow that as well.

"Ensign." Ma'at used a pleasant conversational tone but the ensign's attention snapped from the tray to hir. "Sir!" Her eyes went from glassy to wide.

"At ease, Ensign."

"I'm sorry, Commander." Eireann dropped her head, her mane of unbraided fiery red curls tumbling over her shoulders with the movement.

Ma'at's curiosity was aroused. "Sorry for what?"

"For being such a lot of trouble." The young woman lifted her head but her expression, normally cheerful, was dismal. Even her mouth was turned down and Ma'at thought s/he detected a trembling of her chin.

"Ensign," Ma'at leaned forward and rested hir long slender arms on the table, "the efficiency of any ship is dependant on the well-being of its crew. You humans have a saying for it: a chain is only as strong as its weakest link."

Ensign Eireann nodded her agreement but her eyes remained averted. Ma'at went on. "If there is something disturbing you, Ensign, you should apprise Doctor Jenks or myself of it."

"Yes, sir."

Despite the monosyllabic response, Ma'at tried again. "I apologize that I found it necessary to bring you to your senses in the kinelift. If that is what concerns you, I hope you will accept that my action was not personal in any way. It will not go on your record. You are not in an official capacity aboard *Boadicea*, as you know."

"Yes, sir. Thank you, sir."

"Is that all then, Ensign?"

Ma'at wondered later if it was because of hir patience that Ensign Eireann confided in hir. S/he didn't know why but, in any case, s/he listened in fascination as Ensign Eireann described how when she got around Captain Forrest she lost all ability to reason properly, yet she was equally sure she was not sexually attracted to the captain.

Inwardly, Ma'at concluded the ensign's difficulty consisted of a rather ordinary case of performance anxiety triggered by heroine worship, and a possible rising uncertainty about her sexuality. The Ensign was very young, after all. Despite Ma'at's Nhavan preference for honesty, there wasn't any way to inform the ensign of hir diagnosis without sounding condescending and possibly affecting the young woman's self-esteem or sense of psychological balance.

So, s/he heard Eireann out, recommended avoidance of the captain — which, after all, was Eireann's own intent — and excused hirself from the table, leaving an emotionally-relieved but strangely uncomforted ensign behind.

Chapter
Five

SUKHA WAS THE first to appear on the bridge of the *Heaven's Bow* following Luluai's call to the captain. "Greetings to all of you." He pressed both sets of his palms together as well as he could, considering the splints, and inclined his head.

"Greetings." the bridge crew chorused back, returning the respectful gesture. Luluai bounded out of her chair and came to murmur sympathetically over his bandaged arms. He playfully tousled the hair of her head with one of his two free hands. "It's not as bad as all that."

The bridge crew smiled their collective relief at Sukha's upbeat confidence. He was injured and must have been apprised of the incident with the other ship yet he acted as if everything was fine. He did not comment on the emptiness of Hasitam's chair. Instead, he walked directly to Nachi's station.

"It's a planetoid, sir." Nachi moved aside so Sukha could see his console readout.

"Could it be the one?" Bajana had just stepped onto the bridge. She strode purposefully to Sukha's side.

"Oh, no. Not a chance."

"But it may be worth a look," Luluai said, excitement plain in her voice. Bajana looked appraisingly at her first officer. Luluai was rarely so excited. Bajana spoke to Nachi. "Establish a standard orbit, Lieutenant." Nachi jumped to do her bidding.

Bajana shrugged. "We need the practice."

"In orbiting?" Sukha inquired.

"Yes. And handling the shuttlecraft, testing ship-to-ship communications, keeping a team organized on the planet's surface, collecting scientific data and samples. We had a few run-throughs at home, but can we do it out here under real conditions?"

"A dress rehearsal," Sukha said.

"Yes, and a confidence builder," she added for his ears alone. Bajana started issuing orders. Luluai puffed up with pride when Bajana assigned her to command the landing party.

"I want you to take the doctors with you," she said. There it was, Bajana thought, the real drawback to the Sirensi twin doctors. They went everywhere and did everything together. If she sent them down to the planet, there wouldn't be a physician aboard to handle onboard medical emergencies should they arise.

On the other hand, they were her best scientists and xenobiologists and she trusted their mature wisdom to notice and report on things younger eyes would overlook. Bajana's natural urge was to do everything herself but she knew it was impossible, not to mention dangerous. Deployment of crew was an art she was still learning.

"Take Pukk and Abjay as your security team and—"

"Captain, if I may—" Nachi interrupted Bajana's commands.

"Yes, Lieutenant?"

"I think you should send me as well."

"Out of the question."

"May I ask why, sir?"

"With Lieutenant Deva confined to quarters and First Officer Luluai leading the planetary team, I should think it would be obvious."

"Yes, sir." Nachi subsided. Put that way, it was obvious. He didn't have a good reason for wanting to go to the planetoid except that the mission promised new adventure and Luluai was going.

"Is that all, sir?" Luluai addressed the captain.

"Yes. Good luck. I'll expect you to be in constant communication."

"Yes, sir." Luluai saluted and, with her head held high, marched from the bridge. Her first command! And she was not going to allow anything to happen that would make the excursion less than military perfect.

"COME IN, MA'AT," Sly grumbled at the lanky figure filling the doorway of the infirmary. "What is it now?" Sly was leaning back in his chair, his feet on the desk and his cobalt blue bodysuit half-unzipped, giving a hint of the firm muscles underlying the sleek dark skin of his chest. His head was back and he was agitatedly rubbing his hands across the tight, low-lying kinks of his mahogany hair.

"Doctor Jenks," Ma'at moved into the room, "it is our responsibility to determine if the captain is fit for command."

"She's fit for command, alright, Ma'at. She's just not as young and chipper as she used to be."

"Do you think the captain is aging more quickly than she was before?"

"Stress, as you well know, can accelerate aging, Ma'at. But I have no evidence that that is happening. It was just a figure of speech. I don't know how Nhavans can be so smart and so dumb at the same time."

"Now, Doctor—"

"Alright, Ma'at. This is what I've discovered." Sly swung around in his chair. "I detect no pathology among the crew. However, everyone's dead tired, no one seems to be hungry, and everyone, with a few exceptions, is acting like long-tailed cats in a room full of rockers."

Ma'at's brow furrowed as s/he pondered this latest Earth colloquialism. Sly smiled to himself. It was the most fun he'd had all day. Ma'at's brow cleared as s/he made sense of the phrase and applied it to the present situation.

"And that's it?"

"Essentially. The only thing I've been able to measure scientifically is eye-hand coordination and reaction times. Reflexes are slipping."

"Then there are physiological markers of this syndrome?"

"Yes. But so far that hasn't told me very much. Those markers can mean anything from excess stress to the beginnings of a serious disorder. The difficulty I'm having with settling on a diagnosis is that the reported symptoms are generalized and possibly psychosomatic."

Ma'at was opening hir mouth to ask another question when the quiet of the room was shattered by the shrill whistle of the intercom.

"Sickbay! We have a collapsed crewman!"

Sly slammed the button. "Where?"

"G Deck. N Corridor!"

"My god, Ma'at," Sly shouted, "that's just down the hall." He vaulted from his chair and sprinted away. Ma'at followed. As soon as he reached the crewman, Sly crouched by the man's side and reached for his medical sensor array. It wasn't there.

"Damn," he cursed and pressed his fingers against the carotid artery in the man's neck to take the pulse the old-fashioned way. There wasn't one. As experienced a doctor as Sly was, he could hardly believe the truth of his senses. The crewman was young and healthy...and not breathing. Sly checked the man's throat for lodged matter. Nothing. The airway was unobstructed.

"Ma'at," Sly ordered, "we'll have to administer manual CPR." Ma'at knelt beside the prone crewman and started methodically pumping his chest. Closing the crewman's nose, Sly breathed into his mouth in the prescribed sequence between pumps by Ma'at. A crowd began to gather.

"Ensign!" Sly roared at the nearest crewman between breaths, "get my medical kit. Have Nurse Acton bring the portable cardiostimulator."

The man was already running. The blond male nurse and the equipment were at Sly's side in a flash. Ma'at moved to the crewman's head to take over the task of breathing into the stilled lungs while Sly and Nurse Acton electrically jolted the crewman's heart. Once, twice. The crewman's body jerked but he did not return to life.

Sly couldn't believe it. Acton had brought along Sly's sensor array and Sly checked for vital signs between each administration of the cardiostimulator. Wary, but unwilling to give up, he motioned to Acton to stimulate the crewman's heart a third time. Nothing changed. With a curt gesture, Sly ordered Ma'at to end hir efforts to breathe for the crewman.

"He's dead," Sly pronounced in disbelief. "But why? Why did he die?"

Ma'at leaned back on hir heels considering the same question. "Simple stress," s/he said with care, "does not, under normal circumstances, cause heart failure. If this crewman had a history of heart disease, he would have been restricted from service in Explora Command." S/he looked up to Sly, who had risen to his feet. Sly's hands were clenched, his mouth a thin hard line.

"I should have been able to save him, Ma'at. I wasn't fast enough."

"Doctor Jenks," Ma'at rose to hir feet, "you did everything it was possible to do."

"Except," Sly's voice was angry, "figure out what's ailing this crew." He turned on his heel and stomped away.

In due time, two medics came down the hall with a stretcher and settled their human burden onto it. The crewman was Arthur Exeter Madison, a shuttlecraft mechanic. Ma'at was sure the medics would take Madison to the infirmary for the autopsy Sly was certain to perform.

There was a statistical chance that Madison had a heart condition that had never been detected. His death could not, at least until after the results of Sly's autopsy were known, be attributed to the mystery illness, if it was an illness, plaguing the *Boadicea*.

Nonetheless, it was disturbing.

LULUAI GUIDED THE *Heaven's Bow* shuttlecraft, the *Lithe Arrow*, to a bumpless landing on the planetoid's sandy surface. As she pulled to a stop, she could see a low range of barren mountains far off in the distance and, here and there, scattered across the empty plain, jagged outcroppings of dull red rock.

Although the *Heaven's Bow's* scanning equipment was not as sophisticated as Sukha would have wished, because ship construction had been rushed, they had all been reasonably certain the atmosphere of the tiny planetoid was within safety ranges for breathing. Still, it was with enormous caution that Pukk and Abjay, her muscular Brahuinna security team, let down *Lithe Arrow's* rampdoor. Luluai radioed the *Heaven's Bow* to report their landing.

"We are about to exit the shuttlecraft, Captain, so we will be out of communications range for a short time."

"Carry on," Bajana said.

"We'll head in an northeasterly direction from our landing site. There's a rock outcropping where we can get rock samples."

"Approved. Contact me the moment you return to the shuttlecraft," Bajana said. "Over and out."

Pukk and Abjay preceded the Sirensi doctors and Luluai down the ramp, squinting at the unfamiliar brightness. It was no wonder the place was a desert, Luluai thought, with a blazing sun like that. Though she had read of such environments in the *Glorious Interstellar Journeys*, this was her first experience of desert. Her own planet was 76% ocean and nearly all of Nirvannini was sub-tropical rainforest.

She was astounded by the softness of the sand as she stepped down into it. It was deeper than the hard beach sand she was familiar with. It cushioned the foot the way a feather mattress did. Her second impression, following closely on the heels of the first, so to speak, was that it was fatiguing to walk on. Her sandaled feet sank deeply with every step.

The doctors, Torilli and Tilorri, had skipped some distance away, like delighted children, and were bending down to collect samples of the planetoid's sand. Pukk and Abjay scanned the wasteland with their eyes for anything remotely dangerous.

The small party trooped toward the rock outcropping. As they came closer, they could see tall scraggly trees inside the circle of rocks. The trees looked like the coconut palms on Nirvannini. Luluai imagined them as the welcoming sentinels of the red rock oasis. If there were trees, there had to be water, even on a world like this. They would be able to collect samples of plant life as well.

Excited, she stepped through a narrow gap between two of the natural stone towers and encountered the real sentinels of the oasis. Luluai and her people were surrounded by humanoids who pointed curved hand-held sticks at them.

Luluai wasn't certain what it meant but in the *Interstellar Journeys*, Indrashtra recounted a story of being encircled in a similar manner on the Many-Splendored planet when he first landed. Only the description of the sticks differed.

Apparently, it was a custom on some planets, but she didn't think it was a friendly one. On Elysiansus, strangers were sung to on their arrival and invited to share a ritual meal of fish and seaweed. She guessed this greeting was somewhat different in character.

JUST AS DOCTOR Jenks had done, Ma'at queried the ship's computers concerning the symptoms of the *Boadicea* malady. The computer was not grudging with its data. In fact, it indicated literally hundreds of diseases because numerous pathologies manifested with one or more of the reported symptoms.

S/he understood why Doctor Jenks was having difficulty making a diagnosis. A distinctive indicator, like a patterned rash or traces of specific antibodies, would have made the task far simpler.

After conducting several hours of research, Ma'at caught hirself drifting off to sleep, even though the computer was canting statistics out loud. Hir concentration was normally of the highest reliability and the lapse bothered hir. It was very late in the evening, but that shouldn't make any difference. S/he was capable of working for long periods without sleep, possessing substantially more endurance than the average human.

As a matter of scientific objectivity, s/he was obligated to consider the possibility that s/he too was subject to the unknown disorder. Giving consideration to that fact, s/he was just beginning a new research tack when hir cabin intercom whistled.

"Ma'at here," s/he answered crisply.

"This is the bridge, sir," Ensign DeVargas's breathy, lisped voice came over the intercom. DeVargas was one of the ship's most popular drag queens, having entertained them all on many an otherwise dull evening. "We are approaching a small planetoid."

"Anything unusual, Ensign?"

"No, sir. I just wanted you to know."

"Proceed with a routine scan, Ensign. I'll be on the bridge shortly. Ma'at out."

Less than ten minutes later, Ma'at strode briskly from the aft deck of the bridge to where Ensign Guadalupe DeVargas sat at his science station. "Have you identified the planetoid, Mr. DeVargas?"

"Yes, sir. It's very small and uninhabited, but on the starmaps as SX257."

"Environment?" Ma'at leaned over the console.

"Yes, Mr. DeVargas, what kind of environment?" Dani had come quietly onto the bridge.

"Captain." Ma'at straightened up with concern.

"I'm fine, Ma'at." Dani waved her hand dismissively. "Please proceed, Mr. DeVargas." Dani settled into her command chair.

"Aye, Captain. The environment is mostly desert, a few eroded mountain ranges. The climate is hot and dry with regular high voltage electrical storms—"

"—probably why it's never been settled," Dani said.

"Possibly, sir."

"Anything else?"

"Valuable mineral deposits, Captain," Ma'at scrolled the screen. "I would surmise the planetoid is too remote to attract the attention of large-scale mining operations."

"Very good, officers. Let us proceed on our course to the Free Sector."

"Aye, Captain." DeVargas returned to his station at navigation and Ma'at settled hir long legs into hir seat at the science station. Less than a minute passed before DeVargas shrieked. "Captain! There's something else."

Dani leaned forward. "What, Mr. DeVargas?"

"An unidentified vessel, sir. It is maintaining a standard orbit around the planetoid."

"Mouneera, let's have her on screen."

"Sir?" Lieutenant Mouneera seemed oddly distracted.

"I'd like a look at that ship," Dani repeated.

"Aye, sir." Mouneera touched a button, looked befuddled, hurriedly voided her choice and fumbled for a new button. There was a long enough pause in getting the visual for Dani to shoot an aggravated glance at her communications officer's back.

She forgot it a moment later when the unidentified ship erupted into full color on the viewscreen and riveted the attention of the bridge crew. It was, without question, the most beautiful ship Dani had ever seen, the *Boadicea* notwithstanding.

It wasn't the ship's structure— she was eerily similar to *Boadicea* except for her diminutive size and single nacelle— but the intricate bas-relief design embedded on her hull was enough to take anyone's breath away.

The design consisted of three groupings of humanoid forms, coppery in the starlight, backdropped by a massive old-style wheel with ornately-carved spokes. The wheel glistened gold against the iridescent metal of the ship's hull, a metal Dani could not identify by sight.

The gold, well, it looked like Earth gold, except that she couldn't imagine even the wealthiest of conglomerates or governments being able to afford to put it on a starship. Not to mention finding craftspeople capable of such delicate artistry.

The central figure was the most impressive. It was of a four-armed humanoid drawing back a hunting bow. The bow's arrow— the tip was of the same gold as that of the wheel—had not yet left its launch.

The figure's finely sculpted chest was bare and all he wore, other than a simple loose cord crossing from shoulder to hip, was a richly-detailed thigh-length loincloth. On his head sat a tall tapering headdress, as elaborately carved as the rest of the figure. His long-nosed face was as serene as a god's. Dani wondered why he looked so familiar and yet, at the same time, wholly foreign.

The carved scene on the right of the central figure was that of a man and woman entwined in a flowing erotic embrace. They looked quite human, not godlike as the archer. On the left was a circle of graceful effeminate beings holding hands and dancing. Waves lapped at their feet and over their heads arched five spheres, each a different size and with different details. Planets? Moons? Dani couldn't tell.

"Extraordinary," she heard Ma'at whisper in fascinated absorption.

"Mouneera," Dani forced her eyes from the beauty before her and turned to her communications officer, "please hail them."

"Aye, Captain, hailing," she intoned automatically but instead of a hail being sent to the other ship, the *Boadicea's* viewscreen blanked and was replaced by an interior visual of the other ship's bridge.

The alien bridge was nowhere near as eye-stopping as the ship's exterior but it made a clean-lined backdrop to what promptly captured Dani's eye: the woman standing erectly front and center.

She was not tall, but seemed it. Chestnut hair lit with a copper sheen fell around her shoulders to her waist. Her skin was a dusky golden brown, her eyes chocolate, her dark lips full. Her high cheekbones and brow were that of a warrior goddess's, or so Dani imagined.

She was dressed in a hip-length tunic and leggings of some rippling material in a rich rust that shimmered with gold threads. The loose-fitting leggings tapered at her ankles and a wide belt of copper, set with saffron-colored gems, encircled her waist.

As Dani watched, she glanced away from talking with another humanoid on her bridge and directly—or so it seemed—into Dani's eyes. Danielle Artemis Forrest was smitten. Whoever this goddess was, she couldn't wait to hear her explanation of what she was doing in this lonely segment of Coalition space, so near the Free Sector.

Mouneera's troubled voice interrupted Dani's musings. "Captain, I'm having trouble with my board. I can't seem to hail them."

"Mouneera," Dani swung aggressively on her, "we need to be able to talk to her! What's going on?"

"I can't find the right button!" The pitch of Mouneera's voice ascended alarmingly. Dani started from her chair, plainly annoyed.

"It's where it always is!" Dani raced toward Mouneera's station, but Ma'at reached it first. The lieutenant burst into tears and Ma'at's cool collected voice stopped Dani in her tracks.

"I think we have it under control, Captain."

Ma'at blocked the communications console and stared Dani down.

"Fix it, damn it!" Dani went growling back to her seat. Ma'at whirled and swiftly patched in a hailing frequency to the other ship. Mouneera struggled to gather up her shattered dignity.

"I can take it from here, Commander," she said crisply.

"Very good, Lieutenant." Ma'at moved back to hir station but not before taking a private shaky breath and making a mental note to return to hir research on the *Boadicea* malady. Things had not yet gotten entirely out of hand but they might very soon. S/he had no intention of allowing that to happen.

"Hailing now, Captain," Mouneera's voice rang coldly across the bridge.

"Thank you, Lieutenant Mouneera." Dani was formal. She would have to apologize to Mouneera later. Later, when she felt more in control, and more like her old self. Obviously, whatever was wrong hadn't been helped by Sly's low-impact remedy of brandy and rest.

The warrior goddess and her bridge still shown larger than life on the *Boadicea* viewscreen. When Mouneera's hail reached them, the woman and her crew visibly twitched. Dani guessed they had been unaware of *Boadicea's* presence.

"Mouneera, are we on their viewscreen?"

"We're transmitting a visual image, Captain. I believe they're receiving it." It was Ma'at who answered.

Dani shrugged and proceeded. "Greetings." She began her usual formal spiel. "This is Captain Danielle Artemis Forrest of the *U.C.S.S. Boadicea*, United Coalition of Star Systems. Who are you?"

"Greetings in return, Captain Danielle Artemis Forrest," answered the richly-timbered voice of the warrior goddess. "I am Captain Bajana Ki of the I.S.A. *Heaven's Bow*."

Well, that explained the archer on the ship's hull, Dani thought. What a beautiful name for something that sailed the skies. "Captain," she continued, "you are within Coalition space. What is your origin and mission?"

"We are on a peaceful exploratory mission, Captain Danielle Artemis Forrest. We mean no harm to your...Coalition. We were not aware we were trespassing on...Coalition space."

Dani felt lulled by her melodic voice. She forced herself to concentrate. "You're not from a Coalition planet?"

The foreign captain shook her head, sending her hair swirling, and gestured expressively with lithe arms which jangled with gold and copper bracelets. "This is the first we've heard of the Coalition. We are from twin planets that orbit the star Dayauus."

"Mouneera," Dani ordered, "auditory off. Ma'at?"

"It is possible, Captain," Ma'at said, "that their solar system lies farther away in the Sagittarius Arm of the galaxy, in a sector of space unexplored by the Coalition. If that is the case, this could be the ship we're looking for. It is similar in design to a Coalition vessel and it would have had to cross a narrow sliver of Khrar space to have arrived at its present location."

"Thank you, Ma'at. The captain is so forthcoming, I think I'll just inquire."

Ma'at raised both eyebrows but said nothing to dissuade hir superior officer.

"Mouneera, hail them again."

"Hailing, Captain. Please proceed."

"Captain Ki, the Coalition has received a report of a rogue ship destroying a Khrar Predator. Can you provide any information about this incident? It occurred in a nearby sector of space that you may have recently crossed."

"What is a 'Predator', Captain?"

Dani frowned. Either this warrior goddess captain was very clever or from very far away.

"A Khrar warship," she responded tartly.

"Khrar?"

"The Khrar Empire borders Coalition space, although there is a Free Sector established by treaty between the two powers. If you come from a more distant arm of this galaxy, Captain, you would have had to pass through both to reach your present location."

There was a hurried, inaudible discussion between Captain Ki and one of her associates, a four-armed humanoid like that of the archer on the hull. Ki faced Dani again.

"Captain Danielle Artemis Forrest—"

"Captain Forrest is a sufficient appellation, Captain Ki."

"Captain Forrest," she repeated and against her will, parts of Dani tingled at the way the other woman's voice sang her name, "we encountered a ship several solar days ago. He engaged us in battle. We are new in space and we made the mistake of destroying the ship. I have confined my helmsman to quarters."

Dani didn't need to turn to feel her first officer's astonishment. "Auditory off, Mouneera. Ma'at, what do you make of it?"

Ma'at let out an audible breath. "Convincing in its forthright simplicity, Captain."

"I should believe her then? That she doesn't know our ways and just 'made a mistake'?"

"As I said, Captain, convincing. There is only one 'fly in the ointment' as you would say."

"What's that, Ma'at?"

"I have taken readings of the *Heaven's Bow's* crew. Some of the readings are alien. Aliens, in fact, for which we have no data."

"Then she's telling the truth."

"Except," Ma'at went on, "the woman you are speaking with is a human."

"Humanoid," Dani corrected automatically.

"No, Captain. Human."

Dani did not move for a long moment. "Crew complement?" she finally asked.

"I can't determine with absolute accuracy but gauging from present readings and ship size, probably as little as thirty crew aboard."

Dani leaned forward to ease the tangled knot of pain in her empty stomach which, like the ache in her calves, was growing worse.

"Could a woman like that be so ruthless as to destroy a Predator and then just bald-facedly tell me she did it? The *Boadicea* is more than ten times her size. What's her game, Ma'at?"

Ma'at shook hir head. "I don't know."

"Auditory please, Mouneera," Dani ordered.

"Auditory on, Captain."

"Captain Ki," Dani raised her voice to assure the other woman's attention, "as I stated earlier you are an unknown vessel trespassing on Coalition space. I must have time to investigate your...eh, claims. In the meantime, you are under 'house arrest'."

"Captain Forrest," that sweet smooth voice flowed back to caress her ears, "what exactly does that mean?"

"It means you should maintain your current orbit, Captain. We will join you in that orbit. And, you are not to go anywhere else. Understood?"

"Understood. However, I have already sent an investigatory team to the planetoid's surface. What about them?"

"I will guarantee them safe passage to return to your ship, but no funny business. Do you understand?"

"Of course, Captain." She looked vaguely hurt and Dani felt a tugging at her heartstrings and parts farther south. Clearly it had been far too long since she'd indulged herself with another living, breathing woman.

She sternly reminded herself that, at the very least, this woman was an independent entrepreneur—a pirate in less euphemistic terms—and, at worst, a spy or a scout for someone, possibly even the Khrar Empire. Did she have a score to settle with the Commander of the *Star Spawn* and so had blown him away?

Although 'Inter-Solar Alliance' and 'Captain' Ki had a military ring to it, she had noted no rank insignia on Captain Ki's or her crew's dress. In fact, her bridge crew all wore different colors. Dani had seen Coalition merchant ships with more uniformity of garb.

The captain's pretended innocence had been a dream of a

performance. If Dani had been watching her on stage she would now be whistling and shouting 'Brava, brava!'.

"Communications off, Mouneera."

"Aye, sir."

"Why is she orbiting this planetoid and why has she sent a team down there? What does she know about this planetoid that we don't know, Ma'at?"

Ma'at patiently reviewed hir science console readings. "The planetoid may have enjoyed a lush tropical climate in the distant past as its current sandy wasteland is underlain by extensive coal deposits. More significantly, there is a sporadic but intensive distribution of bauxite containing rich caches of aluminum oxides."

"Aluminum oxides?"

"Corundum, Captain. In everyday terms, rubies and sapphires."

"Rubies and sapphires," Dani said. "Well, that explains a lot." Unhappily for Dani, it cinched her suspicions about Captain Ki. The warrior goddess clearly cared for beauty and seemed capable of dropping big bucks on it.

"And here, as in some places on Earth," Ma'at exposited, "almost laying about for the taking. Large-scale or expensive extraction methods would not be required to—"

"—make a massive fortune in a very short time," Dani finished for hir. "Are there life readings on the planetoid?"

"Yes, Captain." It was DeVargas who spoke up. "Mickites, Ectosians, Humans—"

"You're joking," Dani said.

"No, Captain."

"What else?"

"Some unidentified alien life forms."

"Ma'at," Dani swung once again in her seat, "I think it's time we carried out our own planetary investigation."

"Captain, if I may—"

"Ma'at, don't argue with me. I'm going." She struggled out of her chair. Her calves felt heavier than lead and the pain in her belly radiated through her torso. Ma'at stood and laced hir hands behind hir back in hir most customary pose. "I'm afraid, Captain, I have very little choice but to argue with you."

"On what grounds?"

"Shortly before I returned to the bridge, Captain, we lost a crewman to heart attack."

Dani would have tumbled backward if she had not been gripping the arm of her chair to steady herself. She felt like throwing up at the same time she knew there was nothing in her stomach.

"Who? And why wasn't I told?"

"Crewman Arthur Exeter Madison. And you were not in

any...condition to be told."

"Ma'at," Dani's voice was savage, "don't take my command from me!" The very walls of the bridge seemed to rock with this pronouncement. Even Ma'at looked shaken by the ferocity that Dani directed at hir.

"Whatever this is," Dani's voice was only slightly more controlled, "I'm not going to let it conquer me."

"Dani—" Ma'at made a tentative step forward.

"Alright, Ma'at, for chrissake! You lead the landing party for me. Take some security people. Find out what's going on down there and then report back as quickly as possible."

Ma'at stood paralyzed as though strung between loyalties. "Very well, Captain," s/he said. "We will make all due haste."

Dani nodded weakly, refraining from an overwhelming desire to grip her stomach. She did not want to alarm her first officer any more than Ma'at was already alarmed.

"Are you sure you—"

"I will manage just fine, Ma'at. I'm surrounded by 250 able officers and crew. Nothing can go wrong."

"On my way, then."

"And, Ma'at—" Dani's reptilian nightmare rose before her eyes.

"Yes, Captain?"

"Avoid reptiles."

Ma'at frowned. "Captain?"

"Go. Just go."

Ma'at left. Dani fell into her chair and gave into her desire to wrap her arms tightly around her stomach. She stayed that way for a very long time.

Chapter
Six

WHEN MA'AT AND hir security team of two materialized on the sandy surface of the planetoid near the *Heaven's Bow's* slim silver shuttlecraft, s/he reached automatically for hir sensor array. It wasn't there. S/he felt a second time, taking care to look. Regrettably, looking failed to cause it to appear. Hir security team, both women, stood with syn-guns drawn, watching hir.

"Commander?" Ensign Eluthea Martinez questioned.

"My sensor array," Ma'at answered, "In my haste, I overlooked it."

"Should we send for one, sir?" Ensign Cindy Samson asked.

Ma'at gazed at the empty sands. Far off on the southeastern horizon, towering thunderclouds reared over a low range of mountains. The life forms DeVargas had scanned should be ahead to the northeast where a cluster of upthrust rocks concealed an oasis or canyon. They would not be out here in the blinding heat. The area around the shuttlecraft was deserted.

"No," Ma'at said, "let's do our job quickly and get back to the *Boadicea.*"

Both women nodded their assent.

"Proceed with caution."

"Very good, sir." As a group they made their way toward the rock outcropping. Ma'at reasoned they would be able to approach without being noticed, scout out any questionable activities on the part of the *Heaven's Bow's* landing party and report back to *Boadicea* without wasting a great deal of time or energy.

At least that's what Ma'at intended. They hadn't reached the rock outcropping before a mismatched band of men, sporting weapons of one kind or another, materialized from behind a dune they'd already passed and ambushed them.

If a Nhavan could be said to kick hirself, Ma'at did. Not so much for forgetting the sensor array as for not remedying the problem as soon as s/he was aware of it. It was too late for self-recrimination, however. Hir security people were forced to hand over their syn-guns and transcons and Ma'at too, though s/he lacked a weapon, was subjected to an inexperienced body search by a slip of a boy.

The boy lifted Ma'at's transcon high in the air with a whoop of triumph and the leader of the band, a pudgy bald-headed human, strode up and greedily pocketed it.

"This one's a Nhawan, 'e is," the leader said in broken Coalition Patois to the boy. "See, e's got tits and a dick, too."

The boy blushed red and backed away.

"Who are you?" Ma'at demanded. "And these others?" S/he gestured at the surrounding bedraggled lot. Ma'at knew not responding as a victim was the first psychological rule in this kind of scenario.

"Don't be a'pointin'," the leader snarled. "I might get nervous. My old syn-gun ain't set to stun. The stun's broke, see."

Ma'at dropped hir arm to hir side, forcing hirself to pretend to a calm s/he didn't feel. "My question remains unanswered."

"Probly's goin' to fer a long time."

There was a nervous giggle from the boy who was staring at Ma'at with guilty interest and a titter of amusement from the band. The leader gestured with the impaired syn-gun at the rock outcropping toward which Ma'at and hir security detail had been heading.

"Move it," he ordered. Ma'at and hir company complied. While they hiked across the hot clinging sand, s/he assessed the armed party out of the corner of hir eye. There were seven in all. Five humans, including the bald leader and the boy, one Mickite and one Ectosian. On the whole, they seemed like human societal outcasts: men who'd gone to seed and taken to less acceptable modes of making a living. Ma'at wasn't certain what that mode might be but, factoring in the mineral resources of the planetoid, s/he could guess.

Despite their lackluster air, Ma'at was careful not to underestimate their potential for violence. Their arsenal was ill-assorted and out of date but deadly enough. Although only the leader had carried a syn-gun at the outset, the two other humans had dropped their knives back into their nylon thigh sheaths in favor of the new syn-guns from the *Boadicea's* security people. The Mickite needed no weapon: his species's belligerence and strength was well-know. The emaciated Ectosian was unarmed and the human boy skipped along with nothing.

The remaining human was the one who most concerned Ma'at. Of the group, he was the least careless in his manner and walked with the centered air of a martial arts master. He wore a black robe and carried no weapon, which only served to heighten Ma'at's suspicions.

Shortly, they walked between red-grey towers of weathered bauxite and were plunged into the contrasting cool shade of a desert canyon. The gap widened into a flat protected area. A few spindly palm trees, offering little shade, reared taller than the surrounding rocks.

A hand-dug well, lined with the bauxite, occupied the center of a grouping of circular huts. The huts had been roughly constructed of the lumpy stones, the roofs thatched with the palm. There were gaping holes in the dried-out thatch.

Off to one side, a large florescent canopy had been erected. It cast an incongruous pink shade on the sand beneath it. Under the canopy sat workbenches and tools. Beside them were stacks of supply boxes and a squat square object that Ma'at thought might be a kiln. A giant mound of coal chunks was heaped behind it. Ma'at recalled that heating sapphires and rubies enhanced their brilliant colors and hence, their market value.

Sitting on the rim of the well, guarded by another Mickite, this one holding a metal baseball bat, were five humanoids. Ma'at assumed they were the crew of the *Heaven's Bow's* shuttlecraft. There were three women. They could almost pass for humans except for what looked like the fluting of gills at the sides of their necks and what appeared to be webbing between their fingers. Two dark-skinned and dark-haired human males sat beside them, nearest to the armed Mickite.

"Greetings." A female voice pronounced. Ma'at didn't see any of the women open their mouth to speak. "Greetings." the female voice repeated. Ma'at looked more carefully. There were no women in evidence except the three at the well and none of them had spoken.

A large man with flaming red hair, accompanied by an even larger black man, exited one of the huts to Ma'at's right. He strode forward and surveyed this new batch of prisoners.

"Quite a lot of visitors for one day," he commented acidly. Fists on his hips, he paced between the two groups.

"A Nhavan," he remarked, seeing Ma'at. "Nhavans are dangerous."

Ma'at did nothing to acknowledge the comment but s/he felt the menace tighten around hir. In front of hir at the well was the bat-wielding Mickite. Behind hir stood the martial arts master.

"Name?" the man said.

"Lieutenant Commander Ma'at, First Officer, *U.C.S.S. Boadicea.*"

"*Boadicea.* I've heard of it," the man's voice was sarcastic. "Minority Fleet. Bunch of queens and bull dykes and in-betweeners like yourself."

He shouted at the leader of the gang that had captured Ma'at. "Powwow time, Jasper. In my hut. Bring the transcons." He strode away.

"Guard 'em," Jasper ordered, though he said it to no one in particular, and then waddled after the big man.

"WHY IN HELL hasn't Ma'at reported?" Dani slammed the

transmitter button on the arm of her chair. "Ma'at," she yelled, "can you hear me? Ma'at, answer!"

DeVargas shifted nervously in his seat and stole a glance over his shoulder at his captain. Something was wrong with Forrest. DeVargas had never seen her so wild, so irrational.

Forrest was cool-headed under stress. It was what made her such a successful leader. But DeVargas didn't see that now. He saw a woman with frenzied eyes and clenched jaw inhabiting the captain's seat. He turned back to his post but not before an involuntary shiver raced up his spine. Forrest...mad?

To his and the captain's mutual surprise, there was the beep of an incoming transmitter contact and DeVargas experienced a flood of relief. That would be Ma'at, cool and controlled, capable of handling any situation.

"What the—" A gruff electronically-transmitted voice was interrupted by a high whine and a mumble of voices. A loud 'thwack' followed and what sounded like branches scraping across the transmitter's sensitive voice screen.

"Give me the goddamn thing!" The voice was so loud on the bridge, DeVargas instinctively scrunched his shoulders around his head to protect his ears.

There were a few experimental clicks, then a voice said, "Alright, hey, who's there?"

Dani grimaced. "This is Captain Danielle Artemis Forrest of the *U.C.S.S. Boadicea.* Who is this?"

"What?"

DeVargas could have sworn he heard Forrest curse in Khrar before she said with forced patience: "You have to let go of the transmitter button to hear us and hold it down to speak." Then, wearily, she repeated her name and the name of her ship.

"*Boadicea,* eh? Well, well. Not the glory of Minority Fleet itself? And her wonder girl captain? You know, if you want to come down, I'm sure we could cure your little sexuality problem."

Dani ground her teeth and forced herself to remain silent. She didn't like being baited twice in two days. If she heard such garbage once more, she was going to retire. The voice, apparently unconcerned with her silence, went on. "We've got some of your people down here, Forrest. A Nhavan, some humans, and some webbed-fingered types."

Dani exhaled in relief. Ma'at was alive and where there was life there was hope. "Who are you and what do you want?"

"My friends call me Rusty. My original name is no concern of yours. What I want is this nice little shuttlecraft you sent your people down to the surface in."

"Shuttlecraft?"

"The *Lithe Arrow* I'm told. Pretty little name. Come on, Forrest, let's not pretend innocence."

Lithe Arrow was a pretty name, she agreed silently. The woman it belonged to was also pretty. The thought was a wistful one. Dani was as likely to be duty-bound to take Captain Ki back to Coalition Headquarters in irons as make love to her.

"Of course not," she responded to Rusty's dig. Obviously Rusty thought Ma'at's team and Captain Ki's team were together. Which meant Bajana Ki might not be in cahoots with this gang on the planet, unless they'd had a falling out or were staging this little negotiation as a smokescreen so she would think exactly that.

"Let me just consult with my people and we will let you know our terms."

"Your terms?" Rusty's voice was incredulous.

"Our terms, Rusty." Dani's voice was heavy. "Try not to forget that I have enough firepower to blow your whole planetoid away. Not my first choice but not impossible either. Forrest out."

"COMMANDER MA'AT."

It was the voice again. Ma'at looked to each side but could see no one voice hir name. No one else seemed aware that anyone had spoken. The faces of hir captors had not altered.

If hearing voices was a symptom of the *Boadicea* ailment, no one aboard had reported it. Ma'at looked forward and, quite accidentally, into the eyes of the youngest female perched on the well. Her gaze was one of great intensity.

Ma'at twisted hir head to look over hir shoulder but there was nothing the woman could be observing behind Ma'at with such fervor. She had to be looking at hir and...she was the one communicating with hir. Extraordinary, Ma'at thought, a distance telepath. Unfortunately, the limit of hir own gift was touch telepathy. Nonetheless, s/he signaled hir response to the other woman's call by raising an eyebrow.

A constrained smile lit the alien female's face. "Thank you," she said into Ma'at's mind. Ma'at tilted hir head in acknowledgment.

"I have a plan," she said. "Listen carefully."

Her plan was that when she gave the signal by pulling at her ear, Ma'at was to take out the unarmed Mickite at hir right, while the woman's two male security people rushed their armed Mickite. The elderly ladies would take down the boy, who was to Ma'at's left.

She telegraphed her hope that Ma'at's two security people would be alert enough to jump the three men guarding them—the large black man had gone over to join the powwow with the other two humans—before they figured out how to use the stolen syn-guns.

"Our advantage is surprise," she told Ma'at. "If we can avoid killing, that would be best."

Ma'at could hardly disagree on that point. It was hir preference as well. They did have a temporary advantage in numbers, and their guards might react more slowly to attack in the absence of their leaders. It was not unreasonable to attempt to get the upper hand while the leaders conferred at a distance and before decisions regarding their fate were made.

Ma'at signaled hir assent to the plan with a light nod of hir head. The female lifted her chin in response and with a sweeping glance gathered the attention of her crew. When they were poised and at the ready, she reached, seemingly idly, for her ear.

It was then that all hell broke loose. Ma'at sidestepped and choked the Mickite, who crumpled soundlessly to the ground. Miraculously, or as the result of long training, the *Boadicea's* security people swung about to take out the guards behind them.

Out of the corner of hir eye, Ma'at saw the Ectosian run away past the huts and heard the boy shriek as the two ladies tackled him. S/he could also hear the shouting of the two leaders, alerted by the scuffle.

The *Boadicea's* security people engaged in hand-to-hand combat with their three guards. Ma'at heard the whine of syn-gun fire and the anguished howl of one of the women. S/he didn't have time to help her. Hir attention was focused on the martial arts master who was advancing on hir with an unflappable smile. The man came to a stop in the sand.

Ma'at waited for him to make the first move so s/he could gauge his level of skill. It must have been high. S/he couldn't recall when s/he had seen such manic confidence in a fighter before a fight was engaged. Particularly against a Nhavan. Sabi maybe. And Sabi was deadly.

Ma'at didn't have to wait long. The man played one of the oldest tricks in the book. He crouched and threw a handful of sand into Ma'at's eyes. Ma'at's hands went instinctively to hir face and s/he felt and heard, but never saw, a blow of deadly force that connected with hir jaw and sent hir spinning into unconsciousness.

"GET ME THE *Heaven's Bow*," Dani ordered Mouneera.

"Yes, Captain." Mouneera triggered buttons on her board and the bridge of the *Heaven's Bow* appeared — without difficulty this time — on the *Boadicea's* viewscreen. Captain Ki was perched in her command chair with her head turned to the side conversing with one of her crew. Dani tried not to notice the aristocratic perfection of her profile.

"Captain Ki," Dani said and saw the woman's head swing

about, startled.

"Who's that?" she demanded.

"Forrest here. Of the *Boadicea*."

"Oh. Hello, Captain."

Dani thought again that it was far too long since she'd had shore leave. Captain Ki's silky voice and warm smile shouldn't make her core melt like butter every time she had dealings with her. Sly would tease her that it was downright unseemly. And Sly would be right. She decided to get down to business.

"Captain, a little problem has developed on the surface of the planetoid we're orbiting."

"Problem? What problem?"

Dani couldn't decide if the foreign captain just loved to play naive or really was. "Your crew hasn't contacted you?"

"Of course not. They're supposed to do some exploring, pick up some samples of vegetation, rocks, sand, that sort of thing. They won't call in until they've returned to the shuttlecraft."

"Don't they have transcons?"

"What's a transcon?"

If she was playing naive, Dani thought, she was awfully good at it. She quickly scanned the other ship's bridge. It looked so much like her own, but smaller and with a more hand-crafted look to it. Instead of metal, the railings appeared to be of a finely polished wood. She would have sworn it was teak.

Obviously, the ship was of comparable technology to the Coalition. In fact, the design was so much like a Coalition one she couldn't believe it hadn't been built in the Coalition. By someone willing and able to spend a lot of money on the fine decorative details. How could Captain Ki not know what a basic piece of equipment, like a transcon, was?

Damn, but Dani wanted her to be as innocent as she looked. Instead, she couldn't keep from drawing the conclusion that she was one of the smoothest, most convincing liars she'd ever met. She felt a hardness come into his chest and throat. Two could definitely play at Captain Ki's game and she had no intention of being beaten at it.

"Captain Ki, my people and your people have been captured on that little planetoid by some other group of people. They have contacted me using one of our transcons and they want your shuttlecraft in exchange for releasing our people."

"Captured? Luluai and the doctors and the security team? Oh, no! By whom?"

"Well, Captain, I was hoping you could shed some light on the 'by whom'."

Captain Ki sat in stunned silence and stared back at her. Dani could almost see the emotions move across her face. First confusion, then disbelief, then a narrowing of her eyes. She leaned toward Dani, no smile or soft eyes in evidence.

"All I know, Captain Forrest, is what you're telling me. How, come to think of it, do I know you're not lying to me in order to steal my shuttlecraft? Have you captured my crew?"

Dani felt like someone had punched her in the stomach. The blow was a complete surprise. "Ho!" Her breath escaped in an astonished whoosh. "Lying! Holy goddess, woman! Who's bluffing whom here? No transcons! You don't know what's going on down on the planet's surface? How do you expect me to believe that?"

Captain Ki's eyes went wide but Dani ignored her reaction. She painfully raised herself out of her command chair and pointed a menacing finger at her.

"Just understand one thing, Captain, I'm not fooled. I can see through the acting job. Just don't stretch my credulity much farther, okay? I've already had enough."

"What are you saying? I haven't—"

"I said I've had enough, Captain. Forrest out!" The viewscreen went blank at Dani's command. Dani collapsed back into her chair and wrapped her arms around her stomach again.

"Captain! They've disappeared!" DeVargas trumpeted.

"Who's disappeared?"

"The security team. Their life readings have vanished."

"What! What about Ma'at?" A sharp pain seared Dani's chest. It was an adrenaline rush born of fear. And fear was not a usual emotion for her. But this wasn't exactly a good time to be losing Ma'at. But then, she chided himself, what could possibly be a good time?

"No...I have a Nhavan reading, very faint. There's some kind of electrical interference, Captain. I can't tell if it's the ship's equipment or if it's being generated on the planetoid. I don't detect readings for Ensign Samson and Ensign Martinez."

"Mouneera, lock on to Ma'at's coordinates and get hir back here!"

Mouneera ran her hands rapidly across her communications console and found the coordinates of Ma'at's transcon. "Captain," she reported, "First Officer Ma'at is not at the coordinates for hir transcon. I can't get a lock on hir."

"Damn," Dani swore. "What about the security team's transcons?"

"Their transcons are at the same coordinates as Ma'at's. But, as DeVargas said, there are no detectable life readings for either of them. I can't tell if it's interference of some kind or if they're just not there."

Dani was in full flight to the doors of the kinelift. From there she issued a stream of orders. "Mouneera, drum me up a security team and find Doctor Jenks. Have them meet me in the briefing room on the double. And bring yourself."

"Aye, Captain."

"Mr. DeVargas, keep trying to raise Ma'at. We don't know if or when s/he will get hir transcon back. You have the conn."

"Aye, Captain."

BAJANA SHOOK WITH rage. She had not only been openly accused of deceit in front of her bridge crew, but Forrest had cut her off before she'd even started to say what she felt like saying to her.

She paced at full boil across her bridge, head bent in angry review of the exchange. Sukha stood nearby, watching her.

"I'm so angry," she railed through clenched teeth, "I could spit."

"So why don't you?" Sukha suggested.

She turned ferociously on him. "What gives you the right to laugh at me or take her side?" She flung her head toward the blank viewscreen and her loose hair flew across her back.

With his aura of calm forbearance, Sukha was already having the effect of dissipating the massive head of steam she'd built up. It annoyed her all the more. She wasn't ready to let it dissipate.

"I am not laughing, Bajana."

"Then what—"

"Whoever these beings are, Captain, we are currently moored here under their thumbs. Anger will not change that."

Bajana subsided into her command chair. "I still don't like it."

"Nor do I," Sukha said. "But look at the facts. We are in their space."

"So?"

"So, at least until we know what is going on, we should behave as proper guests would behave in the home of a difficult host."

Bajana's mouth curled with distaste. She felt like a child again, with Sukha's logic leading her unrelentingly to the conclusion he intended her to reach.

"They must out-man and out-gun us ten or more to one. We need to use our wits in these encounters not our infinitesimal brawn."

That stung, Bajana thought, but she conceded that she deserved it. She got up and started to pace again.

"However," Sukha went on, "the most significant factor we must take into account, Bajana, is that our people are trapped on that planetoid. We have no way to rescue them as we have only one shuttlecraft so we must rely on the good will of this Forrest to help us negotiate with the captors."

"How did they get down to the planet?" Curiosity

overshadowed Bajana's anger.

"Who?"

"Captain Forrest's crew. The crew she claims is down there and also captive."

"Their own shuttlecraft?"

"But then the captors would have spoken of two craft. Why negotiate for one when you can have two?"

"Perhaps they only need one."

"No. I think Forrest is lying."

"About what?"

"About the whole thing. It's some kind of trap, Sukha! Don't you see?"

"What kind of trap? We can't possibly have anything Forrest would want."

"Nachi!" Bajana ignored Sukha and spun around looking for her navigator. "We need to—"

Strangely, Nachiketas Buono was nowhere in sight on the bridge. He had been there just a few minutes previously. She made a mental note to reprimand him for leaving his post.

"Bajana, think this out," Sukha tried again, "How did the captors get hold of whatever one of these communications devices is so they could contact the *Boadicea* if they didn't take it from the *Boadicea* people by force?"

"Oh, hell, Sukha! The whole thing was staged."

The Shivani would have characteristically crossed his double set of arms in thought except for the immobility of the pair held in place with splints and a wrapping of herbs. The dressing was starting to stink and needed to be changed. Unfortunately the doctors were not aboard.

"For the sake of argument, I will concede the point," Sukha responded, "but why stage such a farce?"

"I don't know. That madwoman is out to get me."

"That isn't much of a motive."

"I know." She sat down again and put her chin in her hands. "But don't you think she's a little crazy? Her eyes, her pallor—"

"We don't have a control group by which to judge what is normal eyes and pallor for these beings."

"True, but I feel something in my gut."

To her surprise, Sukha agreed with her. "I do too, Bajana. But it is not a sensation of malice. Rather of something wrong, something out of whack."

"Hrumph," Bajana grunted.

"But I'm more concerned about you. This being is doing a good job of making you act crazy."

He had never let on but his greatest worry in her teenaged years had been that, like all Brahuinna, she would 'fall in love' and he would lose her to the biological urges of her race. He had wisely accepted that it would be useless to prevent such a happening and so he had merely anticipated the inevitable.

But it had not come to pass. Bajana's awakening had been late and then it moved steadily, not with the wild abandon to sex hormones that Shivani had come to expect from the Brahuinna. She had sought out the company of Brahuinna women and men when she choose and then always, to his relief, come home and returned to her work.

Was this Danielle Artemis Forrest going to be different? Except for the lighter skin coloring, Forrest looked to Sukha like a Brahuinna. Why she should look like a Brahuinna was a conundrum Sukha had not had time to puzzle out.

"Sukha, that's not fair," Bajana said.

"Love affairs are your private business," Sukha returned. "Ensuring they don't disrupt your performance as captain is mine."

"Love affairs!" she sputtered. "How could you suggest such a thing?"

"Bajana, your reaction to this being is extreme."

"It's hate, Sukha! Not love!"

"One can transform into the other more easily than non-interest can become either."

"This being is an enemy."

"An opponent in the field of relatives perhaps, but no being is an enemy. You should be wary of any being who makes you lose your perspective." Sukha's voice had the hardness of steel.

Bajana would not have taken this from anyone but Sukha, her father. Her mouth had gone dry and she struggled to steady her voice.

"Father, I assure you I have not lost my perspective or my control. My job is to defend this ship and rescue our crew. I will do whatever is necessary to accomplish those ends."

"Short of violence?"

"Of course. Violence is what has gotten us into this mess."

She rose from her seat and bowed formally to him. "If you will take the helm until I can locate Nachi?"

"Of course, Daughter." Sukha moved to Bajana's command chair. "As always," he said, "I respect your ability to handle this crisis in your usual cool-headed manner." It was his way of soothing over the hard words.

"Thank you, Father." They bowed to each other again and then Bajana Ki entered the exit spiral. In its privacy, she muttered to herself that Sukha could believe whatever he wanted. Cool-headed or some other way, she was going to get Danielle Artemis Forrest.

Revenge, after all, didn't have to be violent.

"DANI, YOU CAN'T do this!"

"Sly," Dani said, "you know I can do anything I damn well please."

"Not this, Dani." Sly paused in his stalking to scowl at Dani.

"Whatever is so wrong with de-materializing down to the planet, Sly? It's not like we haven't done this sort of thing before." Dani leaned forward in her chair and laced her hands together on the table.

"You're not well."

"Okay, I'm tired, I'm achy. I'm feeling better though," she lied.

"That isn't all, Dani."

"You've discovered something?"

"No, I haven't made any progress with this disease," Sly flung his arm in frustration, "or whatever it is, but—"

"What the hell is the matter, Sly?"

"We lost a crewman to heart attack, Dani. A young, healthy crewman."

"When? Why wasn't I told?"

"Captain," Mouneera interrupted, "you were told. Commander Ma'at mentioned it just before—"

"That's enough, Mouneera! Of course, I remember." Dani sprang out of her seat and paced away from them. Sly cocked his head at Mouneera, the question in his mind written plainly across his dark frowning face. Mouneera raised her eyebrows but didn't have time to speak before Dani paced her way back.

"So, Sly, what is it? What is this illness?"

"The autopsy shows Crewman Madison died of biventricular myocardial failure, Dani. He had advanced pulmonary edema. But I don't know what caused it."

Dani leaned her hands on the back of a chair and regarded her Chief Surgeon. "Sly, you're the best doctor in the Fleet."

Sly shook his head. "I've never seen anything like this, Dani. Everyone's affected differently. Some crew people are just grumpy, some have slowed reflexes, some are having memory problems," he gave Dani a hooded look, "some don't seem bothered at all. Remember Yeoman Candy Vasquez?"

"The one just getting over that bout with Precullian fever?"

"Yes. She's over the fever but I hadn't certified her fit to return to duty yet. Now she's suffering from hallucinations and is back in the infirmary."

"You'll figure it out, Sly."

"Vasquez won't make it if I don't figure it out soon. But until I do, Dani, I don't want you traipsing off to god knows where trying to rescue Ma'at."

"I'm not just rescuing Ma'at. I have to find out what that woman on the *Heaven's Bow* is up to. I'm trying to prevent an interstellar war here, Sly. She's at the heart of this intrigue with the Khrars and whatever is going on down on that planetoid. I intend to find out what it is. So, I'm going."

"No!" Sly's fist slammed the table.

"Sly, look. I'll have three security people with me and one medical tech fitted up with almost as much medical gear as you have in your surgery."

"I don't like it."

"We won't even be gone for more than, say, half an hour." Dani produced her best snake charmer smile.

Sly equivocated. Maybe a short jaunt was exactly what the captain needed. Maybe she needed to get this woman off her mind. But what Mouneera had revealed unsettled him. How could the death of a crewman slip Dani's mind?

"Sly, we'll take every precaution." Dani observed the doctor's hesitation and was clinching the sale. She would go anyway but she preferred to have Sly's blessing.

"Alright, Dani, but if you aren't back in an hour, I'm hauling you back no matter where you are." Sly laid his palms flat on the table and glowered at her. "And don't think I won't do it."

"Just the kind of quality decision-making I'd expect from the officer I'm leaving in charge." Dani grinned maniacally, snatched up her sensor array and, in a twinkle, was out the door.

Sly exchanged dismayed glances with Mouneera.

"Cripes," he bellowed, "now she's positively jolly."

MA'AT AWOKE TO the sound of a thumping beat. Disoriented, it took hir awhile to comprehend that the measured drumming was someone cuffing hir, first on one cheek and then the other.

Ma'at opened hir eyes. The physical pounding stopped but the swirling sensation in hir head did not. S/he was on hir knees with hir hands tied behind hir back. Someone behind hir was supporting hir body.

Jasper glared at hir in annoyance. "The queer's awake, Rusty," he said. "Finally."

Ma'at inferred it had taken some sustained hitting to bring hir around. The big man with the red hair came from behind Jasper.

"Very clever, Commander Ma'at, your little maneuver," Rusty complimented ironically, "but essentially unsuccessful. You'll notice you've lost some people."

Ma'at surveyed to the right and left. Twisting hir head made hir jaw pound and brought a wave of nausea into hir throat. The young telepathic female, hands also tied behind her back, knelt on Ma'at's right and the old ladies on her left. Ma'at's security women and the *Heaven's Bow's* security men were not in evidence. S/he had to take Rusty's word that they were dead.

Rusty spoke again. "As two of my best men were killed in this ridiculously unnecessary skirmish, the group has decided that you will pay with your lives. This, I would like to point out, is not my first choice, as I would rather exchange you for that charming little shuttlecraft. However, I was out-voted."

Rusty regarded the tight faces and resolutely crossed arms of his men, who enclosed the kneeling captives like the sharpened pales of a fort. Keeping the peace in a gang of half-violent ne'er-do-wells was never an easy task. Leopardi, who had lost his twin brother Roland in the fight, was particularly volatile.

From long experience, Rusty knew at what point it became self-defeating to countermand the wishes of the mob. He wasn't going to sacrifice his leadership for the sake of a couple of officers from someone else's crew who had, in any event, committed murder.

"Mr. Rusty," the telepathic female spoke up, "do whatever you want with me but please let these elderly sisters go. They should not have to pay for what I have done."

Rusty sniggered. "I hate bloody pleading heroes. However, as I have since learned these old ladies are doctors, I plan to put them to good use."

"As for the two of you, I'm certain you will enjoy the fate this pack of wolves has devised for you. It will be, as they say in all the comic books, long and slow. I'm sure you've figured out by now that we're mining gems —"

"—Ah," murmured Ma'at. It was as s/he had suspected.

"—and we don't have time to waste torturing feckless visitors. But I think you'll find they've come up with the next best thing."

"Luke!" Rusty called. The man who had delivered the blow that sent Ma'at into unconsciousness stepped forward. "I don't want the Nhavan putting up a fight when they tie hir. We don't need any further losses."

Luke grinned sadistically. "My pleasure." He looked Ma'at dead in the eye. "I don't get much opportunity to abuse Nhavans and I can think of so many ways to do it. It's unfortunate we don't have the time."

Ma'at unflinchingly held the man's gaze. Jaw clenched and eyes narrowed, Luke swung the flattened edge of one hand to connect forcefully with Ma'at's temple. Luluai, telepathically linked to hir, perceived Ma'at's attitude of still anticipation...then blinding pain...then blank nothingness.

DANI FORREST WAS not right about being gone half an hour. When she and her team stepped up to the de-materialization discs, they experienced the usual de-matter effect of feeling briefly empty of being, sort of an instant Zen-type of experience. A moment later, they shimmered back into existence and on to the de-matter discs from which they'd started.

Dani demanded a re-try. This time the experience was less pleasant. Dani felt a gripping at her lungs and throat as though they would be torn out of her body. This was followed by a sensation of being in a sea of static electricity. Every hair on her body went rigidly erect, pulling skin and muscle after it. The strung-apart sensation ceased abruptly and she again found herself on the de-matter disc, not having gone anywhere.

Dani charged the mystified de-matter tech. "What the hell's going on?"

"I don't know, sir. It's some kind of calibration problem."

"Goddamn that Niko!" Dani felt limp and sore and nauseated.

"We've had strange equipment malfunctions since the ion storm, sir."

The intercom whistled. Dani impatiently slammed the button.

"What now?" she demanded.

"There's a severe thunderstorm, Captain, in your pre-selected de-mat site. It's too dangerous to materialize into."

"Alright, DeVargas. We'll hold off for the moment."

"Mister," she ranted at the de-matter tech, "get some engineering people up here to fix the de-matter on the double. I want the malfunction solved now! Understood?"

The tech blanched. "Understood, sir."

"We'll try again later. Team dismissed!"

Chapter
Seven

ENSIGN CAITLIN EIREANN took Commander Ma'at's advice to heart. She not only avoided the captain but all other crew as well. The only person she had seen was Doctor Jenks. At his request, she had reported to the infirmary and completed a battery of motor skills tests. She came out with flying colors and, although she expected him to congratulate her, he had just frowned over the results.

Because of his medical background, she had wanted to ask him about making a fool out of herself around Captain Forrest. But he'd been so forbidding and preoccupied she hadn't been able to broach the subject.

After that, she had taken to roaming the ship's corridors at odd hours so she wouldn't run into anyone. She had no official tasks or responsibilities on *Boadicea*. Her skills in linguistics seemed to her like the most useless knowledge in the world.

And just when she most desperately wanted to get off *Boadicea*, she heard about the ship's change in assignment. She was stuck aboard, friendless and at loose ends. Caitlin was sure she was the most despised crewperson in *Boadicea* history.

So what, she thought, staring up at the ceiling of her cabin. She needed to be doing something useful. Hiding in her cabin and sneaking around was starting to drive her mad. Maybe linguistics wasn't as useless as she thought.

Caitlin rolled off her bunk and headed out the door. The *Boadicea's* computers must be rife with languages she hadn't had a chance to study in more than a cursory manner at the Academy. She would invent linguistic research for herself. She might even meet someone friendly in the language lab.

And if she didn't make any friends, what difference would it make? She was already rock bottom in popularity. Things couldn't, after all, get any worse than they already were. Or so she thought.

SOMETHING STUNG MA'AT'S face. It was a cold ticklish sting. Instinctively, s/he raised a hand to wipe it away. Hir arm didn't move. For one shattering moment, s/he thought s/he was paralysed. Then s/he realized hir arm—both arms—were bound to a stake above hir head. S/he was laying on the ground. Experimentally, s/he shifted hir legs. They too were tied in place.

S/he opened hir eyes and rolled hir head to the left, hir jaw aching in protest. Hir temple throbbed ominously where Luke had slammed hir. A steep dune of drifting sand met hir gaze.

The stinging was the first drops of rain falling around hir in the desert. Clever, Ma'at had to admit, crude but clever. Their captors had staked them out and left them to the desert elements. It was an absurdly simple solution to the problem of guarding them. And as a torture intended to punish and kill it had few equals.

Ma'at came from a desert culture. In the rare cases s/he had read of the imposition of such cruelties on Nhavan, the victims had not lasted long.

The rain was building in its intensity. Ma'at felt the drops as needle-sharp jabs against hir chest. It burned when it should not have. Stiffly, s/he lifted hir head. Hir captors had taken hir gold tunic shirt and boots. No doubt they had difficulty tying hir feet securely with hir boots on. But hir tunic? That was mere sadism. S/he wondered if Luke had proposed the idea.

Hir naked torso was a flaming sunburned red. Sunburn rarely afflicted a Nhavan, acclimatized as they were to the intense wavelengths of Nhavan's sun. Of course, walking about without ample covering was not a common practice on Nhavan either.

S/he dropped hir head back to the sand and twisted to look to the right. The movement painfully stretched hir already over-extended arms. A few feet away, Luluai, the telepath from the *Heaven's Bow*, was also staked out. With her fair coloring and light tunic, Ma'at had difficulty making her out against the undifferentiated tan of the sand but s/he didn't think the alien turned at Ma'at's movement. It seemed unlikely she would be dead already. Unlike Ma'at, she was still fully-clothed.

The rain was now a cold hard splattering. In Ma'at's experience, desert storms were rarely placid drizzles like the soft nourishing rains of agricultural areas. They were cloudbursts of raging violence. Ma'at contemplated the sky. The billowing tableau of blue and purple thunderheads flashing with lightning was visually stunning, but potentially deadly.

The full power of the storm moved directly overhead. Rain fell with a thoughtless drenching savagery, the tattoo of sound a deafening pounding. S/he found it difficult to breathe against the unrelenting pressure and no amount of twisting and turning allowed hir to protect hir naked sunburned skin.

The best s/he could do was close hir eyes and turn hir head to one side to keep from drowning. Even so, water flowed into hir nose and mouth. S/he shook hir head repeatedly, gurgling and sputtering.

The deluge slackened and the clouds swept on to dump their

lavish bounty elsewhere. Fortunately, lightning had not struck hir. When the rain slowed to a sparse few drops, s/he turned hir head skyward and opened hir eyes.

The hot air had cooled dramatically with the downpour. Ma'at estimated the temperature had dropped at least 20 degrees Celsius, not an uncommon occurrence. In a desert, there was too little plant growth and air moisture to capture and retain the day's heat.

S/he knew the oncoming night, chasing directly as it would after the cooling storm, would be a far more dangerous form of exposure for hir than the blazing hot afternoon s/he had just unconsciously endured.

Ma'at had less capacity even than a human to resist cold as hir skin and internal organs had evolved to do just the opposite: cool the body and preserve moisture. It was going to require all of hir concentration to maintain a high enough internal body heat to survive the night.

Ma'at heard a soft luxuriant sigh to hir right. S/he rolled hir head to look at Luluai. The female smiled languidly back at hir.

"The rain," she said into Ma'at's mind, "so refreshing."

"You are a creature of the water," Ma'at answered without speaking aloud. S/he had no capacity to transmit thoughts at a distance. If the alien heard hir unspoken answer it would be due to her telepathic abilities, not any Ma'at possessed.

She acknowledged Ma'at's remark with a nod. "Yes. My people are amphibious. I nearly died in the heat but now I feel so much better."

Ma'at dropped hir head back to the wet sand. S/he didn't want the female to know of hir concerns for the night. Then Ma'at heard her in hir mind.

"You are afraid?" she asked. Ma'at thought it was an unusual breach of telepathic etiquette to listen in on hir thoughts. Did the alien feel the gravity of the situation justified the intrusion?

"I'm not afraid," Ma'at said. "For you the heat was more dangerous. For me it's the cold."

"Oh," she said, dismayed. "What can we do?"

"I'm not sure what 'we' can do but I'll attempt to preserve my body heat as best I can."

"I am to blame," Luluai said. "I caused this by proposing the escape attempt."

"You made a sound decision, Commander."

"I'm only a Lieutenant. I failed in this mission. I brought about the death of six beings, and now, we too will die."

"How long have you been in space, Lieutenant?"

"This is our world's first space mission, so everyone is new. We've only been in space for two Shivani years."

"Even taking into account your inexperience, you proposed a viable course of action. If you had not, I would have made clear my opposition when you suggested it."

"But all this death and destruction. It is so foreign to our experience. First that ship Hasitam blew up, and now this."

"Then it's true your ship has not previously encountered Khrars or the Coalition as your captain told Captain Forrest?"

"Yes, of course it's true. Captain Ki does not lie."

"Interesting on both counts," Ma'at said. "In my personal experience I have found that humans lie as a matter of course."

"Humans?"

"Captain Ki is, according to our scanning equipment, a human."

"Scanning equipment?"

"I take it that although your ship resembles a small version of *Boadicea*, you don't have syn-guns, transcons, or scanning equipment."

"I've never heard of these things before, except that Captain Forrest mentioned the transcons, which I concluded must be a hand-held transmission device. I don't think Sukha has any secret technologies on board. We all know our ship backwards and forwards."

"That's extraordinary," Ma'at said. "What occurred while I was unconscious, Lieutenant?"

"There was a lot of discussion on how to torture and kill us." A wave of revulsion accompanied her words as they flowed into Ma'at's mind. Ma'at understood. Not only did the alien female seem unaccustomed to the very idea of violence, but as a distance telepath, her unshielded capacity to experience their captors' barbarous thoughts would have been disconcertingly high.

"I'm sorry, Luluai," Ma'at said, using the alien's name. "Do not continue if it distresses you."

"No. If I talk about it, maybe—" she floundered to a stop.

" —it will haunt you less."

"Yes. At least you understand."

"I am a touch telepath, Luluai. Experiencing others' emotions can be a torment even when they're not violent."

"Okay," she took a deep breath. "They discussed burning us alive in a fire made from that coal. It almost won out but was nixed in the end because it would have meant guarding us till nightfall. They didn't want to build a fire in the heat."

"One would think syn-guns would have been the simplest solution," Ma'at commented, preferring not to think about the fire either.

"Oh, they discussed that at length too. But it was decided they didn't want to waste syn-gun charge in the event of an attack, I suppose by your ship. Also, it did not meet most of the group's view of a sufficiently slow and agonizing punishment for us."

"Anything else?"

"There was an argument between Rusty and Jasper. Your team's transcons disappeared around the same time we were trying to escape. At least, they were missing after the melee was over."

"That sounds like theft. Or sabotage of Rusty's negotiation with the *Boadicea*. Unfortunate."

"I'll say."

The missing transcons and breakdown in negotiations was problematic. It meant *Boadicea* couldn't simply locate hir and de-mat hir back. Despite that, Ma'at could not imagine Captain Forrest failing to institute a rescue mission if it was possible to undertake. At this point in time, Ma'at had no way of knowing how rapidly, or in what direction, the illness aboard *Boadicea* was progressing.

"Were you alert during this staking out? How far are we from their camp?"

"Yes, I was alert," she shuddered, "although I wished I hadn't been. I begged Luke not to take your tunic and sash but he just laughed at me. Their camp is over the dune, past you."

Ma'at looked to hir left. S/he couldn't see the pillars of rock that ringed the miner's camp, or any other indication of their presence.

"We're too low to the ground to see the rocks," Luluai read hir mind, "but the camp is quite close."

"And yet," Ma'at said, dropping hir head back to the damp sand, "we're not guarded."

"I don't think we need to be. They rammed these stakes deep into the ground with some kind of air-powered hammer before they tied us. I thought you were already dead because the noise didn't wake you."

"The blow to my temple must have been...severe."

"I've never seen anyone do anything like that with their bare hands." Luluai shook remembering how her link with Ma'at had blanked out. "That was horrifying. I thought he killed you."

"I'm better now." Ma'at was not lying but s/he knew s/he was exaggerating. S/he experienced a rush of vertigo every time s/he twisted hir neck to look at Luluai.

"Lieutenant, we must do what we can to effect our own escape. Such as trying to work these stakes out of the ground."

"Not to be ungrateful, Commander," Luluai said, "but I hoped you would have a more ingenious suggestion. I've pulled and pulled on these stakes for hours with no result."

The despairing tone of her voice in Ma'at's mind made Ma'at twist once again to look at her. Tears ran down Luluai's cheeks and she stifled a sob. "We will never free ourselves that way, Commander Ma'at."

IT DIDN'T TAKE long for Bajana Ki to gather a few necessities from her cabin and make her way to the *Heaven's Bow's* hangar deck. The shuttlecraft, of course, was gone but there was a smaller craft, *The Chariot*, a rotund workbee intended for short repair jaunts around the exterior of the ship. Bajana knew enough about its capabilities to feel certain it would make it to the planetoid's surface.

She stepped inside the glassed viewing station above the hangar deck and pulled up short. The deck's bay doors were opening and the small workbee craft was taxiing its way out of them. Bajana lunged for the hangar deck's control console and slammed the 'close bay doors' button but she was too late. The little craft skimmed narrowly through the closing doorway and vanished from her sight.

Nachiketas Buono set in a course for the dull brown rock that hung beneath him in space like an over-sized beach ball. Even if he hadn't been too busy maneuvering *The Chariot*, he would never have dared to look back to catch the chagrin of his captain.

There would be time enough for her hurled imprecations at his court-martial. Unless he was successful, of course. Nachi was nothing if not romantic. He was sure the gods governing love were on his side and would aid him in his star-crossed mission. There would never be a court-martial.

RUSTY, JASPER, AND Luke, the security man the miners gave a wide berth to, were already deep in discussion when Corky lifted the decaying pigskin flap screening the open arch of Rusty's hut. As he did, their voices died abruptly away.

There had been a misguided colonizing effort on the planetoid in the 22nd century by a group of celibate religionists. They had brought cereal seed and pigs and were the builders of the stone huts. Ethically opposed to procreation, the people had died off in a generation. Porcine descendants, gone feral, foraged in the rugged mountains to the southeast.

A heavy earth smell rose from the clay floor, which was slick from the late afternoon deluge that had cascaded through the gaping holes in the palm thatch. The dank coolness of the hut, like the stony chill of the mine tunnel, was refreshing after the scorching heat of the desert outdoors.

"Gentlemen, come in." It was Rusty's voice in the half-dark, mellifluous with welcome. Corky was suspicious. The welcome sounded false even though it was meant to put them at ease. It was evident he and Barrrk and Porter had interrupted a more private discussion between Rusty and his top two dragoons.

As soon as they were seated on the floor, Jasper blustered officiously, "Alright, you three, listen up. Rusty here's made a change in plans."

Rusty's head nodded in confirmation, eyeing each of the new arrivals in turn. When he scrutinized him, Corky thought Rusty's grey-green eyes would bore right through him. It was like an examination without words. What in heck was going on?

Corky shot a furtive glance at Porter and Barrrk. Porter seemed to be asleep, which Corky knew he wasn't. It was Porter's way of pretending disinterest and forcing the other party to give away too much in talk. Barrrk, unimaginative to the core, shifted restlessly, waiting to hear what their new orders would be.

Across the hut, Luke sat cross-legged with his spare frame erect against the wall, inscrutable as usual. Luke had the kind of presence that gave Corky the creeps. He felt Luke was watching his every move.

Rusty had finished his silent evaluation. "We have a shuttlecraft now, in case you hadn't noticed."

"Even if *Boadicea* doesn't know we're taking it," Jasper gloated.

Rusty gave him a dirty look. "Shut up, Jasper. It's a stroke of luck. It will carry the six of us to the nearest Spaceportal." After, Rusty thought to himself, the gems now in the kiln finished cooking, Hans finished cutting, and he had, under cover of darkness, liberated the staked prisoners. He could accomplish all of that by midnight of the following night but only if he did some of the gem faceting himself. There was no way to push Hans without arousing his suspicions.

Corky counted. There were six of them in the hut. He was one of the six. But why him? He'd never shown any particular loyalty to Rusty and certainly not to Jasper. In fact, he imagined he was viewed as a bit of a pain in the butt about certain things.

What was going to happen to the miners who hadn't been called to this meeting? Bubz, Leopardi, Hans, Snooker, Tam, the boy whose name he could never remember. It was something long and weighty for a child. Jeremiah and Roland were dead so it wouldn't matter to them. But what about the others?

"Each of you must keep this absolutely secret," Rusty said, seeming to read Corky's very thoughts. "We can't take everyone."

"But what's going to happen to them?" Corky blurted. "I thought we were all going to be paid for our work and de-matted off the planet by 'The Boss'." This change in plans smelled bad to Corky. He liked clean getaways, no messes. That was what he had signed on for, not murder and treachery.

"Now, Corky," Jasper said, "don't be gettin' your knickers in a twist about this."

"Right, Cork. You're a very important member of this team," Rusty emphasized. "We need your expertise in electronics and mechanics in case something goes wrong with the shuttlecraft."

"But what about 'The Boss'?" Corky persisted. "Isn't he coming?"

"Of course," Rusty said. "This is just a way for us to snag a couple of pieces without 'The Boss' knowing. You see, we can get a better price without going through a middleman like 'The Boss'.

"But—"

"We're gonna give 'The Boss' his share," Jasper chipped in. "It'll work out fine, see?"

"Are you with us, Corky?" It was Rusty again.

Rusty and Jasper were not the only ones whose eyes were riveted on him. Corky saw that Luke was taking a special interest too. His hard eyes, bent attentively on Corky, were replete with menace. It flashed through Corky's mind that if he wanted to live to see another day, he'd had better stop raising objections.

"Alright," he stammered, "I'm with you." Though it was cool in the hut when he came in, his body felt hot and he could feel fresh sweat starting under his armpits.

"Good," Rusty's voice, as always, was smooth. "Let's move on. Barrrk—"

"Yessir!" Barrrk wasn't called Barrrk without reason. Everything he said came out loud and staccato. His eyes bulged to an abnormal degree even for a Mickite, giving him an air of frenzied bellicosity. The question just put to Corky was reiterated.

Corky slumped back against the wall and felt the heat wrought by tension flow out of him into the cold stone. He only half-listened to Barrrk's unsurprising answers, his thoughts drifting away from the hut.

He wished he was home. A place where there were flowers and tall pine trees and snow-capped mountains that he could see from his back door. His horse, Zorba. Tawny, and the twins, Sherry and Shelly...

But that had been another life, a life full of color and laughter. He was so tired after today's labors, he couldn't bring the romanticized scenes to his mind. Hardest of all was remembering the faces of Tawny and the twins. They were fading to sepia, like old analog photographs.

He wondered if the authorities were still looking for him. Of course, there was no statute of limitations on murder. He knew it was self-defense but the circumstances were so twisted he would have had to serve time. In his own oddly righteous way, Corky believed he should go free, in accordance with the truth. When it came to it, he would not have been willing to plea bargain. So running had proved the only solution.

The meeting was breaking up. Barrrk and Porter had already

straggled to their feet and Jasper threw Corky a nod to clear out too. Rusty and Luke didn't budge. Corky uncramped his legs and hunched out the door.

The weather had cooled after the storm as it did every afternoon and the sun was sinking close to the western horizon. Night would fall quickly now, and with it, the desert's near-freezing cold.

Corky shivered and pondered the fate of the prisoners. Were they already dead? He hoped mercifully that they were. Should he check on them? Maybe free them?

He mulled it over and even took a step in the direction of the dune where that violent midday event had taken place. Then Luke lifted the flap over Rusty's door, came out into the garishly colorful rays of the sunset, and stood watching him.

Corky knew deep down inside he was a coward. He'd known it for years. He could think great thoughts but when it came right down to it...well, when it came right down to it, he went along with the others or took the easiest way out. Tonight wasn't going to be any different. Cowed, he wheeled the other way, toward the hut he shared with Tam and Snooker and the boy, and shambled away across the sand.

ENSIGN GUALADUPE DEVARGAS was serving a second straight duty shift on the bridge and developing a hypoglycemic headache. He surreptitiously nibbled at a contraband GalaxyBar, staving off the headache and keeping his eye peeled for falling crumbs so Lieutenant Mouneera wouldn't dress him down later for eating on the bridge.

GalaxyBars, consisting of bits of dried fruit glued together with honey and rolled oats, were his favorite snack. When the captain de-matted him to Spaceportal seven to make arrangements for Muhammed's and Niko's care, he had bought a case and smuggled it to his cabin.

He scanned the viewscreen, and for the hundredth bored time, his eyes roved over the delicate body of the *Heaven's Bow*, floating languidly ahead of the *Boadicea* in space. DeVargas yawned and repeated his hypnotic survey. It was enough to put him to sleep.

Then something caught his eye. A silver blaze shot from the side of the *Heaven's Bow*. A ship! DeVargas slugged his intercom button with the first feeling of dutiful fervor he'd had in hours.

Captain Forrest answered promptly from the briefing room. "Forrest here."

"Sir!" DeVargas shouted excitedly into the speaker, blasting Dani's ears.

"What is it, Ensign?" Dani's tone was snappish.

"Sir," DeVargas repeated, "a small craft has just left the other ship. It has set in a course heading for the planetoid."

"What?" Dani stormed. "I can't believe those people! Who do they think they're dealing with, an idiot?"

"Captain?"

"Have that woman—"

"What woman, sir?"

"The captain of the *Heaven's Bow*. Have her and whoever else happens to be idling about on that bridge of hers de-matted over here immediately. I'm getting to the bottom of this!" There was an audible bang that sounded like Forrest's fist hitting the table.

"But, sir—"

"Right now, Ensign! Have a security team meet them to escort them to the briefing room."

"Very well, sir. DeVargas out." DeVargas trembled inwardly as he called Security and made the necessary arrangements. At least he would be safely on the bridge and not in the de-matter room when he guessed what was going to be one outraged ship's captain arrived there.

Fortunately for him, DeVargas's imagination did not approach the reality. Bajana would have charged and cheerfully bludgeoned to death the first *Boadicea* crewperson that swam into her focus if she had not been so disoriented.

She had returned to the bridge of the *Heaven's Bow* and was decrying Nachi's defection to Sukha when she experienced a plummeting in her stomach and a wobbling of her knees. Her body tore apart.

She screamed but it was a soundless scream lost in the nothingness that had swallowed her. Her body coalesced again but her quivering legs refused to support her and she crumpled onto a circle that had mysteriously appeared at her feet.

The circle was covered in something that smelled foul and it took her a moment to realize she had retched up the contents of her stomach. Sukha glimmered eerily out of the corner of her eye. Then he solidified and moved to kneel beside her, cradling her against his body.

Only a trembling of his hands gave away his own disorientation. Bajana lifted her head to ask him what had happened and saw black-shirted beings, that looked, except for their different heights and colors, like Brahuinna men and women. Their legs were spread and they were pointing some kind of hand weapons at her and Sukha. Bajana had seen hand weapons before but only among the lowest classes of Brahuinna on Nirvannini. It never occurred to her to equip her crew with them.

The tallest of the men produced a hand-held device and spoke into it. More rapidly than seemed possible, panels set into the walls slid apart, and the darkest-skinned man Bajana had ever seen appeared.

"Damn it," the man said, "what's gotten into Dani anyway? De-matting people without even a hint of warning!" He dropped to one knee and waved a flat grey hexagon in front of Bajana's body. The hexagon didn't touch her, for which she was grateful. It made a bleeping sound and the man glowered at its tiny screen as if challenging it.

"You'll be fine," he said, patting her on the shoulder and standing up. He reached down to grasp her hands and lift her to her feet.

"Mild disorientation," he explained, steadying her. "I couldn't agree with you more, frankly. I hate the damn thing myself."

"What?"

"De-matter." He gestured with his chin at the dias from which he had helped her step down. She looked back at the stepped platform with its grouping of flat circles. A woman in a white body suit was already cleaning up Bajana's mess with a suction tool.

"I'm sorry it made you sick," the man went on.

"What is it?" she asked.

"What? The de-matter? You mean to tell me you've never de-matted before?"

Bajana shook her head.

"Well, Dani sure as hell isn't going to hear the end of this from me! It could have made you really sick. Particularly without any idea of what to expect."

"We were not warned, that is true." Sukha spoke for the first time.

"May I scan you as well?" The man flashed his hexagon and Sukha nodded his agreement. He ran the device up and down in front of Sukha's body and when the box bleeped, he seemed puzzled by the results. At least, so Sukha thought, from the tensed facial lines between his brows. The man stashed the hexagon into a shoulder holster.

"Bad break?"

"Bad break?" It was now Sukha's turn to be puzzled.

"Your arms."

"Oh, not really. Simple fractures. The Doctors Torilli and Tilorri say I will be healed in a fortnight."

"A fortnight?" The man's eyebrows rose up his forehead. "That's good healing time. We don't have that. Perhaps your doctors can come for a visit and teach me a new thing or two."

"You're a doctor?"

"Of course. Didn't I introduce myself? Such bad manners. My

name's Jenks. Doctor Sylvestre Adam Jenks." Sly extended his hand.

"A pleasure." Sukha pressed his palms together and bowed very slightly. Then, uncertainly, he reached out his lower left hand to touch the doctor's. To his surprise, the man grasped it firmly and moved it up and down in a vertical pattern.

"That's a handshake," Sly explained, seeing Sukha's bemusement. "I realize you folks are new around here but you must have met other Coalition—"

"Doctor, if you would be so kind," Bajana broke in, "as to tell us where we are."

"De-matter Room A, G Deck, *U.C.S.S. Boadicea*," Sly said.

"We're aboard the *Boadicea*?" Bajana could not keep the outrage from her voice.

"Now, now," Sly soothed, "I can understand your feelings. What with being whisked over here without so much as a 'by your leave' and all."

"How could she do this? I recognize we are strangers but surely it is rude to just—" she swung her arm expressively as if to include a whole universe of wrongdoing "—do whatever it is she did to get us over here. She is insufferable!"

Sly cocked a startled eyebrow. If he had been Ma'at he would have thought of the upcoming encounter with Dani as 'interesting'. Being Sly, he just began to worry instead.

"Captain Ki," Sly inclined his head, "if you will follow me, you can tell her personally what you think. She's expecting you in the briefing room.

Chapter
Eight

LUKE MAINTAINED HIS pose of impassivity until he saw that Corky had reached his hut and gone inside. There was no one else about. Tam was cooking dinner at a central campfire and Luke could hear some of the men guffawing as they ragged Tam about the hash he had burned into inedibility that morning. The tone of the banter told him they had already started on their evening's beer.

Certain no one was observing him, Luke hurried out of the camp. He topped a dune northwest of the huts then circled back behind the towers of rock that ringed the camp. One of them sloped down on the far side. The angle provided good cover and made it possible for someone to spy out the camp's activities while remaining unseen. It was also the highest spot in the area.

Feeling in the twilight for the hand- and toe-holds he knew well, Luke scaled the rock. He wasn't out of breath at the top. He was in excellent physical condition. After checking the camp — he could see Snooker standing off to one side of Hans and Porter, not quite joining in their friendly patter — Luke sat down on the rock with his back to the camp. First, he checked the left pocket of his robe. All three of the *Boadicea* transcons were still safely nesting there.

He had temporarily disabled them so that *Boadicea* could neither locate nor communicate with anyone. It was careless of Rusty to leave them in his hut after he talked to *Boadicea*. In the confusion following the captives' escape attempt, it had been easy to palm them. They would come in handy later.

Luke reached into the right pocket of his robe and pulled out a vidscreen transmitter-receiver. Its range was limited but it didn't matter. It was time to give 'The Boss' a call. He knew where 'The Boss' was and it wasn't far away.

DANI ROSE AGITATEDLY at the entrance of Doctor Jenks, Captain Ki and Sukha Jabala into the briefing room.

"Captain Ki —"

"Captain Forrest," Bajana snapped, "what is the meaning of this outrage?"

"That," Dani muttered sardonically, "was going to be the very question I was going to ask you."

"Me!" Bajana shrilled.

"I think, Dani," Sly intervened, "this was Captain Ki's first experience with a de-materializer."

"Oh!" Dani's eyes went round with surprise. "I'm sorry, Captain. However," her voice grew harsh, "I told you to stay put and you disobeyed me!"

"Disobeyed you? How?"

"A small craft left your ship for the planetoid just a quarter of an hour ago."

"That," Bajana spat out, "was an unauthorized excursion by a young and hot-blooded crewman."

"It is nonetheless, as Captain, your responsibility to control your crew and prevent them from violating house arrest."

"Captain," Bajana lifted her chin and her eyes flashed, "I am well aware of my responsibilities as commander of my vessel. Do not presume to lecture me."

"Uh, Dani," Sly broke in, "perhaps we could all sit down and discuss this as civilized people."

Dani stepped back from the table and clenched her fists to bring herself under control. Her emotions were out of hand. This wouldn't be the first time she'd used anger to manipulate a situation or probably the last. But this was anger she wasn't controlling. Sly was right. She needed to get a grip on herself and, by extension, the situation.

"Of course," she capitulated, forcing a smile. "I'm sorry for the rudeness. Please sit down, Captain and..." Dani scrutinized the being standing beside Captain Ki. Except for the extra pair of arms and the bluish tint to his skin, he could have passed for a human. His aura of self-possession reminded Dani of Ma'at and she found it difficult to resist liking him.

"I am Sukha Jabala, Chief Engineer of the *Heaven's Bow*, Captain."

Ah, Dani thought, an engineer. She always got on well with engineers. Well, one engineer in particular: the missing Niko. They were so practical.

"If I may, Captain," Jabala seated himself and took the initiative, "we are well aware that we are in the jurisdiction of some power of which you are a representative. We have no desire to offend."

Dani silently added 'diplomat' to the list of Jabala's likely talents.

"But we find ourselves at a loss. We are on a peaceful exploratory mission. We are new to this sector of space. We are unfamiliar with the customs and —"

"I hear you, Mr. Jabala," Dani interrupted, "but you must understand that it is difficult for me to accept that you have a vessel that, in design, is a near replica of mine and you have humans aboard that vessel and yet you pretend no knowledge of the Coalition, the Khrar Empire or simple technologies like the de-matter and the transcon. What do you expect me to make of such an enigma?"

"Parallel development, Captain?"

Dani's eyes narrowed. She knew as much about the odds of parallel star system development as the next starship captain. But was it applicable here or was Jabala manipulating knowledge he knew Dani must possess?

"And the humans?" Dani gestured meaningfully at Captain Ki.

"Humans? Ah, the Brahuinna," Sukha said. "That is a very long story indeed."

"I can imagine," Dani said drily. Manipulation seemed the likelier possibility. Jabala was no fool.

"Captain Forrest," Bajana said, "as you seem disinclined to believe Sukha that we are on a peaceful exploratory mission, what is it you think we're doing?"

"Okay," Dani consented. "It's pretty simple. You're mining sapphires on that planetoid and trying to keep it a big secret. So secret that you were willing to destroy a Predator that came snooping in a little too close." Dani leaned menacingly towards Bajana across the table.

"Now, you're trying to finish up the job and clear out as quickly as possible. But, I showed up and so you have created a clever little ruse to keep me occupied and stall for time. Just the time you need to gather the gems and make good your escape."

Bajana and Sukha exchanged baffled looks.

"What ruse?" Sukha asked.

"Capturing my crew and getting your miner friend Rusty to involve me in a faked negotiation for your shuttlecraft. But something's gone wrong. We can no longer raise him by transcon."

"Why," Bajana said with deliberate care, as if talking to a small child, "would I trade your crew — that I have supposedly captured — for a shuttlecraft that is already mine? It doesn't make any sense."

"Oh, yes it does," Dani retorted. "Your miners have double-crossed you. You've lost control of them and now they want your shuttlecraft so they can make good their escape. That's why I can't reach them. Weren't you going to pay them enough?"

"Captain," Bajana rose from her chair, "this is madness."

"So," Dani also came to her feet, "you're sticking to your sweet but improbable story?"

"It's the truth!"

"'Methinks the lady doth protest too much,'" Dani quoted.

"What?"

Dani circled the briefing table and stared hard at her visitors.

"As you have broken a lawfully-imposed house arrest and refuse to confess what you are up to, I'm ordering you, in accordance with Explora Command regulations, to be confined to the brig until such time as you see fit to tell the truth."

"Dani—"

"Sly, you stay out of this!" Dani silenced the doctor. "Security!"

The security people who had been standing guard at the door approached the table. "Show our visitors to their accommodations," Dani directed.

"You can't put me in your brig," Bajana said. "I need to be on my ship!"

"Why," Dani asked with threatening sweetness, "are you expecting a communication from someone, Captain?"

"Gods, no! I'm the *Heaven's Bow's* commander! Would you leave your ship uncaptained, Forrest?"

Dani drew back. Captain Ki had touched a far deeper chord than she knew. But it didn't change the facts. She nodded to the security team. They surrounded their charges and marched them to the door.

"Wait!" Bajana cried out.

"Ah—" Dani exhaled, relieved. "Put some fear into you, did it?"

"No." Bajana's voice was frosty. "You'll regret this, Forrest. No doubt about it. I have every right to return to my ship and my crew. What you are doing is an outrage!"

Dani cocked an eyebrow.

"However, as you are forcibly retaining me on your ship, I do have a request."

"Yes?"

"You pulled me and Sukha from the bridge of the *Heaven's Bow* without warning. There's no one in command since Nachi deserted. I would like to order Hasitam Deva, whom I had confined to quarters, to skipper the ship in my absence."

Dani smiled politely. "Consider it done, Captain."

She nodded again to the security contingent. They hustled Sukha and Bajana out of the room. The consequent silence was a short one.

"I have never in all my years aboard this ship seen you behave so unreasonably, Dani." Sly stood up. "It's going in my report."

"Be my guest, Doctor." Dani wore a truculent expression.

"Dani. You're running amok. This is serious, not silly. You're ill. I can take your command from you."

"You should do whatever you think fit, Doctor. But if this is a plan you intend to implement, you had better do it. Because I assure you if there are any further outbursts from you during official engagements with these entities, I will consider you insubordinate. Is that clear?"

It was a bald-faced challenge. Dani's eyes were as hard and unbending as steel. Sly took a last look at his long-time friend and stamped from the room.

DUSK WAS FADING into darkness and the temperature descended precipitously in the trough between dunes where Ma'at and Luluai lay staked. A twilight breeze had sprung up adding to the chill. Despite the deepening gloom, Luluai saw that Ma'at was shivering. Her own arms had been trembling for hours from the muscle strain but this was Ma'at's whole body.

"Are you alright?" she asked in concern. Ma'at was focusing on instituting Nhavan mind techniques to negate pain. It took effort but s/he needed to be free of pain in order to focus hir remaining energies on preventing hypothermia.

"I...must...focus," s/he answered mentally. Hir teeth chattered and hir arm and leg muscles twitched out of control. Those twitches were burning calories, making insidious inroads into the core of body heat s/he was regulating with hir mind. If s/he could keep hir internal organs from going below a certain temperature, s/he would survive.

"Maybe I can help somehow," Luluai telegraphed. "I'm not an experienced telepath, but —"

"You're very good," Ma'at answered. "I cannot project as you do, at a distance."

Luluai shook her head in denial. "The others are much better."

"The others?"

"Full-blooded Sirensi, like the doctors. I am only a half-breed Sirensi."

Ma'at heard the bitterness in the alien's voice and wondered what she had experienced in her young life to make her feel so badly about herself.

"Is that bad?"

"I'm worthless. I was always worthless and now I have gone and proved it." Luluai started to sob.

"Luluai," Ma'at interposed, hir voice striving to offer comfort, "don't cry. Rest now. Preserve your energy. You'll need it to survive tomorrow."

ADMIRAL GORDON JAMESON was tossing back a second full glass of Earth wine, scarce as it was in this hinterland near the Free Sector, when a repetitious prickling at his thigh told him a private transmission was coming in on his miniaturized black market transmitter-receiver. Worn under clothes, the device was inaudible and undetectable.

Jameson searched his mind for a plausible excuse to escape the dinner party that Harold Masterson, the Spaceportal commander, had insisted be held in his honor. Around the long table sat the most distinguished entities in residence at Spaceportal sixteen, who were drunkenly working their way up to a third round of toasts.

Jameson would have preferred his visit to the Spaceportal to be neither remembered nor remarked upon. But anonymity was not easy for an admiral, even an off-duty admiral, to achieve. He had concocted a story for Masterson that it was one of his lifelong ambitions to explore the remotest nooks and crannies of Coalition space. Masterson had agreed that Jameson couldn't get much more ass-end than his Spaceportal.

The fabrication spawned a rumor that the Admiral was writing a book, probably his memoirs. He was thronged with base hangers-on, each eager to offer an opinion on everything from fashion to Coalition military policies.

Jameson settled in his mind on the oldest of all excuses. "Have to go to the little boy's room," he whispered to the whore seated on his left, careful to offer her a leer promising future favors. Her pasted-on smile widened to assure him of the same courtesy but the hard look in her eyes didn't waver. Jameson, grinning genially and patting his stomach to assure the assembled guests he held nothing against them or the food, pushed back his chair and departed.

Once in the privacy of the grandest guest quarters the base could offer, he slipped off the illegal device strapped to his thigh. A series of dots and dashes lit the miniaturized screen. Jameson read them with ease. Morse code might be ancient but it still had its uses. He responded with an answering series of his own.

The screen blanked and the muddied outlines of a robed figure appeared. The transmitter was capable of conveying images in full color but the light was poor on the transmitting end. It didn't matter. The code told Jameson it was Luke. The audio cackled. He bent close to the speaker.

"The *Boadicea* is here," Luke informed him.

"*Boadicea*? Shit!"

"With some help from yours truly, these unprincipled ruffians captured First Officer Ma'at. I haven't seen Captain Forrest. Frankly, I'd have expected her to have de-matted down by now on a glorified rescue mission."

"Damn! They're supposed to be chasing after some rogue ship. Why are they there?"

"I don't know. There is some other ship here. We captured some of their crew first."

"Khrars?"

"A mixed bunch, but no Khrars. I don't know what their game is. Rusty is stealing their shuttlecraft to escape with the cache. You'd better come soon, Admiral, or there won't be anything left."

Jameson read the chrono on the headboard. It was a little after 1900 hours. He would have to wait until the following morning to leave. Anything else would look suspicious and be ungracious to Masterson.

"I'll head there at 0900. Is there any way for you to get Forrest out of the way before I get there?" A harsh sound came over the receiver. It took Jameson a second to recognize it as Luke's laugh.

"For enough pay, Admiral, I can do anything."

"Do it, then." Jameson didn't have to think twice. The image of his son, Gordon Jr., standing crisply at attention in his Explora Command cadet's uniform, rose before his eyes. Jameson had only his son. A son who had the talent and drive to ascend into the highest positions of power in Explora Command.

But Forrest had taken all of that away. Forrest, who, during an invited stint of teaching at the Academy covering true-to-life command scenarios, had so impressed the young man, that he had 'come out' to his board and asked, when he graduated, to be commissioned to the *U.C.S.S. Boadicea*.

And if that weren't bad enough, Forrest had killed him. The Battle of Telemak, a mere six months later, where Forrest stupidly lost thirteen officers and crew and seriously damaged her ship. Jameson felt the usual rage burning in his stomach. Gordon Jameson Jr. could have out commanded Forrest any day of the week.

"How much are you willing to pay?" Luke asked.

"How much have the miners brought to the surface?"

"Heat-treated and cut...8 million plus. It's no concern of mine what you hope to make though, Admiral. I will take my pay directly out of what has already been processed."

"Alright. But how much?"

"250,000 credits worth."

"250,000 credits just to kill Forrest? I'm only paying you a tenth of that to act as security and liaison."

"Murder requires careful planning. How do you want me to do her?"

"The more painful the better."

"Perhaps, Admiral, you should do it yourself."

"No, far too dangerous. I can't afford to be implicated."

"Maybe, or is it that you're a coward? Forrest is not an insignificant adversary. She's bested better men than you."

"Goddamn it, you cesspool slime, you wretched sack of—"

This time, Luke's laughter was light and amused.

"Sleep well, Admiral."

CAITLIN EIREANN WAS the only person in the *Boadicea* language lab. The lab was on G Deck. In addition to the language lab, G Deck housed the science labs, the main briefing room, the main de-matter room, the infirmary and the brig. It was late evening.

Day and night were artificially simulated aboard *Boadicea*. Crew were rotated through three eight-hour duty shifts during the ship's 24 hour 'day'. Even in the evening, there were crew assigned to work in the language lab but, with the illness, more and more crew people failed to show for duty shifts. The single crewperson who had reported for duty, a chatty Korean woman named Nancy Kim, had left to take her dinner in the mess.

But Caitlin was so wrapped up in her research she would not have noticed if the room had been full of people or as empty as a tomb. She pored over the results of a series of linguistic analyses she had requested the computer to run on the language data acquired from the *Boadicea's* two spoken contacts with the *Heaven's Bow*.

The ship's computer had self-rated the accuracy of its translation of the *Heaven's Bow* language into Coalition Patois at 87.8%. Caitlin thought this was a high degree considering the computer freely admitted the language of the *Heaven's Bow* was not resident in the *Boadicea's* vast language database.

Unlike the portable translators, which worked by sensing brain wave frequencies — making it useful for rough translations when encountering non-humanoid species — the ship's language computer worked on an older, but more reliable, principle. It created a translation for an unknown language by searching known languages for similar structure, grammar and vocabulary. For the computer to indicate such a high degree of success meant the *Heaven's Bow* language followed the structural patterns of a known language or languages in the database.

Caitlin wondered if the linguistic ease with which the two communications had taken place was one of the intuitive reasons Captain Forrest doubted Captain Ki's assertion that the *Heaven's Bow* was unfamiliar with the Coalition. It was hard not to wince reviewing her second exchange with Captain Ki. She had not been pleased.

Nancy Kim, privy to the ship's grapevine, had told her that Captain Forrest had de-matted Captain Ki and another *Heaven's Bow* crewperson to the *Boadicea* and they'd since been thrown in the ship's brig. Caitlin speculated if it would be wise to tell the captain that the language of the *Heaven's Bow* people was not in the *Boadicea's* database of languages.

Rumor had it that the captain had become irritable since the capture of Lieutenant Commander Ma'at and hir security team on the planetoid. And Caitlin was *persona non grata* as it was. She didn't think she was going to risk the captain's ire on the little she'd learned.

In support of her decision she reminded herself that the fact that the structure of the *Heaven's Bow* language could be syntactically approximated was not in itself meaningful, or even astounding. After all, humanoid languages, no matter how much they differed in grammar or vocabulary, followed certain elemental rules of structure. These rules were dictated by the biological and neurological limitations of humanoid design.

But there was a result from the data that both astounded and perplexed her. A total of ten words from the two exchanges were not only close relatives of words in the *Boadicea's* language database but were from two linguistically-reconstructed Earth proto-languages. Six of the words were related to words in Proto-Brahui, an Earth Dravidian language, and four were related to words in Proto-Indo-Aryan, an Earth Indo-European language.

It had been drilled into Caitlin's head as a student that the presence of linguistically-related words in different languages could be explained by one of only three theories. The first was a single parent language shared by the languages under consideration and from which they had jointly derived, namely a proto-language. The second was the borrowing of a word, usually along with the item, from a neighboring language. The third was convergence. Convergence, simply put, meant 'accident'.

Convergence was the only one of the three explanations Caitlin could eliminate right off the bat. Linguistic theory held that the presence of a hefty handful of words similar in sound and meaning to another language could not be construed as an accident because the comparison of vocabulary across languages was what established language relationships in the first place. Caitlin thought it a safe bet that a 9% word match was outside the statistical norm for linguistic accident.

The other two explanations were much thornier considerations and led down paths unimaginably tortured with conjecture. As a theory, borrowing implied physical proximity but the *Heaven's Bow* people claimed to be from outside the Coalition, not to mention thousands of light years from Earth. As for a shared parent language, that was worse, because it not only implied proximity but a shared and lengthy developmental history.

Caitlin decided it was time to find out everything she could about the *Heaven's Bow* language and the people who spoke it. She'd never heard the brig was off-limits to crew. A quick quiet visit...who had to know?

Nancy Kim hadn't returned from dinner. Caitlin signed off the computer and slipped out of the lab.

A HALF HOUR after Luke's sign off, Jameson was still pacing his quarters. He hated Luke as much as he needed him. But a soldier of fortune became an expensive liability in the end. The man was too dangerous to kill directly but Jameson knew he was going to have to find a way to get rid of Luke.

Then there was the problem of Forrest. Could Forrest connect him to the illegal mining of SX257? He didn't think so. No one but Luke knew of his involvement. Rusty had never met Jameson and knew only that Luke worked for someone ambiguously titled 'The Boss'. Luke had hired Rusty. Rusty had then hand-picked the miners, men with pasts that didn't bear scrutiny, making them unlikely to cause waves.

But how was Jameson going to play his cards if Forrest wasn't dead by the time he arrived at the planetoid? Forrest would hardly fall for the 'memoirs' line. Jameson's mere presence in the neighborhood would smell suspicious to Forrest. On the other hand, Jameson put great stock in Luke's assassination capabilities. He was a professional. If anyone could knock off Forrest, it was Luke.

Anyway, Forrest hadn't looked well when Jameson last saw her. Hopefully, she was still unwell. Tired out, not as alert as usual. It didn't hurt to hope. With Forrest dead, Jameson won every way he looked at it. First off, he would have his revenge.

Second, he could appear in the role of the happening-by hero who stops to comfort the paralyzed-with-grief crew of the *Boadicea* for their tragic, inexplicable loss. As ranking officer, he would assume temporary command.

Third, he could avoid paying off the miners. Strictly in accordance with regulations, he would arrest them for their illegal activities and cast them into the brig of the *Boadicea*. He would hide as much of the booty as possible before turning over a sizeable, believable chunk to the authorities.

He would not only escape the web of intrigue he had spun but would go home covered in glory at the helm of the *Boadicea* proving, once again, that when the going got tough, the queens ran and real men had to come in and take over.

The only worm in the apple was Luke. But that too, on reflection, should prove easy to swing to his favor. He would put Luke in irons for the murder of Forrest. A short session with a Khrar memory-eraser before the *Boadicea* reached Spaceportal sixteen would eradicate any urge on Luke's part to implicate Jameson.

The scheme was perfect because it took every contingency into account and left Jameson smelling like a rose. Like many a military mind, he could hardly wait to set his strategy into motion. He rubbed his hands in glee. A knock at the door interrupted his gloating.

"Admiral?" It was a sensuous female voice.

"Come," he said and the door slid open to reveal the hard-eyed lady of pleasure. She stepped into his cabin and the door whispered closed behind her.

"Everyone's wondering where you are, Admiral. They want you to come back to the party." She affected a disappointed little moue with her mouth.

"And you?" He knew why she had come.

"I think this is much nicer." She settled onto his bed, stretched her long, well-muscled legs out for his inspection, and leaned back.

Jameson smiled, ordered the cabin lights to dim, and began unbuttoning his shirt.

CAITLIN SAW THERE was a security person on duty in the foyer of the brig. He was black, husky, and intently reading something on his computer display. Caitlin slid her hands into the pockets of her emerald green jumpsuit and sauntered across to his console.

"What's up?" he asked, lifting his head and giving her a casual smile.

"Hi," she smiled back, doing her damndest to appear insouciant. "I'm Caitlin Eireann."

"Jeremy Buckster." He extended his hand.

"I'm doing some language research, Jeremy." She said, shaking his hand. "Can I talk to your prisoners?"

"Oh, sure. As long as you stay out of their cells. The bar-less doors make it easy to talk to them from the cell foyer. The lady, Captain Ki," he gestured with his thumb, "is in the cell on the left. The cell next to it has Sukha Jabala, their Chief Engineer or something."

The cells he pointed out were compact door less rooms, the lighting dimmed for sleeping. Each held a bunk, a limited-menu shipcook unit, a wall-inset computer console, and a small screened area near the back wall. For the head, she guessed.

"Just don't forget," he warned, "if you reach across the threshold, the forcefield will knock you on your butt."

"Okay. I won't forget."

"Especially if it happens, you won't." He grinned and shifted his attention back to his console. She raised on tip-toes and peeked over. He was playing a video dogfight game with holographic biplanes. Absorbed in his game, he had already forgotten her existence.

Caitlin moved away from the console and across to the cells. She had never been in a ship's brig before, or talked to a prisoner. She ventured tentatively toward Captain Ki's cell. A feminine figure with long hair lay curled on the bunk, her face to the wall. Caitlin figured she was asleep. She turned to look into the other cell and felt her breath stop in amazement.

Perched in a cross-legged posture on the bunk, hands folded in his lap with the palms up and his eyes peacefully closed, was a man who looked to her like a Hindu sculpture of a god. His limbs and face were androgynously slender, his skin gave off a bluish tint in the dim light, his silver hair was wound into an oriental-style topknot and — Caitlin blinked and swallowed — he had two extra arms.

Chapter
Nine

FOR THE UMPTEENTH time, Doctor Sylvestre Adam Jenks rubbed his bloodshot eyes with his fists. He wanted to sleep, even if just for a couple of hours. He would have allowed himself to do it too, if he could be sure he would wake up again. But he wasn't sure.

He could not recall a time when he'd been so worried and so tired and so little able to do anything about either. He had scrolled, screen by screen, through masses of data on every disease that could manifest with the characteristics of the illness affecting the *Boadicea* crew. Like everyone else, he was being affected, which was not making it easier for him to retain what he was reading.

It didn't help that the presenting symptoms could be interpreted as belonging to scores of diseases. Most members of the crew were experiencing symptoms that were so generalized he couldn't settle on a diagnosis. After all, who worked for Explora Command who didn't undergo bouts of irritability, upset stomach and insomnia? It was part of the job.

It did have some markers that reminded him of sypotis, a blood disease he'd suffered on Par. Like this, that had caused fatigue, weakness and neuralgia. But no one on the *Boadicea*, including himself, was showing the abnormal proliferation of blood cells that was characteristic of sypotis. He had ruled it out.

Complicating matters, the intensity and type of symptoms was different for a few people aboard. Most of the crew, like Captain Forrest, was suffering largely from generalized interferences to peripheral nerve function. But Crewman Madison had died of congestive heart failure. And Ensign Vasquez had now developed a palsy of the muscles controlling the eye and lapsed into a coma. Sly didn't know what made Madison and Vasquez different.

Or what made Ensign Eireann different. The eye-hand coordination battery he had subjected her to indicated she was unaffected. Ensign DeVargas showed no decline in coordination either.

Sly started on a new tack. Could something, say an infectious agent, have attacked the ship before they picked up Eireann at Spaceportal seven where they'd left Niko and Sabi? On the other hand, DeVargas had been the only crewperson to go ashore at Spaceportal seven. Had Eireann escaped the exposure and DeVargas developed an immunity? Sly thought that was a pretty far-fetched notion, but stranger things had happened.

And what if, gods and goddesses forbid, it was a sexuality-linked disease? It was true that 20th Century AIDS had been shown in short order to have nothing to do with sexuality but it had retained the stigma of being a gay disease for decades and the gay community had suffered tremendously. It had even, at its very outset, been called GRIDS: Gay-Related Immune Deficiency Syndrome. Sly had never forgotten that little historical tidbit from medical school. Applying that scenario, the fact that Eireann had no symptoms made sense but the fact that DeVargas had no symptoms didn't. DeVargas was as flamboyant a queen as they came.

Whatever it was, Sly needed to find an answer soon, before he succumbed to total exhaustion. And before Vasquez, who was showing a frightening decrease in blood flow to her brain, died. And before Dani Forrest and the rest of the crew collapsed and the *Boadicea* was left to float eerily, like a ghost ship, among the stars.

What Sly should or should not do about the captain weighed heavily on his mind. It was one thing to declare Dani unfit for duty, but who was going to replace her? Ma'at was missing and he was rapidly becoming unfit himself.

The intercom whistled. "What now?" he groused. Time was running out as it was. He didn't need interruptions.

"Doctor Jenks? This is Ensign Eireann."

Speak of the devil, Sly thought.

"I'm in the brig visiting with Sukha Jabala," she said. "You know, the prisoner?"

What in hell was Eireann doing horsing around in the brig? If she was that much at loose ends, he could put her to work searching the database for diseases. Despite his aggravated state of mind, he forced himself to sound professional.

"Yes, Ensign?"

"Well, he asked if the dressings on his arms could be changed. They're starting to smell."

Sly remembered the humanoid's arm dressings had been odiferous in the de-matter room. But after his run-in with the captain after the briefing, the matter had skipped Sly's mind.

"I had forgotten about the problem of Mr. Jabala's dressings, Ensign. It's some sort of herbal concoction. I'll come down with some splints and fresh bandages." A simple medical activity like changing a dressing might give his brain just the break he needed.

"Oh, thanks so much," Caitlin said. "If you're busy, sir, maybe someone else could come instead?"

"We're very short-staffed, Ensign. Besides, I want to have a second look at this patient. He needs all the standard inoculations. I hope you haven't had much contact with him or his cellmate. Jenks out."

If Sly had been a bit more fancy free, he would have already brought Sukha Jabala into the infirmary for tests and scans and inoculations. Jabala was a humanoid the Coalition had never met up with before and Sly was curious to learn how he differed from other humanoids.

SUKHA JABALA WAS so casual and friendly Caitlin quickly got past her initial astonishment over his appearance. His questioning her about how to get medical assistance had been such a manageable request it had relaxed her. After all, she had half-expected him to behave like a god...well, however a god behaved anyway.

She had introduced herself, told him she was interested in learning about his language and culture and explained why. Sukha Jabala's eyes had lit at her explanation.

"There is much I could learn from you as well, Ms. Eireann," he said. "I have been waiting for just such an opportunity as this."

It seemed to her, with his calm expectant manner, he might literally mean he had been waiting for this moment. But why?

"Really?"

"Absolutely." He smiled. "You say you've discovered correspondences between my language, Atravayasana, and a cluster of planet Earth languages?"

"Yes. It doesn't make any sense, of course. I don't know if you know anything about linguistics but there shouldn't be any correspondences, let alone several."

"Where exactly is this planet you call Earth?"

"Well, it's the third planet from its star in a solar system called Sol in the Milky Way galaxy. We're in the Milky Way galaxy right now, of course."

"Of course," he said, fixing it in his memory. "Do you have star charts on board?"

"Yes. We couldn't navigate without them."

"Can we access them?"

"I don't know." Caitlin felt she was in over her head. She didn't know what Captain Forrest would think of Mr. Jabala's request. As a temporary assignee aboard *Boadicea*, she had only the most elementary security access to the *Boadicea's* computer banks.

Not to mention she didn't know what information would be considered sensitive. There had been no statements from Explora Command regarding the status of the people from the *Heaven's Bow*. There were no formal diplomatic relations, no —

"Apparently not," Sukha's mildly amused voice interrupted her thoughts. "What information can we access, Ms. Eireann?"

She shrugged. "I think we would be safe looking at standard, unclassified, textbook-type data. That would give you some notion of Earth."

"It sounds like a start."

Doctor Jenks blustered into the brig foyer, his medikit under one arm. "Jeremy."

"Sir!" Jeremy stopped playing his game and stood at attention.

"I need to inoculate these prisoners. Can you drop the forcefield?"

"Yes, sir." The forcefield buzzed as Jeremy flicked it off. "Go ahead, sir." Sly nodded his thanks and went into Sukha's cell.

"I'm not 100% sure you won't react to these substances, Mr. Jabala," Sly said, not even looking in Eireann's direction. "You may feel a little sick. But it's for your protection. We could carry a host of diseases for which you might have no natural immunity."

"The injection provides this immunity?"

"Yes. Before this medical technique was developed, whole cultures were wiped out when an invading culture arrived. Sometimes the invaders were wiped out by the transmission of disease in the reverse direction."

Sly touched the hypo against Sukha's left shoulder. The shoulder was broader than a human's but less muscular. Sly pondered whether Jabala's overall slenderness was a structural design compensation on the part of the humanoid body for providing an extra set of limbs.

An interesting theory. If he could obtain proof for it, he could write a paper for one of the medical journals on the topic of these new humanoids. He was eager to find out how the joints worked to allow for the independent movement of two arms.

"Alright," he said, going around to Sukha's other side. "Let's have a look at this." While he splinted and re-bandaged Sukha's right arms, he looked closely at Sukha's skin. He thought the blue tint might be created by multitudes of near-surface capillaries. Without taking a sample, he couldn't tell if the blood would prove to be red or blue or purple.

When he finished, Sly commented, "This is healing very well, Mr. Jabala. Could I meet with your doctors to find out what herbs they're using?" He pointed expressively to the pile of dark, smelly bandages. "Maybe we have something synthetic that would be comparable."

"The Doctors Tilorri and Torilli would be delighted, Doctor. And to learn your medicine from you as well. Right now, they're on the planetoid but I'm sure as soon as this mixup is straightened out—"

"Well," Sly grumbled, "it isn't getting very far very fast." Tiredly, he stepped away from Sukha's bunk to exit the cell. "I need to inoculate Captain Ki."

"Doctor?"

"Yes?"

"Forgive me if I'm wrong, but I sense there is something wrong aboard. You seem so...exhausted. Your captain...so erratic. We do not know what is normal for you, of course, but—"

"It's some kind of sickness," Caitlin blurted out. "No one knows what it is yet. Most of the crew has it."

"Thank you, Ensign," Sly said sarcastically.

"If there is any way I can help, Doctor, I would be glad to."

"I'm not sure how you could, Mr. Jabala—"

"Sukha, please."

"Sukha. But thanks for the offer." Sly tucked his kit under his arm and stalked next door to Captain Ki's cell.

AS THE NIGHT progressed, Ma'at's mind got lazy at its task. At intervals s/he would wake from a hazy seductive state in which surrendering to death was presented to hir mind as a natural and acceptable inevitability. Ma'at wasn't afraid of physical death. But s/he did not know into whose safekeeping s/he could entrust hir inner essence.

S/he could not touch anyone to convey it. If s/he could not pass on hir soul nature, it would be as if s/he had never existed. This thought disturbed hir. Death was one thing, annihilation another.

Ma'at knew s/he must accept the fact that s/he would not survive the night. Oddly, when s/he did, s/he began to feel warm. A different kind of warm than that engendered by the hard struggle of hir will. That warmth had been paltry, niggardly, almost mocking. This warmth was comforting and without effort.

It flowed from the center of hir torso down hir legs to hir stiffened toes and up hir agonized arms to hir functionless hands. It seemed to massage hir, almost release hir from hir bonds. Ma'at knew it was death masquerading as release.

S/he heard a voice, filled with sunshine and flowers, in hir mind. S/he was a child again, in hir mother's garden on Nhavan. S/he remembered hir mother, Osi, as a strong active personality and hir father, Wic'a, as a quiet gentle individual. Both were still alive and living on Nhavan.

Nhavans, when they mated, negotiated either a maternal or paternal role in relation to the activities of conception, child-bearing and nurture for each child. Because of the manner in which their biochemistries interacted, the child-bearer, once the child was born, turned over the role of wet-nursing to the parent who had acted as sire. These arrangements were re-negotiated for each subsequent offspring. Ma'at had one full sibling (although hir parents' roles were reversed for that child) and six half siblings from different matings of both hir parents.

Ma'at, inferring s/he was dead because of the intensity of hir fantasy, played contentedly in the Nhavan sun. Hir mother attended happily to a climber rose. The uplifting harmonies of the Nhavan harp, played by hir father, streamed out of the house, perfuming the air with celestial music.

"Ma'at," the voice in hir mind caressed, "be warm. Play in the sun. Be warm, be warm."

BECAUSE HE LACKED sufficient data to make the necessary calculations, Sukha Jabala could not begin to guess what the odds were of coming across humans from the Planet of Many Splendors in the *Heaven's Bow's* first encounter with other beings. Realistically, he had expected to be in space for generations before chancing upon even the smallest clue to the origin of the Brahuinna.

Yet the planet Ensign Eireann was describing fit the bill. It was in the solar system detailed by Indrashtra and, according to Eireann, was the only naturally habitable planet in the system. In stupefaction, he watched the blue and green visual of Earth, spinning on the computer screen set into the wall.

Earth was not unlike what Nirvannini looked like from space, except that Nirvannini's land masses were bunched around the planet's equator and were little differentiated, a terrain composed of rain forests and terraced farms climbing the humus-rich flanks of eroding volcanoes. Nirvannini's climate was sub-tropical.

Earth, on the other hand, featured far greater variety in both climate and geography. And that too matched Indrashtra's descriptions.

"Well," Caitlin leaned her arms on the back of the chair Jeremy had scrounged from the mess hall and lifted her chin toward the screen, "what do you think?"

"It is very beautiful. I must tell you that I think ancestors of my people, the Shivani, led by an adventurer named Indrashtra, visited your planet in the far distant past."

"You're joking." Caitlin tried to grin but her mouth didn't quite make it. Despite the linguistic match and Mr. Jabala's appearance, she wasn't ready to believe anything so radical. As if reading her thoughts, Sukha asked, "Why did I startle you when you first saw me? I've never been told I look threatening."

"You reminded me of something."

"What something?"

"Alright, I give in. Computer," Caitlin ordered, raising her voice, "give me a full-color visual of the Hindu god Indra." The revolving planet was replaced by an elegantly-rendered full-color painting of a four-armed humanoid riding on a bedecked and bejeweled elephant, hoisting aloft a different object in each of his slender hands.

Caitlin heard Sukha's sharp intake of breath. "I see," he said. "This is an Earth god? You have no four-armed humanoids like myself on your planet?"

Caitlin shook her head. "No. Now, if we look at a depiction of the Lord Krishna, an incarnation of the god Vishnu, you will see that, although he is not usually portrayed with four arms, he is frequently shown having blue skin." The computer complied with a picture at Caitlin's request. "Like yours."

"We are not gods, Ms. Eireann."

"No, I know. It just adds weight to my linguistic findings. If there was a cultural contact between your people, the Shivani, and humans at some time in the past, that visit could have had some kind of nascent influence on the subsequent depictions of these gods. It doesn't mean the humans doing the depicting thought your people — the Shivani — were gods, of course."

"It seems unlikely. Indrashtra certainly did not record any such responses on the part of the humans he met on the Planet of Many Splendors."

"My limited understanding of Hindu religious art," Caitlin said, "is that it is symbolic rather than representational. Extra arms or faces or eyes are indicative of powers the god is reputed to possess. As I mentioned with Krishna, he is not always depicted the same way. Sometimes he has black skin instead of blue skin and four arms — though he's rarely shown that way — instead of two."

"Nor," she went on, "is Indra. Sometimes he has two arms instead of four. Different representations indicate a different manifestation of the god which, consequently, elicits different meanings and responses from worshipers."

"It is an exquisite and intriguing art form," murmured Sukha, his eyes still on the painting of a garlanded youthful Krishna playing on the flute, standing with one ankle crossed gracefully over the other.

"So now you know why I was taken aback. We will never know if Indrashtra's visit had any influence on these symbolic representations. When, by the way, is this visit reputed to have taken place?"

"Well, according to *The Glorious Interstellar Journeys of Indrashtra*, he left Nirvannini in the Shivani Year 52279. His account attests that he reached the Planet of Many Splendors in 52379 and that he left there in 52397. He reached home in 52479, exactly two hundred Shivani years after he'd left."

"We'll have to convert. How long is a Shivani Year?"

"It's 182 and a half days."

"Well, that's half of an Earth solar year. Is your 'day' twenty-four hours?"

Sukha nodded. "It is close, but not exactly."

"We're just estimating anyway. What Shivani Year is it now?"

"It's 62437."

"Alright, so Shivani Year 52379 was 10,058 Shivani years ago or 5029 Earth solar years ago. Using the Earth's calendar, this is the year 2269 C.E. Doing the subtraction," there was a long pause on Caitlin's part, "means Indrashtra reached Earth—if Earth is the planet—around 2760 B.C.E."

"Does that mean anything to you?"

"Not off hand. Can you give me some more details of his journey? For instance, where did he land?"

"According to his account, near a small village on a river tributary called the Sutlej. The village was called Chak Purbane Syal by the inhabitants."

"How can you be so sure?"

"I know most of *The Glorious Journeys* by heart."

Caitlin shrugged. "Computer, please provide information on Chak Purbane Syal." If there is any, she thought to herself. She didn't expect an answer. After all, Sukha's data was more than 5000 Earth solar years old. So when the computer's screen began to scroll with data about Chak Purbane Syal, she unconsciously raised a hand to her mouth.

"Jeezus."

"What is it?" Sukha asked.

"Chak Purbane Syal was a pre-Harappan settlement on the Sutlej River. The Sutlej is a tributary of the Indus River on Earth. This location fits the linguistic matching I told you about. Proto-Brahui, a branch of the Dravidian language, was spoken in the Indus River Valley, although no one knows how early, and some linguists think it broke off from Proto-Dravidian much earlier than the other Dravidian languages."

"So Earth is the planet." Sukha's voice was soft with reverence.

"Maybe. We need more clinching evidence to say for certain. But if it is, this discovery could be more than the answer to your questions. You see, Mr. Jabala, very little is known about the Indus River valley civilization and its cities. Scholars have fought for centuries over differing theories about its origin, its government, and its demise. The written script the Indus peoples invented has never been deciphered so most scholars have had to base their theories solely on non-literate artifacts."

"Most scholars?"

"A few scholars feel the *Rig Veda*, one of humankind's oldest writings, is the written record of the Indus Valley civilization, implying we do have a written record. But the majority hold the *Rig Veda* to be the story of successive migrations of a nomadic people called Indo-Aryans who invaded the Indus Valley from vast grasslands to the northwest."

"Regardless of which theory is correct," she continued, "the oldest extant copies of the *Rig Veda* are written in the Sanskrit language."

"Not, I take it," Sukha pensively clutched his chin and leaned forward, "in this undeciphered Indus script?"

"Right. Technically, Indus-Sarasvati. There are thousands of steatite seals inscribed with glyphs but no extant documents written in this script. Whether it is more closely related to Dravidian or Indo-Aryan scripts, such as Brahmi, which is a pre-cursor of Sanskrit, hasn't even been agreed on. However, it is generally agreed it was a very advanced civilization for that time period in Earth's history."

"Why is that?"

"Well, for instance, the average city dweller, rich and poor alike, had a bathroom — toilet and shower — in the house. The contemporary civilizations of Sumer and Egypt didn't have anything of the kind. Hell, medieval and modern civilizations didn't always have that. The cities of Harappa and Mohenjo-Daro had city sewage and drain systems, refuse collection, uniform weights and measures, overland and seagoing trade —"

"Hmmm," Sukha murmured again. "Indrashtra's account only mentions small villages and nomadic peoples. Not vast cities."

"Well, based on the time you gave me, it looks like your Indrashtra arrived a generation or so prior to the construction of the great cities. Harappa and Mohenjo-Daro are so alike it is believed they were meticulously laid out before being built, which makes them the first known human experiments in city planning."

"Fascinating."

"Fascinating and exciting! If any of this is true it could add dramatically to what we know about this civilization, about this period in Earth history, and about these languages. It would be unprecedented original scholarship."

"Mr. Jabala," Caitlin said, her face tense with appeal, "I must read Indrashtra's account. I must know everything you know."

"Call me Sukha, Ms. Eireann. I must know everything you know."

"Only if you call me Caitlin. An equal collaboration?"

Sukha nodded. "Agreed."

NACHIKETAS BUONO WAS looking for a soft place to land. *The Chariot* wasn't styled for landing and had no landing gear. He had strained the small craft to make good time but it had been slow going. Nachi wanted to arrive before dawn so his arrival would go unnoticed but the planetoid's hot sun was already climbing over the horizon as he searched for a suitable spot to touchdown.

He had seen the *Lithe Arrow* from the air and the huts nearby. At the altitude he had maintained to avoid detection, they were uninformative circles dotting the sand but he was reasonably sure the encampment would prove to be where Luluai and the others were being held.

For ease of access, he didn't want to land too far from the encampment. On the other hand, he couldn't risk landing close enough to be discovered. In the end, he chose a site a little over a kilometer west of the camp behind a sand dune so high it could have hidden six workbees.

After securing his craft, Nachi scrambled up the dune, edged his head cautiously over the top and peered around. There was no one as far as the eye could see. In the far distance he could just make out the tip-tops of the spears of rock surrounding the huts. In broad daylight he did not expect to march into the encampment but he did intend to scout it out. He had to determine if the shuttlecraft was guarded. He would need it to fly everyone back to the *Heaven's Bow*.

Nachi crawled over the dune and rolled down the steep side. The process raised a smidgen of dust but not enough, he concluded, to be noticed. He continued this procedure until the spears of rock looked, by eye, to loom a few centimeters over the dunes. As a result, he calculated that the shuttlecraft, which was parked to the southwest of the camp, should be about a kilometer to his right.

He turned in that direction, walking in the trough of a dune. It was already hot, far hotter than any weather he'd ever experienced. Fortunately, his tunic was of a synthetic material that had been designed to repel water and whisk away sweat. It didn't, however, lower the temperature. Only on a few of the hottest days of high summer were soaring temperatures a problem on Nirvannini. He stopped to take a sip of water from his waistpack, then continued on his trek.

The glare of the sun on the sand burned his eyes. He longed for the cooling fronds of a nabanda tree to stand under. Nabandas were famous on Nirvannini for creating their own cool moist breezes. They didn't, of course, but it sure felt like it on one of those few sweltering days. He needed one here.

He climbed out of the trough to get his bearings and sighted the *Lithe Arrow*. The slim silver shape looked undamaged but it stood at the center of a flurry of activity. A being with a wide snout, like a pig, stood guard near the rampdoor, holding a sizeable club.

A well-built man with red hair was pointing at a shiny rectangular box. His mouth was open in a shout. An enormous black-skinned man was bending over the box. Nachi was too far away to hear voices but presumed they were trying to move the box.

To his horror, the red-haired man swung his head around and looked right at Nachi. Nachi ducked behind the dune. Had the man seen him? He counted to 100 then slowly, hugging the sand, brought his eyes up over the edge.

The two men had the box halfway up the rampdoor of the shuttlecraft. No one was looking toward the dune. Nachi figured he hadn't been seen. If he had, the men would probably have stopped what they were doing and come in his direction to investigate.

Nachi slid back down the dune, took a huge swig of water and contemplated his situation. It was hot. He was tired; he had been awake for hours piloting the shuttlecraft, and his stomach was growling.

It would be pleasant to eat some of the cooked rice he'd stashed in the workbee. He only had dry snacks in his waistpack. And although it would be hot in the little shell, it would at least be shaded.

Also, he was going to need a hand weapon of some kind with which to knock out the pig-snouted guard. He wasn't going to be able to take out someone that large and strong with just his hands.

Just because the Shivani preached non-violence, didn't mean he hadn't been in a few brawls with them as a kid. He had come to appreciate the value of Brahuinna hand weapons. With or without a weapon, he had a better chance of success if he sneaked up on the guard in the dark.

Nachi decided to walk back to the workbee, have a good lunch, a long nap, and start out fresh at dusk.

Sometimes waiting was the best strategy.

WHEN MA'AT WOKE up, the sun was rising over the mountains. The first warm rays flowed over hir head and chest. Hir body soaked up the warmth but, oddly, s/he wasn't as cold as s/he had been early in the night. S/he had never been so stiff, though. As painful as it was to shift hir arms even a fraction of a centimeter, s/he tried it. Nothing had changed. They were still staked above hir head.

S/he wasn't shivering anymore. Could the sun have warmed hir so rapidly? Hir arm muscles weren't even twitching. Of course, trying to lift more than a feather would be a Herculean task. Hir muscles had gone beyond exhaustion to useless limpness. S/he turned to see if Luluai was still nearby. S/he was surprised to see her head was turned to hir and she was watching hir.

"Awake?"

"Yes." Ma'at said it with a sense of wonder. "I don't know what happened. I was so cold and then—"

"I did it." Ma'at heard the pride in Luluai's voice. Ma'at twisted hir head to see her better and the movement made hir pant with exertion.

"You were nearly dead," Luluai made an effort to tone down her triumph, "and I...well, I've never done anything like it before, but—"

"What?"

"I kept you warm telepathically."

Ma'at dropped hir head back to the sand and gazed up into the eggshell blue vault of the morning sky.

"You sent me to Nhavan where it was warm—"

"Nhavan? I just sent you message after message to stay warm and alive. You must have chosen the scenery yourself."

Ma'at remembered hir voice now: Be warm, be warm, be warm.

"How did you know I was...dying?" S/he twisted again to look at Luluai.

Luluai made a gesture with her shoulders that passed for an apologetic shrug. "I didn't mean to hurt or offend you. I went into your mind—"

"You kept me alive, Luluai," Ma'at's voice conveyed the depth of hir gratitude. "But I don't understand why you made such an effort to save me. By using up your strength, you put your own survival into jeopardy."

"I could not do otherwise. I took...lives yesterday. It was good to give one back. Perhaps—"

"—you can rebalance the wheel of karma?" Ma'at finished for her.

"Oh, if only I could."

"In my own culture, we have a philosophy called 'do no harm'. Since such an ideal is not achievable in the real world of error and tragedy and mortality, we practice the philosophy of 'do the least harm'. You have not only done that, Luluai, but gone far beyond it by saving my life. It is not necessary to do more."

"But I took the lives of so many."

"It is not a matter of quantity, but of intent and action."

"I can never make up for it."

"Remorse is not healthy, Luluai. Try to let it go."

"Okay," she said. "I will try."

"Good, you'll need to preserve your energy, especially your psychic energy, to survive the day."

"Yes. It's already getting hot."

"Yes," Ma'at agreed. "Try to sleep." S/he lifted hir head again and looked across at the young Sirensi. Her face was strained with exhaustion and flaming with sunburn. It irked Ma'at that s/he was not a distance telepath. It would not be possible to keep the alien alive with thought as Luluai had done for hir.

Hir emotional side would have given a lot at that moment for the ability to send Luluai images of splashing oceans, cool waterfalls, and fern-dappled rainforests. Hir mind reasoned s/he would have to find another method to keep her cool.

NACHI HAD BELIEVED himself unobserved but Luke had seen the glint of silver in the sky as Nachi skimmed high over the camp and, with his eyes, followed the glint as it raced toward the west. It had eventually vanished from his sight over the dunes. That could mean it had flown on or that it had landed.

But Luke was not a person to wonder. Without a word to another soul, he trekked after the object. It would be too good to be true if yet another shuttlecraft was available for the taking. Since his conversation with Jameson, he had been formulating a plan to steal the *Lithe Arrow* in order to carry out his assignation with Forrest. It was tricky because he needed to accomplish it before Rusty managed to steal it. A second shuttlecraft would simplify everything.

Luke had convinced Rusty it would be best to escape the planet under cover of darkness after the miners who weren't included in the escape plans had gone to bed. When they awoke in the morning, they could decry their fate to an empty sky, or possibly Jameson.

Rusty had been lying to Corky about paying off 'The Boss', of course. Rusty had every intention of stealing the whole shooting match and getting off-planet before anyone stopped him. The presence of two starships floating overhead had Rusty in a sweat.

It didn't take long to locate the round silver ball, parked in the trough of a deep dune. In his mind, Luke complimented the pilot on the location. If he hadn't seen and trailed after the object, Luke was sure he would never have come across it. He doubted anyone in the camp would stumble on it accidentally.

This thought added to the ease with which Luke believed he could steal the craft without anyone, except the pilot, noticing. But the pilot would be easy to take care of. Luke gave it no more than a passing moment of reflection.

Luke slipped cautiously around the back end of the ball. It was plain from the size of the thing that it was intended to be manned by a single person. He heard no sounds and saw no activity. Considering the time it had taken him to track it, he assumed the craft had been on the ground for a little over 45 minutes. That meant the pilot was already out exploring the neighborhood.

Abandoning the need for stealth, Luke walked around to the craft's rampdoor and examined the entry command console. On the *Lithe Arrow*, there was a keyed pad which required knowledge of the code to open the door.

Doctor Tilorri, who seemed unaccustomed to lying, had provided the code to Rusty when he asked for it. Torture or threats hadn't been necessary. Luke concluded the old gal was too smart to waste her remaining life energy on something as useless as resistance, considering the circumstances.

Luke saw the same keypad on this smaller craft. He was sure he could get the access code from the pilot, although it would no doubt require a bit more persuasion. He would rather not force the door as he didn't want to damage the craft's ability to fly him to the *Boadicea*.

Luke had himself been putting away a few baubles here and there as insurance against Jameson's failure to pay up, which was now certain. Jameson might fancy himself an underworld crime boss, but he lacked the required ruthlessness.

It took one kind of ruthlessness to claw one's way up the ladder of the military hierarchy and another entirely to move successfully in the world's underbelly. A world-weary bitterness and the lust for wealth were insufficient credentials.

The stones Luke had fingered were ones that, when set, would sell for nice but not noticeably high credits. Enough, on top of his 250,000 in blood money, to justify this current adventure.

As for Forrest, Jameson didn't know Luke would have agreed to kill her for the sheer challenge of it. It was an exercise in ingenuity. No one had ever been able to 'do' Forrest, although it had been tried. Luke would be the one to bear the honor, even if it would remain a secret honor, except within LiShanNa. His brother assassins would celebrate his success.

Luke had calculated Jameson could not reach the planetoid before nightfall, and quite possibly not until long after that. He didn't intend to be there so he didn't care.

He had given Jameson the coordinates for a de-mat into the miners' camp. If he and the miners opted to kill each other, more power to them. If the miners were already gone and Jameson, who had advance-funded this illegal mining enterprise, came up empty-handed...well, *c'est la vie*.

And his getaway? Luke had made another call after his call to Jameson that had arranged for that. Like a magic trick, he would escape directly from the bridge of the *Boadicea*.

Chapter
Ten

ALTHOUGH SHE WAS only next door, Sukha couldn't see Bajana. Coming to the rescue, Jeremy showed him how to contact her via the computer. Despite his ingrained patience, Sukha was chomping at the bit to tell Bajana about his discussion with the Language and Cultural Attache.

She had not answered his call and he presumed she was asleep. He had eventually dropped off himself. Now, gauging the increasing brightness of the automated lighting in his cell, he gathered it was morning.

He washed and punched up a whole wheat muffin and something titled orange juice from the shipcook, a second device Jeremy demonstrated for him. Sukha had no qualms about using the shipcook once Jeremy pointed out that vegetarian entrees were easy to identify. They were starred with an asterisk on the display. He also taught Sukha the names of the three daily meals.

The *Heaven's Bow* did not possess food replicating capability. She carried sufficient backup food stores to last 48 Shivani years for her small crew of 30. But most daily meals came from the deck devoted to hydroponic food production. Indrashtra had mentioned the existence of food replication with which his ship had been equipped, but the technology was not recorded and, as far as Sukha knew, had disappeared from Shivani knowledge.

As an engineer, he had listened enthralled to Jeremy's admittedly non-technical explanation of how the shipcook created an enticing array of foods from a chemical soup of fats, proteins, carbohydrate chains, vitamins, minerals and trace elements.

That this technology, and others unknown to him, might become available to Nirvannini captivated his imagination. If nothing else, he could bear home news of other technologies to gratify the I.S.A. stockholders.

Under normal circumstances, Sukha exhibited the qualified cynicism and mental control appropriate to his age and learning. But so much had happened in the last 12 hours he was ready to run and shout at the top of his lungs with the bursting excitement of an adolescent. To keep busy, he tried Bajana again. This time she answered.

"What time is it?" she asked groggily.

"Early morning, Bajana. You are more disciplined than this."

"I think I'm suffering from disorientation. Phew. I could stand with a shower."

"The facilities don't extend to that. But there is a sink. It could be worse."

"Yes." She yawned, dragging herself from her bunk. "I'll wash up as well as I can."

When she returned to his computer screen, looking fresh and more like her usual self, Sukha demonstrated the shipcook for her. She punched up a bowl of oatmeal with raisins and a cup of coffee. Neither of them knew what these were but they were listed as vegetarian choices under breakfast.

"It's some kind of grain," she said, after chewing a few mouthfuls. "Thicker than rice with a sweeter, mealier taste." Rice was the pre-eminent grain on Nirvannini. Terraced paddies of it covered nearly all of the arable land. Bajana took a sip of the black coffee.

"Zow! Bitter! It's like our korkor."

"Probably a stimulant. Bitter often indicates the presence of alkaloids."

As Sukha watched Bajana consume her unfamiliar meal with gusto, he was reminded of the time, eight years before, when he had to bully her to take even the smallest mouthful of food. She had been listless and inattentive, touchy to a fault.

At first he thought it was a change related to her Brahuinna female biology. Then Nirvannini's official news agency reported that the cluster of symptoms Bajana exhibited had appeared almost universally among the Brahuinna. Shivani had been immune to the disorder.

"Sukha, your thoughts." Bajana scraped the bowl for the last bite of the oatmeal. She pushed it aside and chugged down her coffee.

"Nothing," he waved away her question. He didn't want to remind her of that time. "I wanted to tell you what I learned from Ensign Eireann."

"Go ahead, Sukha. But then I want to talk about how we get out of here. I must return to the *Heaven's Bow*." She crumpled the empty cup in her fist and tossed it down the chute marked 'disposal'. Then she punched up a second cup.

"Are you sure?" Sukha questioned. "You don't know how strong the effects of the first will be."

"The stronger the better, Sukha. Maybe," she said, "you should have some yourself. You may need it."

THE FEW HOURS of deep sleep s/he had enjoyed as a result of Luluai's efforts had revitalized Ma'at's energy. S/he pulled experimentally at the stake above hir head. It didn't budge and a sharp pain raced down hir arms at the attempt.

It was going to be a long day, much longer than the day before. Today there would be no water, no food and no release from the sun. And just as the night had been life-threatening for hir, the day would be deadly for Luluai.

Ma'at gripped the stake and went to work in earnest, ignoring the searing pain that shot through hir muscles. Hir shoulders bunched in agony every time s/he yanked at the stake. Pain messages from the nerves in hir beaten jaw and temple tugged insistently at hir consciousness. Hir naked chest simmered. Ma'at knew if s/he laid there all day, despite the reflective capacity of hir skin, s/he would have 2nd degree burns by nightfall.

S/he took a breather and checked on Luluai. The Sirensi looked to be asleep. Ma'at watched the measured rise and fall of her chest to reassure hirself she was alive.

S/he went back to work. Despite hir Nhavan physiology, the exertion and the hot sun began to take their toll. Unlike a human, s/he didn't sweat to cool hir body. Instead, hir blood circulated like a coolant against hir skin to radiate heat away from hir organs.

S/he began to develop a rhythm. Pull on the inhale, rest on the exhale, pull on the inhale, rest on the exhale. The work began to take on a power and life of its own. All s/he had to do was participate. S/he had pulled and rested, pulled and rested for at least an hour when Luluai began to moan and twist, wresting with her bonds.

Ma'at stopped to take a break, contorting hir complaining neck to look at her. Tears flowed down Luluai's flaming red cheeks. She licked at cracked lips. "I won't make it Ma'at," she groaned miserably. "I won't make it through this day."

Ma'at gave in to a moment of regret. I can't save her either, s/he thought. The stake, as near as s/he could tell, had not loosened perceptibly. S/he laid hir head back on the sand and went at it again.

LIEUTENANT PATRICIA MOUNEERA had felt worse in her life but she couldn't remember when. Her joints ached, her feet burned, her mind wandered, and her communications board gave her nothing but grief. All the buttons were where they had always been, as the captain had been so rude to point out, but she felt a lingering sense of confusion.

She had dragged herself to the bridge in response to DeVargas's craven appeals for relief. He had sworn to her he would only grab a meal, take a catnap, and be back in a jiffy. Mouneera was the sole senior officer left on her feet who could fill in on the bridge.

Ensign Harley Hammerstein, who had taken Sabi's position

since that helmsman's medical quarantine, looked wobbly to Mouneera. Like a dog guarding the manager, he had snapped at her when she suggested he take a break from duty.

Mouneera figured he was viewing the job as a proving ground and she wasn't to the point of ordering him to take a reprieve. As near as she could tell, he was doing his job properly, which was to keep them in a synchronized orbit with the *Heaven's Bow*. Another junior officer, Ensign Sue Mata, ceaselessly scanned the science console, keeping her eyes peeled for any hint of trouble.

Mouneera had confidence in the able junior crew. These were the people who would, in all likelihood, command the *Boadicea* some day. It was good for them to get a sense of what it was like to be in charge in a real situation. Well, virtually in charge. Anything they did could be countermanded by her. Any real danger would require her to consult with Captain Forrest.

Shortly after coming on to the bridge, she called the *Heaven's Bow* at Captain Forrest's request and told them it was Captain Ki's order that Hasitam Deva be released from cabin arrest and given control of the *Heaven's Bow* bridge. The *Heaven's Bow* communications officer, a young olive-skinned, dark-haired human named Makka No, had smiled her relief at receiving a transmission from the *Boadicea*.

"We were so worried," she told Lieutenant Mouneera. "We didn't know what had happened. Captain Ki and Sukha just disappeared."

Mouneera knew it would be violating regulations to comment on the status of the prisoners but her heart reached out to the frightened girl and she did her best to reassure her. "Captain Forrest is a very good captain," she said, "I'm sure everything will get worked out very soon. Please don't worry."

"I will give Hasitam his orders right away," Makka No answered. "And please," she said, "call me the moment you know anything."

"Of course," Mouneera agreed.

The kinelift doors whooshed opened and Mouneera turned to see Ensign Eireann coming on to the bridge. She had hoped it would be DeVargas returning to his station.

"Hi, Lieutenant," Eireann waved cheerfully. The casual tone irritated Mouneera. She felt sorry for the ensign and her inability to fit in on the *Boadicea* but this was the bridge after all, not the rec deck or the mess hall.

"What can I do for you, Ensign?" Mouneera's voice was chilly but the effect was lost on Eireann.

"Sukha Jabala and I," —Mouneera thought it sounded awfully friendly, considering Sukha was officially an enemy—"are conducting some cultural research. We need some data from the *Heaven's Bow* in order to proceed. I thought maybe you could call them and request it."

"Have you talked to the Captain about this?"

"Uh, no. But I'm going to."

Mouneera's eyebrows angled steeply. "Ensign—"

"I mean as soon as we have some conclusions. There's no point in talking to Captain Forrest until I have something to tell her, is there?"

"Maybe not. But has the concept of permission for these activities ever occurred to you?"

The other woman's face colored a bright red. "I, uh—"

"Let's just call the Captain, shall we?" Mouneera hailed the briefing room.

"Yes?" Forrest sounded irritated. Mouneera knew she was in conference with the only engineering tech who was experienced enough, and still lucid enough, to analyze the de-matter's calibration patterns.

"Captain," Mouneera said, "Ensign Eireann informs me she is conducting some cultural research on the *Heaven's Bow* people. She has been meeting with one of your detainees and they would like to transmit some data that they need from the *Heaven's Bow*."

"Cripes, Mouneera! Can't she stay out of trouble?"

"Captain, she is standing right here."

"Captain," Eireann put in, "I am staying out of trouble. All I need from the *Heaven's Bow* is a copy of some of their historical scripts. It's for language analysis. It's nothing classified."

"Hrmph." There was a long pause while Dani considered the request. Something—*anything*—to keep Eireann busy and out of her and the rest of the crew's hair might be worth it.

"Alright. Mouneera, you can request it. But I want you to check over the incoming transmission with a fine-toothed comb to ensure there is nothing that could in any way represent a danger to *Boadicea*."

"Will do, Captain."

"Good. Forrest out."

After giving the details of her request to Lieutenant Mouneera, Caitlin rushed from the bridge to give Sukha the good news. A different guard, her stringy mouse-brown hair pulled back in a regulation bun, was on duty and she was a good deal less casual than Jeremy had been. She demanded to know by what authority Caitlin was visiting the brig's occupants.

"Captain Forrest has okayed it," Caitlin said, "You can take my word for it."

Chief of Security Cory Markett, a suspicious-minded woman,

had no intention of taking the ensign's word for anything. It was whispered among the crew that Eireann was a troublemaker who was sure to run awry of the captain eventually and get herself thrown in the brig, no matter how perky and charming she might be. Conscientious security personnel took note of rumors of this type.

"Yes, it's alright, Markett." Forrest wearily explained in answer to the security chief's call. "As long as she doesn't go into their cells. Her clearance to the ship's computers is limited. She can't access any information vital to ship security."

"Very good, Captain."

"That doesn't mean," Forrest continued, "you shouldn't keep a close eye on her."

"Noted, sir." It would be her pleasure, Cory Markett thought.

"Forrest out." Dani sighed. She had enough problems without Eireann. For one thing, despite repeated tries, DeVargas had not been able to raise Rusty or anyone on the planetoid in order to further negotiations. Maybe the miners' figuring out how to answer the transcon the first time had been a fluke. Or maybe they had lost interest.

Dani didn't want to contemplate the later possibility. She didn't think Ma'at or the *Heaven's Bow* crew were in immediate danger from the miners, the lack of Samson's and Martinez's life readings notwithstanding. She still didn't know if the ship's equipment was operating properly or if some kind of planetary electrical interference was skewing the readings. But she did know that Rusty had to know he wasn't going to get what he was angling for if he started killing off Forrest's crew. It was not in his best interest.

Sending down a shuttlecraft to rescue Ma'at and hir company was one possibility but not one she was ready to put into action. Not only were there too few able crew to draw on for such a mission but she wasn't half sure anyone would stay well long enough to make the journey to the planetoid, let alone effect a rescue against armed men.

The crew was dropping like flies as a result of the ailment that Sly couldn't diagnose. She knew she was getting worse. Her feet burned as if she was walking barefoot on hot sand at the beach. But she didn't want to worry Sly any more than he already was with a complaint about yet another bizarre symptom.

The de-matter was still under repair. The tech, John Sibell, had promised Dani he would institute the new calibration changes immediately and let her know the results. Dani knew Captain Ki and Sukha Jabala had de-matted over more or less safely. Captain Ki had been shaken but she claimed it had been her first time to de-mat, so there was no way to know if she had suffered from normal aftershock or if it was as a result of the de-matter calibration problem.

Until the equipment was certified shipshape, it was too risky to de-mat to the planet. De-mating Ma'at and hir team back was a moot point. Without their transcons, Mouneera and DeVargas couldn't get a lock on them.

If only they had been allowed to stop at Spaceportal sixteen and have *Boadicea* overhauled before they made their way to the Free Sector. And make one small delivery of a certain loose cannon.

What would Eireann do next?

LULUAI BEGAN TO talk and it was a strange sound. At first, Ma'at thought she was hysterical. Then s/he realized the Sirensi was singing. Her voice was ragged and the elusive melody was broken by stretches of wheezy gasping, but it was a song. As near as Ma'at could interpret, Luluai was singing her lifestory. A cultural rite? S/he didn't doubt Luluai believed she was dying. Just as Ma'at needed someone to accept hir soul nature, Luluai might need to tell of her life's experiences preparatory to death.

Ma'at listened as s/he tugged at the stake above hir head, hearing both Luluai's voice and in hir mind, picking up those fragmentary images of the alien's life that were strong enough to be telepathically transmitted.

In the beginning Luluai's voice was lilting, sweet with the memories of early childhood. As she grew in years, the flowing cadence was punctuated by howls or whoops of delight and warbled bursts of excitement. When she came to tell of adolescence, her voice sharpened with rancor. Ma'at felt Luluai's dismay at realizing she was not like the rest of her people. S/he was not sure how Luluai was different from other Sirensi but Ma'at perceived that Luluai believed she was different. Luluai's burgeoning awareness of the significance of her difference from those she loved and played with made her voice heavy. The cant became a dirge.

In a melancholy key, she lamented the loneliness that became her constant companion. Then the notes began to swell like the climax in a symphony, until, with a wail of frustration, Luluai reached the turning point of her young life: she decided to leave Elysiansus.

A new movement took hold, thumping with the stiff qualities of a march, as she recounted her journey to Nirvannini and her early days there. After a time, the beat loosened and notes of shy happiness crept in as she found herself adjusting to living among a diversity of people in another culture's cities. With pride, she crowed about her accomplishments, about the hard work she invested in learning sciences no Sirensi had ever mastered.

Despite her exaltation, the last verse seemed to exhaust her.

When she started to tell of the journey of the *Heaven's Bow*, her voice was a hoarse whisper and Ma'at noticed there were long, utterly still, pauses between verses. She was beginning to slip away into death. The effort of singing had drained what little remained of her life energy.

Ma'at's energy was oozing away as well, soaked up by the merciless sun. Hir quivering arms existed in another dimension. Hir awareness of them was that of an ethereal dislocated numbness. They did not belong to hir and s/he did not know what powered them as they rhythmically contracted and released, clasping and pulling at the unmoving stake.

CAITLIN PACED IN her cabin waiting for Lieutenant Mouneera's go-ahead. In addition to the text of *The Glorious Interstellar Journeys of Indrashtra*, she had requested, at Sukha's insistence, a source manuscript called the *Vedka-Atra*. He had refused to tell her anything about it. "Be patient," he counseled, "I do not know if it will be of value to you."

Patience had never been one of Caitlin's virtues anyway but now she was practically vibrating with anticipation. She considered she might be on the threshold of one of the greatest linguistic discoveries of the era. She tried to sleep, she tried to play games on the computer, she ate a chocolate bar she had stashed under her pillow. Finally, she just sat down on her bunk and gave into an overriding desire to bite her nails down to the quick.

Lieutenant Mouneera, cool and competent, buzzed her. "Your data has been cleared and is in the ship's computer, Ensign."

"Great! I owe you one, Lieutenant."

Mouneera snorted gently. Right, she thought to herself. Eireann probably wasn't so bad. Just unseasoned and a bit more impetuous than the usual crew member on *Boadicea*. It took all the new personnel some time to settle in. Eireann's problem was that she wasn't thinking about settling in. It was hard to blame her since she wasn't staying.

"When you sign on, you'll see the access code for the data," Mouneera said. "And Ensign—"

"Yes?"

"Good luck." It was unexpected and Caitlin was touched.

"Thank you. Thank you very much."

MA'AT WAS SO absorbed in catching the last of Luluai's soliloquy, a pained gurgly whisper, that s/he didn't notice the stake give way. Hir arms flung unaccountably upwards, the stake adhering to hir sticky palms. S/he stared for a moment in bafflement at hir raised arms before hir mind accepted the facts of hir senses. As relentlessly as s/he had worked to uproot the stake s/he had not realistically expected to see it in hir hands.

Ma'at forced apart hir blistered palms and the stake slipped from hir grasp and fell against hir chest. S/he hardly felt the dull thud. S/he swept it away into the sand and sat up. Blood rushed away from hir head and the desert swung and bobbed in front of hir eyes. It was difficult to remember s/he had ever enjoyed such a position. When hir head cleared, s/he lifted hir bound wrists to hir mouth and, pulling with hir teeth, worked to loosen the knots.

When the bonds fell apart, s/he reached down to untie those securing hir feet. S/he had so little sensation in hir fingers s/he could not feel with them. S/he had to direct the slow, pained activity of hir hands with hir sense of sight. The process seemed to take forever and s/he gritted hir teeth in concentration. When it was done, s/he crawled across the sand to Luluai.

Luluai took no notice as Ma'at freed her hands from the stake. With care, Ma'at eased her arms down to the sides of her body. S/he untied her feet, then crawling painfully back to her head, leaned hir ear near her mouth. Her quavering song had long since ceased. She lay still, her eyes closed against death, but Ma'at felt a faint exhaled breath against the sensitive sunburned skin of hir cheek.

"Lieutenant," s/he grasped the Sirensi's shoulder and gently shook it. S/he got no response and s/he knew the Sirensi was unaware of both hir presence and their sudden freedom. Kneeling beside her, Ma'at took note of their location. The miner's camp was behind hir. If s/he twisted around, s/he could see just the tips of the surrounding rocks. It would be futile to sneak into the camp in broad daylight in search of the doctors. In hir weakened condition, a light bop on the head would be sufficient to fell hir.

Unfortunately, crossing the desert was no more savory an idea. Aside from the heat, which hung shimmering in transparent waves in the motionless air, s/he had no food or water. S/he had no knowledge of the planetoid's desert creatures but s/he had never been in a desert that lacked them, particularly poisonous ones, and hir feet were bare. S/he wasn't even certain s/he could walk.

Ma'at gazed across at the low line of mountains edging the southeastern horizon and sought to gauge the distance. Two hours walk? Three? Four? S/he twisted to look at the camp then turned back to eye the mountains.

Cautiously, Ma'at got to hir feet. A hot prickling, like the stabbing of a thousand razor-sharp knives, raced through hir thighs and down hir calves. Knowing rationally it was blood cascading harmlessly into atrophying muscles made the experience no less painful. S/he reeled with vertigo. After a long uncertain minute, the searing pain in hir legs was replaced by a numb throbbing and the spinning of hir head settled into mere shakiness.

Ma'at took a deep breath and let it out. S/he hadn't fainted. It meant s/he had a chance of making it. S/he knelt again and, putting hir arm beneath Luluai's back, lifted her to a sitting position. Without a sound, the Sirensi pitched sideways and rolled limply on the sand.

Ma'at's teeth ground together in despair. S/he estimated the likelihood of surviving a crossing of the desert, taking into account hir physical state and the environmental conditions, was less than 20 percent. If s/he had to carry Luluai, s/he calculated that number descended very close to zero. Carrying her would make for very slow going, vastly prolonging every life-threatening element s/he faced: heat, thirst, fatigue, hunger.

But s/he could not leave the Sirensi to die. S/he slid hir hands under her back and legs and, in a crouch, hefted the Sirensi's body onto hir naked sunburned shoulders. S/he raised up slowly, swaying dizzily as s/he adjusted Luluai's unconscious form across hir back.

S/he calculated she weighed 45 kilos to hir 70, a heavy but not unmanageable burden under normal circumstances. But today...just as with the stake, s/he sternly reprimanded hirself, s/he must think only of the goal, not the journey.

S/he swung about to face the mountains and took an initial unsteady step. In the mountains there would be water. Luluai was a water creature. Water might revive her. Ma'at started walking.

"SUKHA, THIS DOCUMENT is immense! It will take months to read, let alone complete a comparative analysis and conduct the research necessary to corroborate Indrashtra's account."

Sukha laughed. "You could hardly expect 200 Shivani years of 'captain's logs' to be diminutive, Caitlin. I have made a study of *The Interstellar Journeys* my life's work. I have much still to learn from this text and I am already 95 Earth years old."

"Which makes you, let's see, 190 Shivani years old?"

"That's right."

"Whew! Well, since we don't have that kind of leisure and I don't even have that kind of lifespan, where do you suggest we start?"

"Clearly we are most concerned with determining the correspondence of Earth, if any, to the Planet of Many Splendors so we should start with Indrashtra's account of his 18 Shivani—or 9 Earth if you prefer—years' contact with the people of that planet."

"Good idea. Computer, please provide text entries from *The*

Interstellar Journeys beginning with Shivani Year 52379." The text was displayed on the giant screen of the brig in side-by-side columns. Atravayasana occupied one column and Coalition Patois, showing numerous untranslatable gaps, filled the other.

"These first entries deal with Indrashtra's landing and accounts of the damage to his ship as well as descriptions of the surrounding land and climate," Sukha said.

"What became of Indrashtra's ship, by the way? After he got back to Nirvannini?"

"At first, it was housed in a museum honoring Indrashtra's adventure. A few centuries passed and the political climate changed. The government repressed Indrashtra's legacy and the ship was dismantled. Pieces of it—the electronic circuitry, for instance—turned up millennia later incorporated into the religious art of a few remote monasteries."

"But they didn't know what it was?"

"There was a secret knowledge about *The Interstellar Journeys* passed down through a lineage of monks at Tal. These monks were Brahuinna, not Shivani. They were disparaged for clinging to what was perceived to be a highly speculative tradition regarding the origin of Shivani religious ideas."

"But you believe this 'highly speculative' tradition is true?"

"Yes. The text of *The Interstellar Journeys* proves it. You must understand that when Indrashtra left Nirvannini on his adventure, he was authorized and funded by the government of his day."

"Hmm. That's interesting. What did his government expect him to accomplish by going out into space?"

"He was sent to seek the existence of other cultures. No one knew if any existed but the hope that they did ran high. You see, Nirvannini was a monoculture and was dying."

"Dying? But they had spaceflight. That's very advanced technologically."

"Yes. Material comforts abounded. But the heart of the culture was dead. There was no philosophical stimulation, no difference in opinions, no ideals to strive for, no reason to live from day to day."

"And Shivani live a long time."

"Yes. Fortunately, Indrashtra not only returned but came home laden with booty. His reappearance revitalized Shivani culture in dozens of ways. There were fresh ideas and fresh pastimes. A new religious philosophy, new food grains, new plants, new animals. But especially, new people to allow for a broadening of the diminishing Shivani gene pool."

"Are there Brahuinna-Shivani offspring then?"

"Not anymore, but there were at first."

"Something went wrong."

"Yes, politically. Not biologically. From what I have gleaned from the rare historical records that were not destroyed, which cover the period two centuries after Indrashtra's return, issues of cultural control began to take an upper hand, probably ignited by population pressures."

"Just not enough elbow room, huh?"

"Our land masses are small and space is always at a premium. But it was more than that. I think repression was driven by the fear that when the Brahuinna eclipsed the Shivani in population, they would eclipse them in political power as well, becoming the ruling elite."

"But, if I understand you correctly, the Brahuinna were already the philosophical and religious elite."

"Precisely. That power was a threat. I think the Shivani of the day rationalized that the religion that had been brought by the Brahuinna was their own invention—after all they had been practicing it for centuries by that time—and were anxious to claim it as their own."

"So—"

"So, Brahuinna priests were murdered and Brahuinna source documents in the original language destroyed. Brahuinna citizens were forced to move to less elite communities, isolating them from Shivani culture. Educational opportunities for Brahuinna children were severely restricted."

"Brahuinna-Shivani marriage was outlawed and racially-mixed individuals were herded onto the most remote and most non-arable lands and left to survive as best they could. The hope being, of course, that they would die out in a few generations. The conditions were so severe they did."

"Whew," Caitlin said. "This is an old story."

"Yes, it is." Sukha looked speculatively at her. "I take it you mean something other than mere antiquity?"

"Unfortunately, yes. This is a story that has been repeated on Earth many times over. Sad, wrong, but ever-repeating. I suppose," she sighed, "to top it off, the repression was covered up?"

"Of course. Until the Brahuinna themselves had no recollection of their origins or their contributions to Nirvannini life and culture."

"Wow. You know, we should get back to the text, Sukha."

"Of course, Caitlin. Let's do."

MA'AT'S PROGRESS WAS slow. It took all of hir concentration to lift a foot, swing it forward, and allow it to sink back into the clinging sand before s/he lifted the other foot and repeated the process. The sand burned the soles and edges of hir naked feet and

Luluai's weight dragged at hir shoulders.

After an hour that subjectively seemed an eternity, Ma'at experienced a second wind. Pain faded from hir mind. Ma'at knew it wasn't a result of the pain control technique s/he had instituted the night before to survive the cold. The relief afforded by that mental exercise had long since passed. Ma'at had not had the time or strength to institute another.

This was an indication hir mind refused to accept any more signals from hir overworked nerves. It didn't matter. Ma'at was still awake and walking. At least Ma'at assumed s/he was. For all Ma'at could be sure of, s/he might have fallen and now be engaged in an elaborate wish-fulfilling dream.

Ma'at had no way of being certain so s/he kept going, taking advantage of hir temporary energy. If Ma'at was actually walking, s/he knew hir second wind would fade in time. It was a last burst of athletic output before hir muscles, nerves and organs refused further effort and hir body forced collapse despite the urges of hir will to survive.

Looking at the sky, Ma'at surmised it was near or just after high noon. The mountains seemed to be closer. Just as had occurred the day before, voluminous white clouds spilled over the low range. As the afternoon wore on, they would build themselves into towering thunderheads and bring rain. But it would be hours before they did.

For the first time, Ma'at became aware of an unrelenting thirst. Hir body was designed to preserve every molecule of moisture available to it. For a Nhavan to become acutely aware of thirst meant impending disaster and s/he knew it. Ma'at accepted the message and pushed on. Ma'at had not stopped once. Ma'at feared if s/he did, s/he would not get up again.

"THERE'S JUST ONE hole in your story, Sukha, and it's a big one." Caitlin looked away from the side-by-side texts she and Sukha were reading on the computer's large wall screen.

"What's that?"

"If the Shivani rulers of ancient Nirvannini were so successful in repressing the contribution of the Brahuinna, how did you ever get into space to seek proof of exactly that?"

Sukha liked Caitlin. She had a quick analytical mind and, like Bajana, was blunt and enthusiastic in her approach to the subject at hand. At least like Bajana usually was. Since they had been captured, Bajana had kept him at arm's length. He didn't know if it was the mere fact of their capture or the conditions which chafed at her spirit. Despite the progress he and Caitlin were making, she had declined to join in their discussion.

"Once I deciphered *The Interstellar Journeys*, I had them published. Quietly at first, and in small print runs. But the work was such a radical revision of the *status quo* that copies began to circulate secretly among highly-placed Shivani. Some of them were sympathetic to the conditions under which the Brahuinna lived and wanted to see change. Some were not. Nonetheless, over time, Indrashtra's adventures attracted more and more attention at all levels of society."

"So much so that I was ordered to stop lecturing and teaching. But it was too late. The time, I guess was just ripe. Once the media got hold of the text, they played up the controversy. That led to an open and vituperative social debate that split Nirvannini into an array of factions."

"I still don't see how that got you into space," Caitlin said.

"The government was losing control of the people and suffering from a devastating loss of face. They were most cowed by a group of Shivani calling themselves the New Progressives. The New Progressives are espousing elimination of any cultural ideas that are 'foreign'—read Brahuinna—in origin. And a 'final solution' to the problem of the Brahuinna."

Caitlin shuddered. "Genocide?"

"Yes. The current government, which has maintained a tradition of peace for thousands of years, is revolted by the notion. As a way of maintaining social stability without sticking their necks out much, they posited a temporary solution. They suggested to the people that before any action is taken, the story of the Brahuinna as related in *The Interstellar Journeys* be either verified or laid to rest as false."

"So here you are."

"So, here I am," he said, "at the mercy of your Coalition."

"I guess we need to decide once and for all if the Brahuinna are from Earth. That's the real question, right?"

"Yes. It is clear—you have already read it—that Indrashtra brought back highly-learned priests and priestesses from some culture on some world. These beings gave Nirvannini such philosophical beliefs as monism, non-violence, and the concept of every person's soul residing in the Great Soul which is at the center of creation and endlessly generates life."

"You know, if Earth is the planet, this is a bit of a twist from the usual."

Sukha frowned. "How so?"

Caitlin giggled. "Well,it's always been a popular alternate viewpoint on Earth that early humans were too stupid to build the great civilizations, like Egypt and Sumer and the Indus Valley, and that they got help from 'superior' extra-terrestrial beings. But you're saying your civilization is based on Brahuinna ideas. The ideas, namely, of early humans from Earth. It's a topsy-turvy version of that theory and it's going to make a lot of Earthers mad."

"Not only ideas, too. Nirvannini received a number of material enhancements from the Planet of Many Splendors as well."

"Oh, yeah. You mentioned plants and animals and pastimes. What were they?"

"It's later in the text but Indrashtra brought back teak and rosewood trees, barley, cotton, and horses. Even chariots. He wanted to bring elephants and water buffalo but he couldn't fit them aboard his craft."

"I'm not surprised," Caitlin said dryly, "those are massive animals. But chariots? Wasn't that kind of primitive for Nirvannini's material culture?"

"Chariot racing became, and remains, one of Nirvannini's favorite pastimes. It is visceral and violent, yet aesthetic. Indrashtra fell in love with horses and chariots. He brought experienced horsemen to care for them. Men from the 'steppes' he says, whatever that is. Not, apparently, the people populating Chak Purbane Syal."

"The Russian Steppes," Caitlin said almost dreamily. "The steppes are vast grasslands," she explained to Sukha. "They were supposed to be populated with nomadic peoples at that time. At least one of those groups, the Sinhasta, are believed to have developed the single-person racing chariot. Their chariots pre-date the heavy war chariots of the Middle East."

"Interesting," Sukha said. "Another corroboration?"

"I'm not sure but I think so. This has to be Earth, everything seems to fit! We must find a way to prove it, Sukha."

"I don't know if the source document I asked you to request, the *Vedka-Atra*, would help but—"

"What is it?"

"The content doesn't make any difference for our purposes. But it is written in the original script brought by the Brahuinna to Nirvannini with a columnar translation into Old Atravayasana. If it matches any known Earth script, it may be a way of proving the connection."

"Computer," Caitlin gestured, her hands trembling slightly, "show us a sample of text from the *Vedka-Atra*." The computer complied and a script Caitlin had never seen before appeared on the screen accompanied by an archaic form of the Atravayasana script she was just learning to recognize.

The symbols were a kind of pictographic scrawl, something between pictures and abstractions. Some were as recognizable as fish or antler's horns, some were unidentifiable shapes.

"Computer," Caitlin asked, her breath coming out in an excited puff, "does this script match any script in the ship's database?"

"There is an 83% match rate to Script AG671."

"Please display."

Obligingly, the computer produced a new column of text, this one showing the symbols comprising Script AG671.

"Computer, is AG671 the script more popularly known by linguists as the Indus-Sarasvati script?" Caitlin's voice rose and her question ended on a squeaky high note.

"That is correct," the computer responded neutrally. Caitlin's face went white. Sukha leaned toward her with concern. She seemed to have stopped breathing.

"Are you alright?"

"Barely."

"Considering," Sukha said slowly and distinctly, his eyes focused intently on her, "that the *Vedka-Atra* includes a translation of this script into Old Atravayasana, it can be translated into contemporary Atravayasana, and from there into Coalition Patois. You could, therefore, decipher the original Indus-Sarasvati script."

Caitlin's vision blurred. The scripts danced on the screen like stick figure children laughing merrily in a game. She lifted a shaking hand to her forehead.

"My name," she said in a dazed voice, "will go down in Coalition linguistic history."

MA'AT DECIDED IT was not hir imagination that the mountains were closer. For one thing, there were thin scatterings of desert plants alleviating the tan barrenness. Patches of scrub sage and clusters of baby-sized barrel-shaped cactuses sprouted along the ridges of the sand dunes. Straggly clumps of blue-grey grass became common. It meant water. S/he topped a dune and thought s/he saw it. S/he saw a distant tree anyway. Tall, almost leafless, one of the hardy palms. S/he looked again and it wasn't there.

Hallucination. The well-known desert experience of the mirage. S/he heard the squawk of a bird and attributed it to the expanding hallucination. The mountains, though, were closer. S/he was convinced of it. S/he anticipated their shade, their coolness, and focused hir mind on it: coolness, coolness, coolness.

S/he climbed torturously down another dune and then trudged out again, shifting Luluai's weight to counterbalance hir own as s/he had done on every trough and every ridge of every dune. Hir shoulders were blistered now as well as burned. There was a twanging pain beneath hir shoulder blades that radiated down to hir ribs. It hadn't been there when s/he started carrying Luluai.

When s/he topped the dune, the palm tree was there again, larger this time. Coolness, coolness, coolness. It was a lovely fantasy.

S/he crept down another dune, crossed its trough and doggedly tramped up the other side. The land leveled out. The palm was still there. It was some distance off and suffused by wriggly waves of heat that shifted weirdly in the dead air, making Ma'at's eyes water and hir head pound.

As s/he got closer, s/he saw there was a natural scoop of rock holding water that burbled out of a spring somewhere beyond, hidden up a narrow canyon. S/he could see the cleft in the mountains that formed the canyon. S/he could hear the water gurgle and smell its wetness.

An exceptionally beautiful mirage, s/he thought, ironically complimenting hirself on the powers of hir imagination. The tree stirred in a desert gust, beckoning hir. Ma'at laughed, a maniacal self-deprecating laugh.

The part of hir mind that was still rational forced hir to keep putting one foot before the other. The irrational part indulged in the exquisite completeness of hir mirage oasis. There were rock outcroppings like those around the miner's camp, protecting hir mirage and making it a pleasant, cool valley. But waves of heat surrounded the whole image, making it dance before hir eyes in its unreality.

Ma'at walked toward the pool of water. Its perfection mocked hir. S/he knew it would dissolve the moment s/he touched it, the moment s/he walked through it. It was such an elaborate wish-fulfilling invention s/he knew s/he was near death.

Ma'at staggered and felt Luluai's body slip erratically to the left, throwing hir off balance. S/he counterbalanced by throwing hirself forward. S/he wasn't certain Luluai wasn't already dead. But s/he had to reach the pool even if it was an illusion.

In another four steps, s/he was in the water. It felt infinitely cool around hir ankles. Nothing had ever felt so pleasurable to hir: not hir parents' love, not Dani's friendship, not the physical bliss shared with lovers, not anything.

Ma'at dropped to hir knees. S/he had no idea how a mirage could feel as real as it looked. S/he shifted sideways and Luluai slipped from hir shoulders. S/he let the Sirensi lay in the shallow water while s/he bent forward for a drink of the pure, cool, crystalline liquid.

S/he saw hir cupped hands, adrip with water glistening in the sunlight, saw them lifting themselves upward toward hir parched lips. S/he felt the cool droplets glide silkily down hir raw throat. S/he lifted another handful and another.

It tasted like water. Ma'at laid down and the coolness, like a balm, suffused the raw skin of hir burned torso. S/he rolled over and the water soaked hir blistered back. S/he saw the rain-heavy clouds over hir head and laughed again.

What was real? What was not? For all s/he knew, s/he had been drinking sand and was now rolling in it like a boisterous, if deranged, puppy.

Ma'at lay motionless on hir back and stared straight up into the gathering clouds until hir eyes no longer seemed a part of hir but were clouds themselves. Hir whole body was becoming clouds. Flat on hir back, s/he was floating upwards toward them. There was no effort involved in it.

From the sky, s/he glanced curiously back down at hir mirage oasis. A long silver cord stretched between hir and hir body, now far below on the ground. S/he wondered what the cord was and where it had come from but only idly, the way one wonders why an acquaintance has changed her hairstyle. S/he could see Luluai laying on hir side, growing smaller. S/he could see the top of the palm tree. It too was growing smaller, and seemed to wave goodbye, much as it had waved hello.

Ma'at faced upwards again and saw a flash of lightning and heard a crack of thunder. Although it was close, s/he wasn't frightened or even startled. S/he felt happy and light. The clouds were welcoming hir. They were not white, but a heavy blue-purple. A comforting enclosing darkness that s/he longed to merge with. S/he could almost reach out and touch them. As s/he did, their darkness pulled hir into themselves and s/he thought no more thoughts.

Chapter
Eleven

WHEN THE EMPIRE learned of the loss of the *Star Spawn*, it dispatched two Ggr'ek-class Predators to investigate. This well-disciplined Khrar fleet had since tracked the ion traces of the vessel that had annihilated *Star Spawn*.

Commander Korsaag of the lead ship *Qa'Hhogh* would have blown away the *Heaven's Bow* the moment he sighted her except for one small difficulty. That difficulty was the presence of the *U.C.S.S. Boadicea*. *Boadicea* might be a Minority Fleet ship in the Coalition, but it and its female captain had a solid reputation for strategic competence. Korsaag's clan sister's husband had been killed in a space battle with *Boadicea,* which did not make Korsaag care to rush into matters without forethought. Also, for the moment, *Boadicea* outgunned him.

His immediate interpretation was that the cozy orbit of the two foreign ships constituted a damning indicator of conspiracy. That made destruction of *Star Spawn* an act of war, initiated by the Coalition. Korsaag called his High Command, reported the circumstances, and requested backup ships.

There was no hurry. *Boadicea* was not likely to detect his fleet's cloaked presence for some time. Preferably not until right before they fired. The engagement, when it came, would be a pleasant one. For the time being, Korsaag sat back to wait.

CAITLIN HAD HEARD the expression 'walking on air' hundreds of times but had never experienced it herself. It felt exactly like it sounded. In her current state of euphoria, she believed she could have willed herself to wing like a bird down the corridor and it would have happened.

The feeling came to an end, however, the moment she reached the *Boadicea's* briefing room door. She was terrified of Captain Forrest. She almost slipped on down the corridor pretending she had nothing to meet with the captain about.

But she stopped herself. That would not be fair to Sukha and the people of the *Heaven's Bow*. She wanted the captain to reconsider their position. She was sure if she could just explain their origin and mission, the captain would understand they were not spies. After all, Captain Forrest was not known as a good starship captain for no reason. She always listened to the other side. At least, that's what Caitlin hoped.

Caitlin stepped into the field of the door's motion detector. The silver plates slid apart to reveal a room empty except for one woman. Captain Forrest's lowered head rested on her folded arms.

"Sir?"

The captain did not respond. Caitlin approached and, fingers trembling with uncertainty, nudged the captain's shoulder. "Sir?"

"What is it?" Dani's head jerked up and she scanned the room, tensely alert.

"It's just me, sir. Ensign Eireann."

"Oh, Eireann." Dani dropped her head back to her arms.

"Can I get you some coffee, sir? Or something else?"

"Coffee? Doesn't work anymore," Dani said. She raised her head and briskly rubbed her face with the palms of her hands. "What's the problem, Ensign?"

"Well, sir—" Caitlin rung her hands and shifted back and forth on her feet. Dani eyed her morosely.

"Ensign, sit down. Stop hovering and get to the point."

Caitlin's mouth went dry. Forrest sounded as irritable as the rumors claimed. She moved around the end of the table and took a seat opposite Forrest. She felt safer with the briefing room table between them.

"Captain, I'm not sure how to begin but I have some exciting news to report."

"How could you have news? Lieutenant Mouneera is responsible for reporting changes in our status. And, thank Goddess, she hasn't reported any."

"Not that kind of news, sir. News of a cultural discovery."

"Cultural?" Dani rubbed her face again and slumped back in her chair. "Do you think I have time to consider cultural news?"

"Maybe cultural is the wrong word, sir. See, the people aboard the *Heaven's Bow* are humans. They're from Earth."

"Ensign," Dani leaned forward and put her elbows on the table, "I know that. The ones that look like humans anyway. As for the guy with the topknot and four arms—"

"Sir. That's the really astounding part. Doesn't he look familiar?"

"Familiar?"

"Doesn't Sukha Jabala, look like a Hindu god?" As soon as she said it, her mouth burst into a triumphant smile.

So that was it. The archer on the hull. Mr. Jabala. "Come to think of it he does resemble some of the religious depictions of the gods of Earth India," Dani said.

"Yes!" Caitlin crowed. "That's right!"

"Wait a minute, you're not saying Mr. Jabala is a god, are you?"

"No. Of course not."

"You should never say 'of course not' in space, Ensign. The *Boadicea* has encountered one or two gods, well, demi-gods at least, in her travels. Nothing is impossible."

"Yes, sir."

"I admit this is interesting, Ensign, but it's trivial at best. It has no bearing on our current situation."

"But it does, Captain. Sukha's people visited Earth many centuries ago. That may be how those artistic representations came into existence —"

" — or maybe not," Dani interrupted, feeling a flash of annoyance. She thought this was even more of a side issue but it was one that always pressed her buttons. "The notion that extraterrestrials influenced Earth's early development has never had any basis in fact."

"But —"

"Not to mention, even I am aware that Hindu religious art is intended to represent symbolic, not literal, depictions of gods."

Caitlin felt she was being beaten back into a corner she had no stake in defending. "What I mean, sir, is that —"

"Ensign, I will give you one last chance to tell me what any of this has to do with the price of rice in Indochina. Or is it tea? I can't remember. But I have a ship to run here. A ship with an ill crew and missing officers."

"Sir, I don't think the *Heaven's Bow* people are spies."

Dani's voice took on a note of threat. "They destroyed — they admit to destroying — a Khrar Predator."

"Yes, but it was an innocent mistake. They don't know anything about the Coalition or Khrars or —"

"Innocent! You just told me there are humans aboard — from Earth!"

"Captain, from Earth of 5000 years ago."

"These people are 5000 years old? We've never met a human race that old, Ensign." For someone so ancient, Captain Ki looked pretty good, she thought.

"Captain. They're not 5000 years old, 5000 years ago. The *Heaven's Bow* people are from another planet, a planet called Nirvannini."

Dani was starting to think Eireann was from another planet. That, or she'd stumbled into Alice's Wonderland, a place where one carried on aimless discussions with overgrown white rabbits. She couldn't recall having had a more bizarre conversation with anyone, even when blasted on Khrar ale.

She decided it was time to bring this most recent episode of the

Eireann Problem to a close. She lifted herself out of her chair, pressing her hands against the table to steady her arms. The look on her face was so threatening Caitlin found herself rising to attention.

"Ensign," Dani said in her most formal voice, "I am ordering you to cease from further communications with the *Heaven's Bow's* people aboard this ship. They are enemies of the Coalition."

"But, sir —" Eireann raised her arms and then, seeing the look of cold fire in Forrest's eyes, dropped her head in defeat. "Yes, sir."

"Further, I am ordering you to stay out of the legitimate business of this ship in its conduct with alien powers. That is the role of briefed and experienced officers. Do you understand?"

"Yes, sir."

"And stay out of my way. Dismissed."

After Eireann departed, Dani fell back into her chair, exhausted. A few minutes passed before she mustered sufficient energy to call the bridge.

"Lieutenant Mouneera here."

"Mouneera, this is Captain Forrest."

"Sir? Nothing to report from the bridge. Status unchanged."

"That's good, Mouneera." Dani's voice was lackluster. It struck her suddenly that she just didn't care anymore. "I want you to send a Priority One message to Explora Command's HQ."

"Yes, sir."

"Tell them we have detained the Captain and Chief Engineer of the ship that destroyed the Khrar Predator. Make it clear that the ship is not a Coalition ship but is from an unallied world."

"I will transmit immediately, Captain."

"And Mouneera —"

"Yes, sir?

"Add to that, that the crew of the *Boadicea* is suffering from an unidentified illness and that we cannot, other than what we have already done, complete our mission. We are requesting immediate medical assistance. Do you have that?"

"Yes, sir."

Thank you, Mouneera. Forrest out." So that was it, Dani thought. It was over. She folded her arms on the table and laid her head on them. She had never expected to go out with a whimper. After all, she was a bang kind of a gal. But then, fate dealt the cards, not her.

Mouneera transmitted Forrest's message to Explora Command's HQ in a fog of disbelief. She could not fathom Captain Forrest admitting defeat. Forrest never said 'die'. She always pulled them through. Pulled them through everything. But this time, everything was over.

A tear rolled unbidden down Mouneera's cheek. She didn't

bother to wipe it away.

MA'AT REGAINED CONSCIOUSNESS to find hir arms were
stretched uncomfortably around a massive post which dug into hir
back. Hir hands were tied. Hir folded legs were numb and hir
leggings were damp. S/he observed s/he was in some kind of
circular walled structure that smelled of animal offal and dank
humidity.

S/he concluded the miners had recaptured hir and tied hir in
one of their huts. S/he must have walked back into their camp. S/he
didn't remember there being a pool in the camp but then there had
been no pool of water. That had been a mirage. S/he had known it
was a mirage at the time.

Where was Dani? S/he thought bitterly.

Why...hadn't...Dani...rescued...hir? Danielle Artemis Forrest,
touted heroine of the Minority Fleet. Danielle Artemis Forrest,
intrepid adventurer, who couldn't get her first officer off a barren
spinning rock where there wasn't likely to be more than one life form
reading on any sensor array as Nhavan.

"Ma'at?"

Ma'at squinted through the shadowy gloom. "Luluai?"

"You saved my life, Ma'at. The water restored me."

"The water? The water was real?"

"Why wouldn't it have been real?"

"I thought it was a mirage."

"Mirage? What's that?"

Ma'at recalled that mirages were desert phenomenon and
deserts were new in Luluai's experience.

"Never mind," s/he said, "how did we get here?"

"When I woke up, it was raining and you were on your back in
the shallow pool. I was working my way towards you when four
humanoids appeared out of nowhere and carried us to this stone
hut."

"So I was walking in circles. I was delirious."

"No, we're in the foothills. We're not back at the miners' camp.
Our hosts are, well, I don't know, but I don't think they're miners."

Ma'at didn't care to doubt Luluai but s/he had a hard time
believing there could be yet another set of humanoids on this tiny
out-of-the-way planetoid.

"You carried me across the desert, Ma'at. I believed I was dead
already. Why did you make such an effort?"

"I wanted you to live, Luluai," Ma'at said simply. S/he knew
there was no rationale to it.

"I am grateful. We are bonded in a special way."

Ma'at felt confusion. Bonding meant different things in different cultures and could imply anything from an aid-obligated friendship to a requirement to join sexually.

"I didn't mean—"

Luluai had plainly read Ma'at's thoughts again. S/he wanted to lay the issue to rest. "Luluai, in your culture, is it socially the norm for members of your race to read the thoughts of others all the time?"

"No."

"I thought not. In most telepathic societies there are rules and forms of protocol governing reading the thoughts of others. Yet, you always read mine."

There was a long mental quiet during which Ma'at thought s/he had so alienated Luluai that their communication link was broken. When Luluai answered, her voice was subdued.

"I am sorry. I can take actions to shut out your thoughts. I didn't because we're in a situation for which I have no experience remotely applicable to help me understand what to do. I've read your thoughts to stay alive and because I know of no other way to communicate with you."

Ma'at struggled with hir answer. S/he understood Luluai's rationalization. S/he also acknowledged Luluai's telepathic abilities had kept hir alive through a night when s/he otherwise would have died. And, although s/he was perfectly well inclined under normal circumstances to value hir mental privacy even above hir life, s/he couldn't justify valuing it over Luluai's life. S/he was also nearly 100 percent certain Luluai had followed every nuance of hir thought.

"Well?"

"I didn't know privacy was so primary to you. Among my race there isn't the kind of individuality that such personal mental reserve implies. We're like one organism, a big extended family. I don't mean we don't shield against reading the thoughts of others. But not because we have private thoughts. It's more a matter of politeness. I mean, we do have private thoughts but...it's a little hard to explain."

"Do you mean you weren't going to learn something from tuning into the thoughts of an individual of your race that wasn't already known in some way by the group?"

"Exactly."

"Interesting. What about yourself? When you were singing your lifesong, I had the impression something about you was different. Some way in which you were not like the rest of your people."

"I'm not," Luluai blurted.

"How are you different?"

"I'm not whole."

"'Not whole'? What do you mean? What makes you 'not whole', Luluai?"

"I have a father."

This seemed to Ma'at to be a *non sequitur.* "I don't understand. You don't like your father?"

"I like him a little. That's one of the worst parts."

Ma'at frowned. "You like him a little but you think that's not good. Is that because...does he mistreat you?"

"I shouldn't like him at all. I need to hate him. No one else has fathers. But I can't hate him anymore. I've tried."

Ma'at knew s/he had lost the thread of the conversation. S/he was exhausted, thirsty, hungry, injured, cramped, cold. Even Nhavans had limits. Perhaps s/he was functioning in a state of delirium.

Luluai had said the oasis was real but hir experience of merging with clouds, which s/he remembered in vivid detail, had to have been a hallucination. Some humans would have termed it a 'near-death experience' but there was no tradition of near-death experiences in Nhavan culture, so s/he discounted it.

"You don't understand what I'm trying to say, do you?"

"No." There was no point in denying it. Luluai could read hir thoughts anyway.

"You have a father, don't you?"

"Yes," Ma'at replied, "of course."

"The Shivani have fathers too, and the Brahuinna. Do all the beings you came here with have fathers?"

"Yes." Ma'at's voice was thoughtful. Surely s/he didn't mean...

"Sirensi don't have fathers."

"Do you mean Sirensi don't have a relationship with their male parent or there is no male parent?"

"No male parent."

Ma'at took in a breath as deep as hir cramped position would allow.

"You reproduce—"

"Parthenogenetically."

Ma'at felt as surprised as s/he'd ever felt. There were no parthenogenetically-produced sentient beings on Nhavan and a limited array on Earth. But nowhere had s/he heard of humanoid life forms reproducing in such a manner. Out of the wealth of hir experience and knowledge, s/he could think of no comparable example.

"And how, if I may ask," Ma'at said, "is this accomplished?"

"When we are ready, we go inside and connect with the inner wisdom of our bodies and 'choose' to create a daughter. It just happens. We know, or actually they know—" Luluai's voice turned resentful.

"You are afraid you will not be able to do this?"

"It's already past the time!" Luluai wailed.

"You are unique among your race, Luluai. Your biology is unique. It may be impossible, but then again, it may not. Perhaps it must be triggered by something, or is set for a different time. If your mother is any indication, members of your race can reproduce sexually as well as asexually."

"My mother! I don't know how she could do this. To abandon such perfection, such unity, such wholeness for...ugh!"

Ma'at was beginning to understand Luluai's distress. She was descended from a race for whom sexual contact was abhorrent or, at the very least, strange or unusual.

Nhavans could enjoy sex in such a variety of modes that the idea of not experiencing sexual relations with other beings, even if only for the specified purposes of reproduction, was something entirely new for Ma'at to think about.

For Nhavans, sex itself, if not pre-negotiated for the purpose of producing offspring, was simply viewed as an engaging pastime that could have as many meanings as the number of Nhavans involved. Polyamory and serial monogamy were accepted with little or no jealousy by most Nhavans.

For humans, on the other hand, Ma'at knew sex was imbued with serious emotional significances and long-term social consequences. A good example was the Minority Fleet itself, which was the direct social consequence of a preference for heterosexual relations by the majority of Earth's society.

Homosexual and heterosexual relations didn't exist as mental constructs for Nhavans. The only differentiation related to sex was whether the bonding was a negotiated one for the purpose of reproduction or not.

"Brahuinnas are like humans," Luluai said suddenly, having listened in on Ma'at's thoughts, "they look at sex like that. Always fighting over it, planning ways to get it, boasting about it afterwards. Fixating on with whom, or how they had sex."

"Shivani, on the other hand, are very controlled, ritualistic, methodical. It's like meditation. They prepare and then—well, I don't know what the emotions are—but I've heard it's very spiritual. I think it's always a heterosexual bonding."

"And your father is?"

"Brahuinna."

"Was this bonding with your father a choice of your mother's?"

"She wanted to."

"But you do not?"

"Never, never, never! It's disgusting. Flesh and flesh...joining...like that."

Ma'at remembered that the Brahuinna aboard Luluai's ship had read on the sensor array as human. That meant that, in essence, Luluai was half-human. She had half a human biology and half a Sirensi biology. Which would predominate and which would determine her sexual nature only her own development could tell. There was no tradition or precedence to go by.

If, however, in Luluai's case, human biology predominated, could her revulsion be a cover for desire, for feelings she could not or would not admit to? With humans, true emotions sometimes exhibited as their opposite.

Luluai was once again listening in on hir thoughts. She snorted. "That is the most awful, disgusting —"

At that moment, the hide curtain covering the door was ripped back, interrupting Luluai's outraged telepathic rejoinder to Ma'at's thought. An orange shaft of sunset sliced through the murk. Into the opening stepped a giant of a humanoid, the heavy curling hairs of his bare arms and legs emphasized to grotesquery by the backlighting of the sun.

A Deimeon, Ma'at recognized instantly, hir thoughts grim. Dani would have said, 'from the Frying Pan into the fire.' Deimeons were of the planet Coskeer, one of the dozens of humanoid cultures that bordered Coalition space. Their culture was rigidly stratified and those Deimeons joining the military — considered the most glorious of all occupations — were held to an almost obsessive code of honor. Although the Deimeonate refused to join the Coalition, they occasionally joined forces to achieve some distinct purpose. Ma'at knew this from personal experience. S/he groaned again, remembering it.

"Afternoon," the Deimeon greeted them both, tongue in cheek. Three smaller Deimeons crowded into the hut. One went briskly to work on Luluai's bonds. The others came across to Ma'at and untied hir.

"Bring them," the big Deimeon ordered when the others were finished. "And don't forget to re-tie the Nhavan's hands."

Hir legs too numb to support hir, Ma'at was dragged across the sand on hir knees. It was strewn with sharp points of volcanic lava which tore at hir leggings and scraped hir skin. S/he felt the pain. A good sign, s/he thought, considering hir body's numbness and hir concerns about delirium.

Hir two Deimeons guards dragged hir to a stop ten meters from the hut and Ma'at found hirself in a circle of Deimeons — seven including hir and Luluai's escorts — facing, of all prosaic things, a campfire. Luluai had been dumped unceremoniously into a space on the other side of the campfire. Her golden skin shown red in the setting sun.

Ma'at looked from face to face. To a man, the Deimeons wore their raven-dark hair long and curling to the shoulders. Earrings flashed in their ears, catching the light of the fire. With mustaches and goatees, they looked much alike. None, though, wore the uniform of the Deimeonate Force. These men were pirates, Ma'at deduced, hir heart doing a flip-flop. Memories flooded hir mind.

S/he looked at the faces again. They were unknown to hir. All except one. That one was across the campfire, his face shadowed because the sun was behind him. He half-crouched next to Luluai and was observing her with interest. She seemed to shrink away from him.

He was clad, like the others, in a tunic and leggings of a luminous velvety green material. A row of showy earrings lined the ridges of both ears. But he was older than the rest of the group, his hair having washed out to a salt-and-pepper grey. Nonetheless his mustache still twirled and his goatee gave him a rakish air. He had obviously been lithe, almost slight, in his youth. Now his shoulders were broad and his face was lined with a feral wisdom...and bitterness.

He was the leader. It was evident the others were waiting for him to speak. He turned his attention from Luluai and his dark shining eyes looked directly into Ma'at's. His voice, smooth as a snake slithering over sand and just as menacing, said:

"Welcome back, Ma'at."

WHEN CAITLIN REACHED the brig, she saw that a drained and thinner Jeremy was on duty. The suspicious-minded Security Chief of the night before was gone. Off duty, Caitlin assumed.

"My god, Jeremy," she said, "you look ghastly!"

"It's the malady," he said, offering her a sickly smile. "I keep throwing up." Caitlin could see he was trying to behave as though everything was normal.

"Here to see your friends?"

"Uh, yeah." Caitlin had come only to tell Sukha she could no longer speak to him. She didn't think the captain would object to her telling Sukha about her banishment. After all, she rationalized, anything less would be discourteous because she had assured Sukha she would let him know of her success or failure in her meeting with the captain.

"Ooooh," Jeremy gripped his stomach with his arm. "Hey, Eireann. Seeing as you're here, could you keep an eye on the place for a minute? I have to go to the head. Please."

"Okay. Sure." Jeremy had already started on a dead run to the door before she finished agreeing. Caitlin felt her own stomach lurch. She had been so wrapped up in her language research she had almost erased the problem of the *Boadicea* sickness from her mind.

Now she began to feel serious twinges of anxiety about the health of the crew. She hardly knew Captain Forrest but she doubted she normally slept with her head on the briefing room table. What, she wondered, was going to happen to them? And to the ship?

Sukha had come to the door of his cell. "Caitlin," he said cheerfully, "good to see you. What did Captain Forrest say?"

"Sukha, things are very bad. Did you see Jeremy?"

"Yes, he's been trotting in and out since he came on duty. Poor fellow."

"No one knows what this sickness is. Captain Forrest has it too. Oh, she said I can't talk to you anymore."

"Then you should go before you are put on report for being here."

"Yes, you're right. I just wanted to tell you. I explained our conclusions to the captain but she didn't...well, she didn't seem to think it made any difference."

"It is out of your hands then, Caitlin. You have done your best. Don't worry over something you can't do anymore about."

"Okay. But now I'm worried about this other thing. Why can't anyone figure out what it is?"

"Your doctor seemed very capable."

"Yes, he is. But he's sick too. Everybody's sick."

"You're not."

"No. It's strange, isn't it?"

"There has to be a rational reason." Sukha's choice of words sounded vaguely familiar to Caitlin but she didn't know why.

"What rational reason?"

"Ever since your Doctor Jenks was here I've been giving some thought to this sickness."

"You have?" Caitlin was incredulous.

"Yes. You see, about ten years ago on Nirvannini, there was a similar widespread illness among the Brahuinna."

"Did people die? A crewperson died night before last."

"Oh yes. Many did. Even Captain Ki came down with the symptoms."

"But she didn't die."

"No, she got well. The cure in fact was very simple and everyone who took it got well immediately. But some intensive research was required to find out what was causing the disease."

"Okay, Sukha, you have me in suspense." Caitlin wanted to laugh but felt too strung up. "What was it?"

"Our planet's main food grain is brown rice. No one knows how the trend started but you know how trends are. One day everyone was eating brown rice. The next day it was *declasse*. A process of milling the rice to remove the husk and convert it into 'white' rice had been developed and white rice became fashionable."

"Earth mills its rice too," Caitlin said, mystified at the turn the conversation had taken.

Sukha nodded and went on. "Unknown to anyone at the time, the milling process in use resulted in the elimination of a vitamin essential to the health of the Brahuinna. No Shivani were affected because we have an adaptation that allows us to synthesize the necessary vitamin in the gut."

"So what happened?"

"The government required that milling processes be developed that would retain the vitamin or that white rice be enriched with the synthesized vitamin. Both are done today and white rice is still widely available and widely consumed. But many people went back to eating brown rice to obtain other trace elements which still get milled out of white rice. Brown rice is all we have on the *Heaven's Bow* for instance."

"So it was a vitamin deficiency disease? I assume the cure was supplementation with the missing vitamin."

"Right."

"Well, that would explain why I'm not sick! I take a vitamin supplement every day. I brought them with me. But I'm new to the ship. The rest of the crew has been aboard for a long time and probably isn't supplementing. Eventually, I would run out of my supply too, if I were aboard long enough."

"Yes. But that doesn't explain why the crew didn't get sick earlier. If I understood Jeremy correctly, all the shipboard food is synthesized. The vitamin could have been missing for only a short time if everyone is showing symptoms now."

"You're right," she said slowly, "now that I think about it, no one started showing symptoms until after the ion storm."

"Could this storm have damaged the shipcook?"

"I have no idea but I think we have to tell Doctor Jenks right away." Caitlin rushed to the intercom and hailed the infirmary. There was no answer. She tried again. And again. And again. She turned to Sukha, her eyes wide.

"What if he's already dead?"

"Are there emergency vitamin supplies in the infirmary?"

"I don't know."

"Perhaps I can come with you and help you."

"Count me in," seconded Bajana from the neighboring cell. Caitlin had forgotten her existence. She turned widened eyes on her. Captain Ki stared expectantly back.

Caitlin looked at Sukha and rung her hands in indecision. She needed Sukha's calming presence. She trusted him. If she waited, the world of *Boadicea* might go madder and deader around her.

"I'll be court-martialed," she said.

"I thought," Sukha said, "your name was going to go down in Coalition linguistic history."

"Yes," she said, touching the button on the console that released the cell door forcefields, "but first I'm going to be court-martialed."

"SHIM'ON? It's not possible!"

"It's not possible because your treachery condemned me to death."

"But you didn't die." Ma'at's mind reeled. S/he knew hir traitorous actions as Shim'on's Co-Commander aboard the Deimeon vessel *Falconkill* could have resulted in only two culturally-acceptable Deimeon choices for Shim'on: execution or suicide.

Ma'at hirself, acting as a Coalition double-agent spying on the war-building Piftoknasa Empire, had barely escaped alive to the *Boadicea*. Even Captain Forrest had not known of Ma'at's role and had very nearly killed her first officer by believing Ma'at's subterfuge as a Deimeonate Co-Commander to be a genuine change in loyalties.

Shim'on had trusted Ma'at completely, believing hir to be delivering the *Boadicea* into his hands. That trust, Ma'at believed, had cost Shim'on his Deimeon honor and, by association, his life.

They had been closer during that adventure than Nhavan age mates. First, as pirates playing alter ego to each other as the legendary pirate Shadow Light, then as Deimeon Co-officers. Then Ma'at had betrayed Shim'on, a man s/he respected and honored. Ma'at would not blame him if he choose to kill hir on the spot.

"I did not allow Deimeon custom to take effect. After your defection, Ma'at, I walked — blindly I must say — to the hangar deck of the *Falconkill*. I intended to follow custom but I wanted to die in space. You remember the *Talon*? I took her out. I had every intention of implementing her self-destruct mechanism."

"My parents were dead. My beloved sister Roma was dead. I had no offspring. It was time to die a noble death. I assumed the officers from the *Falconkill* were watching, waiting for the explosion."

"As I got farther from the *Falconkill*, the dark vastness of space swallowed me. Drew me. I could not initiate the self-destruct sequence. My fingers would not go near the button."

"One litany played over and over in my mind: My parents were dead. My beloved sister Roma was dead. I had no offspring. Then I asked myself, why should I die too?"

"I was a genuine outcast now. I had been a successful pirate — we had been successful pirates, Ma'at. Why should I not return to that profession?"

"Of course, I could not return to our haunts on the planet Coskeer, which had been cleared of pirates. But many out-of-the-way planetoids, like this one, presented themselves. Many ships, rich with booty, presented themselves. I have been egalitarian, Ma'at. I have robbed Deimeons, Khrars, and the Coalition with equal fervor."

There was cheerful rumble of agreement from Shim'on's men around the fire. Shim'on laughed with them. The last of the light, now a paling turquoise, enriched the green of his costume and caused a flash of recollection for Ma'at. The recollection was of a fantastic tale of piracy s/he'd overheard in the rec room of the *Boadicea*.

"You're Robin Hood."

"Yes," Shim'on laughed. "That's my Coalition nickname. I'm a legend all over again. Robbing from the rich, giving to the causes I choose. As a name, Shadow Light was too obvious and...too painful. I would have been captured by the Deimeon Empire in a few months if I'd gone back to calling myself Shadow Light."

"I understand."

"No, Ma'at, you don't understand. I buried Shadow Light."

Ma'at saw the chameleon-like change in his manner and heard the menace in his voice again. It held a loathing unnerving quality. Ma'at too had been Shadow Light. They had been Shadow Light together. *I buried Shadow Light.*

"Why green?" Ma'at stalled.

"The color of Deimeon blood, Ma'at. The blood we spilt on several occasions. The blood you betrayed."

There was no question about the menace now.

"What do you intend to do, Shim'on? You could have killed me when you found me. I could hardly have offered resistance."

For the first time, Ma'at saw indecision touch Shim'on's face, the pirate swagger momentarily blanketed by something else, something deeper, something unadmittable. Was it that love for each other that had kept Shim'on trusting Ma'at all those years ago? Was the bond still there?

Ma'at admitted hir attachment to Shim'on had been strong: but it had been stronger for Dani Forrest and the *Boadicea* and the Coalition. Yet hir bond with Shim'on had been like no other relationship. It had held exhilaration and danger and Ma'at had given hirself over to the sheer sexual drive of hir body, sharing hirself uninhibitedly with Shim'on and Shim'on with hir. S/he and Shim'on had been lovers, lovers without a responsibility or a care in the world. Lovers pushing the envelope of sensual experience.

Seeing Shim'on now was the opening of an old wound for hir. A reminder of the guilt and remorse Ma'at had locked deeply away in hir mind, never to reflect on again. Ma'at knew s/he had no choice those many years ago, but to do what s/he had done. Shim'on had been the casualty, the cost, the payment price. But betrayal was like no other sin. It could not be repaired or forgiven. And Ma'at was the betrayer.

Almost as if reading hir thoughts, Shim'on's eyes turned dark. Ma'at could not read them. Even the fire had burned down to smoking grey embers in the cobalt blue twilight. The men were unnaturally still, alert.

Shim'on turned his attention again to Luluai, kneeling at his side. He reached out to stroke her golden hair, now a tangled dirty mess from the conditions of her and Ma'at's two captures. Though s/he couldn't see Luluai's expression in the shadowy light, Ma'at thought s/he saw her chin tremble.

"Tell me who your friend is, Ma'at," Shim'on said softly.

"She is Luluai, First Officer of the I.S.A. *Heaven's Bow.*"

"A Coalition ship? I have never seen such a beauty aboard a Coalition ship."

"Not a Coalition ship," Ma'at said carefully.

Shim'on pushed Luluai's hair back from her cheek and then let it fall forward again. "She has gills, Ma'at. Isn't that a little unusual?"

"Very, Shim'on." Ma'at's jaw tensed. If Shim'on chose to assault the girl as revenge for Ma'at's long-ago betrayal...

"Not from the Coalition?" He eyed Luluai with even more interest.

"Shim'on, this is not...like you. You are a Deimeon. You did not — we did not — take females as spoils."

"I am not of any race any more, Ma'at. I am an outcast and a pirate. Real pirates take females as spoils. It would do you good to keep that in mind."

"Very well. What do you plan to do with us?

"Finally, a practical question from a practical person. That depends on you."

"How does it depend on me?"

"We've been watching your friends, the miners, off and on for several days. They've mined, heated, and faceted quite a valuable cache of rubies and sapphires at this point. It's the right time for a raid."

"You want my help."

"We need a distraction, Ma'at and you're the perfect decoy. They might kill you, of course, but it would be out of my hands."

Ma'at forced hirself to not react. Shim'on went on:

"I'll even try to keep it fair: I'll tie only one hand behind your back. No hobbles on your feet. As you are fearless and strong, the fight should keep them occupied for just the right amount of time."

"A suicide mission."

"Call it what you like. You've actually been in the camp. You can also provide me with the details of the layout and where they have most likely stored the stones. How many weapons they have, who the dangerous ones are."

"No," Ma'at said. "I will not."

"Little John," Shim'on called across the fire to the hairy giant that had ordered Ma'at and Luluai dragged from their hut.

"M'lord?" Little John queried, sitting up from a half-sprawl.

"Do you think this female is pretty?"

"Very pretty," Little John said. There was a raucous smirk from one of the pirates who had untied Ma'at's hands and a general tittering and anticipatory shifting of weight from the men around the fire.

"Even with the gills, Little John?"

"No problem for me." The tittering turned to a lecherous murmur.

"She's yours. Don't be too greedy though: share her with the other men. Everyone should get a turn."

Ma'at didn't need to be a distance telepath to feel the shudder of horror that passed through Luluai's kneeling form.

Chapter
Twelve

LUCKILY FOR CAITLIN, no one loitered in the G Deck Corridor and the infirmary was only a short lope from the brig. They would not be seen. If they were, she could hope the observing crewperson was sick enough to think the four-armed Sukha was a hallucination brought on by the disease.

Caitlin burst through the infirmary's lab doors trailed by Sukha and Bajana. "Doctor Jenks?" The lab was empty and there was no answer. She stuck her head into the Chief Surgeon's office and called again, "Doctor Jenks?"

She could see him slumped over in his chair, head resting on his desk, impervious to her. "Doctor Jenks?" She went up to touch his shoulder and felt sick. Hadn't she just done this with the captain? Repeating the same action was eerily unsettling. She knew then that the captain and the doctor were dying.

"Groww arwway," Sly grumbled.

"Doctor, I have Sukha Jabala here. He thinks he knows what the disease is."

"Grro," Sly repeated, his cheek pressed against the smooth surface of the desk. Caitlin shook him hard.

"Doctor Jenks, you must listen! We have to save the crew."

Sukha stepped forward. "Doctor," he said, "I think the disease is beriberi."

Sly's eyelids flickered open then shut. He inhaled, made a chewing motion with his jaw and swallowed. "Very very what?" he mumbled distantly.

Sukha looked at Caitlin, his brows drawing together in a frown. "Doctor," Sukha leaned closer, "beriberi. The absence of thiamine, the B1 vitamin."

"Thiamine...vitamin deficiency?" Sly's eyes were open but unfocused. "Hasn't been a vitamin deficiency disease in two centuries. Unlikely as plague or smallpox," he grumbled, losing interest. "Shipcook takes care of that, long-term injectables...the crew is up-to-date on its injections."

"I don't know what you mean by injections, Doctor," Caitlin said, coming up on the other side of him. "But, as for the shipcook, we think the ion storm damaged it somehow."

Sly seemed to be sleeping.

"Doctor," she shook him again and then again, but got no

response. He had passed out cold.

"What do we do?" She looked in real fear at Sukha.

"Two things," he said and turned to look over his left shoulder. "Bajana, could you...Bajana?"

"Oh, god," Eireann squealed, turning "where is she?"

"I don't know," said Sukha, his eyes clouding.

"I'll go look. I have to track her down."

"Yes, of course," said Sukha, "I understand. But first, Caitlin, how do I contact the *Heaven's Bow* from here?"

"We can't. Only Mouneera on the bridge—"

"Go to this Mouneera on the bridge then. Call the *Heaven's Bow* and ask Makka No to ask Poornah Ba, the cook, to make rice in as many pots as he has with lots of extra nutritional yeast and de-mat it over here as soon as it's ready."

Caitlin pursed her lips and whistled. "I hope to goodness Mouneera agrees to send a message like that."

"Yes, me too. We have a small supply of injectable vitamins aboard as well. Ask that it be de-matted first. I just don't think there's enough to go around your crew. That's why we'll need the cooked rice."

"Then I have to track down Captain Ki."

"Yes," he agreed sadly.

"And you will be—?"

"I will try to rally the doctor. We need his expertise."

"A COMPASSIONATE CHOICE, Ma'at." Shim'on grinned, his teeth flashing in the uneven light given off in his hut by a hanging lantern. "For her at least."

"It's a simple matter of survival, Shim'on." Ma'at had no intention of telling Shim'on what a gang rape would mean to Luluai. Considering her unique biology, there was no way to calculate the physical or psychological impact of such an event. It might be enough to kill her and so s/he felt hir decision rested as much on reason as it had when s/he'd decided to carry Luluai across the desert.

"I don't care how often you Nhavans claim otherwise, the lot of you are just as driven by gut instinct and archaic notions of honor as we Deimeons. Sacrifice yourself to save an alien girl you hardly know and aren't planning to sleep with? Pshaw, Ma'at. That's pure sentiment!"

Shim'on, Ma'at remembered from their shared past, had a devious talent for honing in on what were arguable flaws in Nhavan's balanced-mind, balanced-body philosophy. It reminded hir of a certain other personality s/he knew, a certain flamboyant

captain who was famous for using tools transcending common fact to
escape from sticky situations. Ma'at admitted to hirself s/he would
not have wanted to argue the reasons for hir actions point-by-point
with Shim'on but it didn't matter. S/he was at peace with hir
conscience in regard to Luluai.

S/he choose not to answer Shim'on's taunt and Shim'on saw,
only because he was looking for it, the subtle compression of Ma'at's
lips and almost imperceptible squaring of hir shoulders. He laughed
and shook his head.

"Very well, Ma'at," he said, "I didn't think you'd rise to that bait
but I had to try it. Let's get down to details."

They were sitting on the packed dirt floor of the largest, and
least odiferous, of the huts. Shim'on had ordered it made into a
makeshift headquarters. Ma'at's shoulder muscles shivered with odd
electrical nerve shocks, hir jaw pounded and the blisters on hir back
and feet smoldered. S/he had never had time to reinstate any mental
pain control techniques.

Still, s/he was grateful for small favors. S/he had been provided
with a spare pirate tunic which s/he now wore loosely over hir torn
leggings. There had been no spare boots so s/he was still barefoot.

Basically a fair man, Shim'on had insisted s/he and Luluai be
fed. After the meal, Luluai had been returned to their hut and
restrained again. Ma'at could be reasonably assured of Luluai's
temporary safety if only because all of Shim'on's band were
surrounding hir in Shim'on's makeshift headquarters.

Unlike humans, Deimeons did not fear hir Nhavan physical
strength, which was matched by their own. So, s/he was sitting,
cross-legged, unbound by either hand or foot. It was a refreshing
change. Nonetheless, Shim'on took precautions. Two of Shim'on's
burliest Deimeon pirates, Friar Tuck and Sir Much, were seated on
each side of Ma'at.

Ringing Shim'on were his other four men, all having taken or
been given pseudonyms related to the Earth medieval ballad of
Robin Hood, no doubt to erase their pasts. There was Little John,
Will Scarlet, The Sheriff and Sherwood. Will Scarlet was apparently
Shim'on's heir apparent. They were all casual enough, weapons
sheathed, but they were there. Even at full Nhavan strength, which
s/he could not be said to be enjoying at the moment, Ma'at doubted
s/he could have escaped Shim'on's hut.

"Our plan is to strike as soon as the miners are drunk enough to
be reasonably incapacitated but not so drunk as to have stumbled off
to their quarters. If they are all still around the fire, causing a full-
scale distraction by dropping you in their midst should keep them
occupied long enough for us to steal the gems without resistance and
be on our way before they have a chance to notice."

"How very un-Deimeon," Ma'at said drily.

"Yes, but as you may recall, very pirate-like. Rob and run is my game, Ma'at. I avoid all but the most necessary murders. Surely you remember?"

"I remember."

"Your murder...I have no control over. The miners can do with you as they please."

Ma'at's shoulders twinged at the memory of what they had already been pleased to do. Shim'on could not know how little relish s/he felt at returning to the miners' camp.

"Alright, Ma'at. I need to know the layout of the huts and where the baubles are most likely to be."

"I will be drawing conclusions based on very limited knowledge, Shim'on."

"Guessing? Why can't a Nhavan just bring themselves to use the word?" Shim'on laughed again. "Guess away, Ma'at. You still have more experience of the camp than we do."

Ma'at shrugged. "As you wish," s/he said, and requested a writing implement.

THE DE-MATTER ROOM was deserted. Bajana didn't know what she would do if she met a *Boadicea* crewperson there but decided she would follow her instincts if she did. She had no weapon so she would have to make do 'using her wits', as Sukha had said on their own bridge just the day before. She did not agree with Sukha about cooperating with Ensign Eireann or saving the crew of the *U.C.S.S. Boadicea*.

In her view, saving them would only mean they would be a stronger and greater threat to the *Heaven's Bow*. They had argued the point for several hours after breakfasting in the brig. Her view had been that slipping away was the best course of action. Space was big: they ought to be able to sneak away and hide in its vastness.

Sukha had reminded her that the *Boadicea* belonged to a larger group called the Coalition and that they didn't know the extent of this entity's powers. His argument was that befriending the *Boadicea* in its current troubles might lead to a diplomatic resolution to their problem regarding the Predator.

She didn't disagree on logical grounds but her instincts were against it. Forrest was too erratic to trust. Even if they befriended her and her ship, it was no guarantee she wouldn't simply blow them out of the skies for destroying the Predator once, as she had said, her investigation of Bajana's claims' was complete.

At the very least, Bajana was sure Forrest would be duty bound to turn them over to this Coalition — whatever it was — who would lock them up and throw away the key. Forrest certainly had not hesitated to toss them into her own brig without trial. Some redress was sure to be called for. They had clearly committed a heinous crime by blowing up the Predator.

No. No matter how many times she thought it through, she came back to escape as the best course of action. After all, how long could the arm of this Coalition be? It wasn't big enough to have reached Nirvannini and Elysiansus. If worse came to worst, they could turn tail and go home.

She knew this argument had created a rift between them, a rift neither of them was talking about. Sukha's eyes were sad when he looked at her. She did not know what it forebode for the future of their relationship. If there even was a future to their relationship, she reminded herself.

In any event, it had been extremely easy for her to slip away from Sukha and Ensign Eireann. She merely backed up when they opened the doors of the infirmary and under the cover provided by the hiss of the door she had turned and raced down the corridor to the nearest section pullout. Conveniently, there had been a Deck Map on the wall and she determined her position relative to the de-matter room. Finding the de-matter room was the first step in her escape plan.

The next was to return to the *Heaven's Bow*. Confidently, she walked over to the room's control console and examined the large array of buttons. Her heart sank. It wasn't a simple manner of turning on the equipment as she had hoped.

She would have to punch in location coordinates in order to go to the right place and not end up de-mating out into the airless void of space. Bajana had no intention of being defeated by this elementary problem. She sat down on the console stool, put her chin in her hands, and thought.

NACHIKETAS BUONO LAY face down on a rock escarpment overhanging the miners' camp. He had been there since early twilight and as the evening wore on, the huts, which had looked grey in the twilight, were now barely distinguishable dark blobs against the greater darkness of the night. He had watched the men eat their evening meal and had observed the cook give two bowls of food to a boy. The boy had scurried off with the food to a hut on the southwest rim of the camp.

Nachi wanted to believe the food was for the captives, the *Heaven's Bow's* crew. But why only two bowls? Were they being required to share out of that small amount? Of course, it could be the cook was just giving the boy extra food. The boy was small but, at a distance, it was hard for Nachi to determine his age. The food could also be for a sick man or for a leader who didn't eat with the other men. Nachi had taken a count of the camp's inhabitants but he couldn't be sure there weren't men he hadn't seen.

Nachi knew he didn't have enough information to make a decision but, once the men had gone to bed, he would search the hut the boy had taken the food to first. He thought it the most likely place the *Heaven's Bow* people were being held.

Within a fire ring made of the misshapen reddish rocks, the men had started a campfire out of a dead palm tree. The light reflected off their faces and conversation was lively with noise and gestures. As Nachi watched, three men he hadn't previously counted emerged from the largest hut and made their way to the campfire. One was the large red-haired man he had seen that afternoon at the shuttlecraft. Of the other two, one was a balding pudgy man who, even in the dark, looked irritable. The other was a slender man in a robe who walked with the light pace of a nightcat.

As the three reached the fire, the men's boisterous clowning petered away into silence. Nachi decided the red-haired man was the leader. As he started to talk, an aura of taut attention seized the group. The cook stopped banging pans. The boy, who had returned from the hut where he'd taken the food, sat beside the cook and watched the big red-haired man gesticulate as he talked.

Nachi knew he'd never have a better chance to search that hut. He slithered backward on his stomach until his feet felt the softness of sand. Bent low, he ran soundlessly to the next looming spear of rock. Edging around it, his body pressed flat, he scanned the fire. The men's attention was still focused on the leader. The hut where the boy had taken the food was now the closest one to Nachi. Keeping low, Nachi ran the 200 open meters to it, and dove through the flimsy piece of hide hanging over the door.

"Eeeek!" squealed two voices simultaneously.

"What was that?" said one.

"Who was that?" said the other. Their voices followed each other like a round of song.

"Shhhh," Nachi hissed. This could be none other than Til and Tor, as he privately called the good doctors. Nobody else talked quite like they did, in that merry carefree cadence.

"It's me, Nachi."

"Nachi! What are you doing here?"

"I'm here to rescue you and the rest of the crew." His eyes scanned the circular space, empty save for Til and Tor.

"Where are they?"

"How heroic!" said Doctor Tilorri.

"Dead," said Doctor Torilli.

Although most Shivani and hardly any Brahuinna could even tell the two Sirensi apart, Doctor Torilli considered herself the more serious-minded of the two. She frowned in the dark at her more flibbertigibbet sister.

"Dead?" Nachi couldn't hide his shock. "Are you sure?"

"About Pukk and Abjay, yes." This was Doctor Torilli.

"About Luluai, we aren't sure." This from Doctor Tilorri.

Nachi grabbed for Doctor Tilorri's uncertainty like a lifeline. Luluai could not be dead. He wouldn't allow it. "Why aren't you sure?"

Doctor Torilli took it upon herself to answer. "She and that being from the other ship—"

"—the *Boadicea*," detailed her sister.

"—were staked out in the desert. We don't know if they're dead or alive," Doctor Torilli finished, her voice full of regret.

"We've been guarded every second and haven't been able to get out of the camp," Doctor Tilorri said.

"Staked? Are you joking? When?"

"Yesterday. Late afternoon." Doctor Torilli's voice was subdued.

"Ohhh," Nachi groaned. "She couldn't have lived through today. It was so...hot. If I'd known I could have searched for her. Saved her."

"We're so sorry," Doctor Torilli said.

"Don't blame yourself," Doctor Tilorri said.

"Shhh." Nachi had heard a sound. He crawled to the door, lifted the hide curtain, and peered out at the fire. Was the gathering breaking up? No, the men hadn't moved but there was some sort of commotion at the center of the fire itself that he couldn't make out. He guessed they would probably break up soon so he needed to work fast.

"The shuttlecraft isn't too far away. About one and one-half kilometers. Can you both walk that far?"

"Of course," they chorused. "But you'll have to untie us first." They presented their bound hands, which he hadn't even noticed. He started on Doctor Tilorri's but had only half-untied her when he heard the sound of a heavy footstep at the door and saw a hairy hand reach in to yank back the curtain.

RUSTY WAS NEARING the end of his impassioned diatribe about the importance of hanging together and finishing the mining job for 'The Boss' when Luke saw his opportunity to slip away. Rusty's speech was an amalgam of half-truths mixed with a glowing avaricious fantasy about how much each miner could expect to make. Rusty assured them over and over they would all be paid in a day or two.

Except for those in the know, who were part of the escape plan and pretending otherwise, they seemed to be swallowing it. Luke knew it was a sleight-of-hand trick to keep everyone happy — until tomorrow. Tomorrow they would wake up and there would be no Rusty and no money.

As soon as Luke was away from the camp, he broke into a smooth, tireless lope. On the way, he felt for the Khrar disrupter at his belt, hidden in the folds of his robe. The workbee operator wasn't going to feel a thing. If he cooperated. Or, for that matter, even if he didn't. Luke prided himself on the clean kill.

SHIM'ON'S PIRATE BAND had a sum total of three surface fighter craft. They were old, Ma'at perceived, and more jerry-rigged than was safe. Despite Shim'on's boasts, he couldn't be making all that good a living. Ma'at knew there was a lucrative black market in surface fighters, each fitted out with the latest in high-tech gadgetry. Why didn't Shim'on have any?

Shim'on ordered his pilots to surround the miner's camp on three sides. Little John and The Sheriff were to land near the *Lithe Arrow* on the southwest and search her for the goods. Will Scarlet and Sherwood were to land on the north and search the three nearest huts. Shim'on and his two men, Friar Tuck who was guarding Ma'at, and Sir Much who was piloting the craft, would land on the southeast. Presently, all the fighters hovered a short but undetectable distance from their landing positions waiting for Shim'on's order to move in.

"Ready, Ma'at?"

Gagged, Ma'at could make no answer to the pirate leader's question and s/he wondered why Shim'on bothered to ask. Shim'on was going to de-mat hir into the camp whether s/he was 'ready' or not. Besides, how did one prepare to be a sacrifice?

Considering the gag, Ma'at surmised Shim'on wanted to buy time on the ground and didn't trust Ma'at not to alert the miners to the raid. Whether s/he said anything or not, Ma'at didn't see how the maximum of a minute it would take Rusty, the miner's leader, to pull off the gag would give Shim'on any breathing room.

To ensure Ma'at didn't remove the gag, Shim'on had overseen the binding of Ma'at's hands and the hobbling of hir feet. The 'one hand free and no hobbles' had been an empty promise. Friar Tuck grabbed Ma'at under the armpits and hauled hir to hir feet. "S/he's ready," he said.

"Coordinates plotted," Shim'on said, "Actualize."

Ma'at heard the whine of the de-matter and felt the familiar sense of disembodiment as the de-mat took hold of hir body. Deimeon technology provoked a heavier, clumsier sensation than s/he was accustomed to, but it was not unpleasant.

It was when s/he re-materialized that s/he thought something had gone wrong with the de-matter. It flashed across hir mind again that Shim'on's equipment was in bad need of a refit. But this sensation was not like any s/he had ever experienced with a de-matter.

Hir bare feet felt as if they were burning and s/he smelled smoke and heat. When s/he had fully materialized, s/he saw s/he was looking into the panicked faces of men standing around hir. One raised an arm and pointed at hir feet, his round open mouth incapable of sound. Several others started to move and shout.

Ma'at looked down at hir feet where the burning sensation had intensified. Flames of a very real fire engulfed them, roared up hir legs and licked at hir borrowed tunic. Shim'on had de-matted hir directly into the miner's campfire.

Leaden with shock, Ma'at began to move, forgetting hir feet were hobbled. S/he tripped and started to fall. S/he twisted in the air, hurtling downward. The mens' reaction was a palpable psychic wave of horror that rushed at hir mind, shaking it to its foundations. S/he knew the instant hir torso touched the flames s/he would be burned to death.

In that long split-second s/he thought: Shim'on could not have meant this. Death at the miners' hands, maybe. But not this.

A pair of powerful arms grabbed hir hurtling torso and flung hir with force across a firecircle of sharp rocks. Their owner leaped on Ma'at's body, rolling hir over and over in the sand to put out the flames.

"My god," Rusty shouted shatteringly close to hir ear. "What in the hell is going on?" He ripped the gag from Ma'at's mouth. "Where in god's name did you come from?"

"Aaaaagh," Ma'at gurgled, uncomprehending. S/he stared in stupefaction at hir legs. The flames were out but hir feet didn't know that. They burned with a heat so hot s/he couldn't feel it. S/he was encircled by booted men. They were familiar but s/he couldn't remember who they were.

A small man pushed his way through the circle. Sopping wet rags dripped across his shoulders. With an efficiency of motion, he wrapped the rags around Ma'at's legs and feet. The cold sent a rippling tremble through Ma'at's body that set hir to shivering.

"Fast thinking, Tam," Rusty said, still panting with exertion.

"Cold saltwater," answered the camp cook. "It's the best I can do with our cooking supplies."

Ma'at's memory, jolted, was returning. The man who had pulled hir from the fire was Rusty. Ma'at's body shuddered, from physical shock or emotion s/he didn't know. In a moment when the surprise had passed, Rusty would remember that Ma'at was supposed to be dead. Staked to posts on the other side of a nearby dune. A slower death, but also a death by fire.

Like a Khrar dreadnought, the thought bore down on Ma'at that s/he was trapped in a nightmare that had circled back on itself, like a loop with no end. S/he was back to where s/he had started less than thirty hours before and the fate s/he had worked so relentlessly to escape was going to repeat itself.

S/he sought to shake off the vivid image of being stretched and slow-roasted beneath the planetoid's hot sun but it was too late. Even a Nhavan nervous system was capable of overload and this one had skirted close to overload too many times in the last few days.

Ma'at's mind surrendered to hir body's shock.

LIEUTENANT MOUNEERA GAPED at Ensign Eireann as though Eireann had lost the few marbles the crew believed she possessed. "Rice? You want me to call the *Heaven's Bow* and ask them to de-mat over some rice?"

Caitlin swallowed hard. "Please, Lieutenant. I know it sounds crazy but—"

"I'm clearing this with the captain, Ensign." Mouneera tapped the intercom for the briefing room.

"Captain Forrest. This is Lieutenant Mouneera, please respond."

She waited but got no answer. She tried the briefing room a second time, and then the captain's quarters, while the ensign paced out her agitation behind her back. Finally, Mouneera called Cory Markett.

"Check in the briefing room, first," she said. "Page me the instant you find her." She didn't have to wait long. Security Chief Markett was not one to malinger.

"Lieutenant," Markett rung back, "she's still in the briefing room but she's unconscious."

"Have you called the infirmary?"

"Yes. But no one answers, Lieutenant. I'm not sure who in the infirmary is still functional and we can't wait for medics. My security team will de-mat her there now. Markett out."

Mouneera, not to be deterred, rammed the intercom for the infirmary. "Sickbay! This is Lieutenant Mouneera on the bridge. Anyone there, please answer!" There was an extended empty pause.

"Anyone." she repeated hoarsely. She had almost despaired of an answer when the intercom beeped.

"Sukha here," said a calm voice.

"Sukha?" Mouneera shot a withering glance at Ensign Eireann, whose head snapped up alertly at Sukha's voice. Mouneera thought she had never seen a guiltier face.

"Yes?" Sukha said.

"Uh, Sukha," Mouneera made her voice as silkily casual as she could, "where is Doctor Jenks?"

"Here," croaked the doctor, his voice so weak Mouneera's mouth went dry with fear. "Lieutenant, get us those vitamins, food. Hurry. Dying...everyone is dying."

"Will do, Doctor. Oh, and Doctor, Security is bringing Captain Forrest—"

"She's already here, Lieutenant. Don't worry, she'll get the first shot. And Vasquez the second. Jenks out."

Mouneera let out a sigh of relief which was seconded by Ensign Eireann. Without turning to look at her, Mouneera hailed the *Heaven's Bow* and made her strange request directly to Hasitam Deva, the helmsman.

"There is cooked rice in storage," he said. "Since you can de-materialize and re-materialize people, I will put a container in every crewperson's hands and they can take the food. You will probably need help distributing it."

"An excellent idea," Mouneera responded. "Many of our crew are too weak to feed themselves."

"Still, it will take maybe fifteen or twenty minutes to get ready."

"Fine," said Mouneera, "but you can send the injectable supplies immediately?"

"Of course. How?"

"Just tell me where they are and I'll plot the coordinates."

"Coordinates? You mean like positions on an x-y axis?"

"Similar. In three dimensions."

"I think I can figure that out for you. Hold on." Hasitam returned a moment later and rattled off a string of numbers for her.

"Got it," answered Mouneera. "Someone will meet the supplies in our de-matter room. Thanks."

"Keep me posted. *Heaven's Bow* out," replied Hasitam, efficiently cutting the transmission.

Mouneera swung about to look meaningfully at the ensign. She had already spun on her heel and was headed for the kinelift doors. "I'm on my way, Lieutenant."

"Caitlin," Mouneera called after her. Caitlin turned back in surprise. No one aboard had yet addressed her by her first name.

"Yes?"

Mouneera gave her a thumbs up sign of approval. "Even if you are court-martialed," she produced a tired lopsided grin, "thank you. You may have just saved this ship."

Caitlin didn't know whether to laugh or cry.

HIGH ALONG THE roofline of Luluai's hut was a small break in the mortared rocks. She guessed it was a hole left by a rock that had given way. Thatch from the roof overhung it, almost completely obscuring it. She had not noticed it earlier in the afternoon because the sun had been in the west.

But now the moon or moons that had risen in the east were so bright some of the light penetrated. It suffused the hut with a dim golden haze and made Luluai long for home. Homesickness was not a problem that had afflicted her on the *Heaven's Bow's* journey until this moment.

On two or three occasions a year, Elysiansus' five moons conjoined to rise one after another over the sea, dappling the waves with the special color of each. On those nights, all the Sirensi sat on the beach and sang special moon-love songs. Many were well-known favorites but always there were new compositions.

Luluai didn't know if she would ever sing those entrancing songs again. Not just because she might die here in this desert but because she would be forever changed even if she lived.

Nothing in her life, her education or her training had prepared her for the sheer physicalness, the gut-wrenching raw emotion, and the mental confusion of what she was undergoing. Even her compensatory tendency to over-achieve had done nothing to help her. In fact she believed it had cost the lives of Pukk and Abjay and the two women from the *Boadicea*.

Luluai calculated the pirates had been gone for at least an hour. The camp was wholly deserted and she didn't even know if the pirates planned to return or if she would simply be abandoned, bound and gagged and left to starve to death on the smelly earth-packed floor of this hut.

The pirate, who had tied her hands behind her after she hungrily slurped down a single bowl of tasteless gruel, had relished telling her about the tusked feral pigs that ranged in the mountains and how they feasted on any edible they could sniff out. He had disgusted her with his ghoulish imaginings and she was glad he was gone.

The only sound was the light breeze, which had sprung up with the moonrise. It rustled the roof thatch and whistled mournfully through the jagged hand-sized gap high in the wall. No pigs had come in search of her yet.

She wasn't sure which was worse, pigs or pirates. If the pirates did return, what fate awaited her? Death, most likely. And before death? If she understood what had transpired, Ma'at had agreed to a suicide mission to prevent her rape.

She marveled at Ma'at's physical and emotional balance. Despite the violent stresses they had endured, s/he far more than Luluai, hir thoughts had remained good. She could not recall one that had been violent or vengeful. If she had asked hir about it, she knew s/he would have told hir such emotions were not beneficial.

Yet when s/he had recognized Shim'on, the head pirate, a tangled flurry of hir emotions, beneficial or not, had burst into Luluai's mind like yoked pairs of galloping horses: Bonding and grief. Guilt and remorse.

Shim'on and Ma'at plainly knew each other from the past. Listening to their exchange, she had learned Shim'on had an old score to settle with Ma'at. Luluai felt certain he would settle it too. She worried that Ma'at would not return alive.

Despite the gag, Luluai choked. Ma'at had been her only lifeline. She had survived, she was sure, due to Ma'at's will that she survive. And now Ma'at was going to die. Die to prevent a kind of violence that, in all likelihood, would happen anyway. Ma'at would not be there to prevent it...or to comfort her afterwards.

Tears fell unbidden from her eyes and soaked her gag. How could anyone, she thought, make such a sacrifice? Despite Ma'at's own suffering, s/he had been nothing but patient with her. Even when, out of fear or desperation, she intruded into the privacy of Ma'at's mind, something s/he clearly held as sacred as life itself.

The crying was making her gasp and her chest hurt from the effort to breath through the gag. She forced herself to stop and take small breaths. In a minute, her breathing was back under control and she felt calmer but her heart was heavy with grief, a grief she knew wasn't going to heal.

NACHI SPRUNG BACKWARDS to hug the rough circular wall of the hut with his back, his hands stuffed tightly behind his buttocks. The beam of an infrared flashlight scanned across him and then moved to pass over the doctors.

"Who are you?" an unfriendly voice demanded.

"Captives of the miners," Doctor Torilli said.

"We can do no harm," added Doctor Tilorri, "our hands are tied. See?" She held hers out for his inspection and Doctor Torilli followed her lead.

"Hrrmph," he grunted. "And this one?" He shown the flashlight on Nachi again.

"His hands are tied behind his back," Doctor Torilli said.

"He's a deaf-mute," added Doctor Tilorri. "He can't hear you or answer."

The man's attention was disrupted by the appearance of another man at the doorway. "Did you find anything, Sherwood?"

"Yeah, but no treasure," the searcher said. He backed out of the hut and lifted the flap to show his friend, "just a couple of trussed-up captives."

"Leave them. Someone seems to have pulled the Nhavan out of the fire and they're still distracted by hir. But they'll start to get suspicious any minute now, even if the Nhavan is too freaked to talk. We have to hurry."

"Right," Sherwood answered, dropping the flap, "some moons are coming up too. Look, Will, three of them. We won't have much cover of darkness soon." Their voices moved away and Nachi jumped to his knees and went back to untying Doctor Tilorri's hands.

"Deaf-mute! Of all the screwy fabrications!" He complained.

"Wasn't that breathtaking!" Doctor Tilorri laughed. Her laugh had a liquid pearly quality.

"Doesn't anything bother you?" Nachi asked in mock disgust.

"No," she giggled, "I'm too old, Nachi."

"You're done," he answered, throwing her bonds on the floor. In a moment, he had Doctor Torilli untied as well. He knew exactly how to get from the hut to the shuttlecraft with the maximum of coverage and a minimum of time. It was a route he had mapped out in his mind as he lay on the rock and watched the camp. But there was now an added complication.

"I take it," he addressed both of them, "that those gents weren't some of your new friends from this camp?"

"Never seen them before," Doctor Torilli said.

"Oh, no," Doctor Tilorri shook her head, "they were looking for the miners' treasure."

"Miners? Miners' treasure?"

"Rubies and sapphires," responded the sisters in harmony.

"That means the camp may well be crawling with people looking for gems and, based on what those two said, in a few minutes it will be crawling with some real unhappy miners too."

"We should make a run for it now," Doctor Torilli said.

"Yes," echoed her sister, "before all hell breaks loose."

"Let's hope it hasn't already," Nachi said. Then he added, almost as a prayer. "If the Preserver is with us, we may actually reach the shuttlecraft alive."

"Let's go," Doctor Torilli said.

"Not a minute to lose," agreed Doctor Tilorri. All three together, they made a rush for the door.

LITTLE JOHN AND The Sheriff landed their fighter near the *Heaven's Bow* shuttlecraft and were the ones responsible for searching it. Unknown to them, they had come at an especially propitious time. The *Lithe Arrow* was momentarily unguarded, Barrrk having departed to attend the meeting around the campfire.

Little John and The Sheriff could hardly believe their good fortune. The craft was open, the lowered ramp practically inviting them to board. Inside, they promptly hit pay dirt. The single metal box holding layer after layer of gems was heavy though. Together, they scraped it across the shuttlecraft floor and half-pushed and half-pulled it down the ramp.

Three shining moons, attached to each other by their gravitational pull in a pleasing triangulation, had risen over the horizon and the pale yellow light they cast softly suffused the sands. Little John could make out his fighter 500 meters away, its body glinting in the moonlight like a hunkering florescent insect.

Together, Little John and The Sheriff bent down for the box, lifted it to their shoulders, and started across the sand, sinking deeply with every weighted step. They had covered nearly half the distance to their craft when they heard aggrieved shouts and turned to see a crowd of men barreling down on them at full speed. Little John looked futilely at the fighter. He and The Sheriff might as well have been kilometers from it. They could not outrun the pack closing in on them while carrying the box. To boot, they were plainly visible in the moonlight, with all the hard work of the enraged miners symbolized by the one massive box riding on their shoulders.

Little John counted seven attackers, three with syn-guns drawn as they ran. He dropped his end of the box and it went crashing to the sand, narrowly missing The Sheriff's foot. He crouched behind it and reached for his syn-gun.

The Sheriff tried to follow suit but the box was not massive enough to provide protection for two men. A well-aimed syn-gun blast catapulted The Sheriff from his half-crouch and hurtled him backwards through the air. To Little John's surprise, his partner didn't vaporize but lay unconscious on the sand. Maybe the syn-gun was only set to stun or was too energy-low to kill a man.

The thought didn't prevent Little John from aiming his own syn-gun where he'd seen the blast originate. He heard the scream of the man as contact was made and one tall dark shape vanished from the approaching mass.

That left six men. He couldn't hold off six men. He figured he would be dead in a few minutes. Then off to his right he heard the familiar whine of a Deimeon laser-rifle. A second shape in the mass of oncoming attackers, this one short and pudgy, vaporized. Four of the remaining five men halted short.

Just one, a Mickite by the pig-shaped snout, came aggressively on. Little John raised his syn-gun to fire and the Mickite joined his newly non-existent compatriots. The four men who had stopped dead seemed to make a group, if undiscussed, decision. They turned and raced back to the main encampment.

Little John laughed in satisfaction. The miners were cowardly weaklings. It was too bad Shim'on had a policy of only killing when necessary.

"Hey, Will!" he waved cheerfully to the Deimeon who was walking across the sand to meet him. Little John might have been Shim'on's right hand man for muscle, but Will Scarlet was Shim'on's right hand man when it came to brains. Little John was grateful Will had chosen the moment he had to show up.

"Look," Little John exclaimed, "the whole shooting match in one box! Let's get it loaded and get out of here."

"On your fighter?" Will Scarlet said.

"Of course, my fighter,"

"No way. What's going to keep you from just sailing off? No, I don't think so. Is The Sheriff dead?" Will waved his laser-rifle at the downed pirate.

"Just stunned."

"Alright, he's your partner. Load him on your fighter."

"But the box, Will. What about it?" Little John's teeth ground in desperation.

"I'll buzz Shim'on. Don't you remember the instructions? The box was to be loaded on his fighter only."

"Alright, whatever you say." Little John remembered it was futile to argue with Will. He grasped The Sheriff by the middle and heaved him over his shoulder. Will stood near the box, watching Little John trudge to his fighter with The Sheriff. He pulled out his transcon and notified Shim'on of their success.

As they talked, Will smiled to himself. Shim'on was pleased indeed. After a most satisfactory conversation, he sheathed his transcon in its hip holster. The moment he did, he heard the distinctive purr of a flying craft starting its engines behind him. He spun around.

The *Lithe Arrow*, her ramp door firmly shut and looking every bit as sleek as her name, lifted off the ground and into the air.

Chapter
Thirteen

THE MOMENT THE kinelift dumped her on G Deck, Caitlin ran at full tilt for the de-matter room. She was out of breath when the doors sensed her presence and slid apart to admit her. Panting, she rushed in just as a transparent box filled with vials of clear fluid materialized on De-Matter Disc One.

The Holy Grail could not have looked so good to Sir Galahad. Desperate not to lose time, Caitlin jumped the steps to the de-matter dias and lifted the box into her arms. Cradling its precious contents, she turned to go.

Bajana Ki stepped away from the de-matter console and stood at the door of the de-matter room, blocking her exit. Caitlin had not noticed her in her rush for the vitamins. The captain was unarmed, Caitlin noted automatically, but the determined look on her face more than made up for it.

"So, Ensign," Captain Ki said quietly, "I see that you're in a hurry."

"Yes, Captain. I am."

"And, I will not detain you. Except for one small easy-to-accomplish favor."

"What?" Caitlin tightened her hold on the box.

"You will de-mat me to my ship. I don't know how to set these controls." She pointed at the de-matter console.

"You know I can't do that."

"You can release me from the brig but you can't de-mat me to my ship?"

Could she? Caitlin fought herself internally. The urgent crisis aboard the *Boadicea* might justify the release of the prisoners—at least that's what she planned to argue at her court-martial—but de-mating an enemy commander back to her ship where she was free to fire on the *Boadicea*? Even with her minimum of military training, Caitlin didn't think that would wash very well with the court.

"I can't," she repeated.

"Then I suppose, Ensign, you are stuck here with me until you see fit to change your mind."

"This stalemate serves neither of us, Captain."

"Agreed. But you less so than me. I can wait. You cannot."

Caitlin squatted on the de-matter steps and pursed her lips in thought. Ensuring the safe delivery of the box was her first priority.

Should she just rush the captain? If she'd been unburdened, she would have simply fought her to get out. But the vials were too fragile to risk. She doubted she was in any immediate physical danger. The captain had not threatened any and neither of them had weapons. Whatever war they fought was going to be a war of wits.

"Alright, Captain," Caitlin stood up, still cradling the box, "you win."

"I knew you would see the dignity inherent in my request and honor it, Ensign."

"Of course. Right. Look, I will go across to the console and plot your coordinates. You'll stand over here on the de-matter disc."

"Wait." Bajana was wary. "How can I be sure you'll de-mat me to my ship and not out into empty space?"

"I don't really have a valid reason to murder you, Captain. But so you can feel sure, why don't we meet at the console and we'll ask the ship's computer to provide the coordinates for the *Heaven's Bow's* bridge? We'll plot those in and, presto, you'll be de-matted over there."

"Ask the computer? I didn't think of that. Very good." Feeling much easier in her mind, Bajana moved back to the console. This ensign that Sukha had raved about was a good person.

"Ah," Caitlin said taking a look at the console, "the coordinates are already plotted in. See?"

"There was nothing there a minute ago." Bajana felt suspicious again. She looked uncertainly at the digital display of numbers.

"No, but, remember this box was just de-matted from your ship. Now, if you'll just go and stand on that central disc—" Caitlin put the box down on the console and reached for the de-mating handle. Bajana Ki snatched up the box and raced for the pad.

"Hey! We need that. You can't take that!"

"No! These are for my crew. We will be many years in space."

"Not at the rate you're going," Caitlin grumbled, mostly to herself. But it didn't really matter. The coordinates she was de-mating Bajana to were the ones that would put her right back on the de-matter disc she was standing on.

While she shimmered temporarily out of existence, Caitlin would be able to call security. It was not her first choice. She would have preferred to just give Bajana the slip, taking the precious box with her, and let the captain fume when she found herself back on the *Boadicea*. But now she had no choice.

"De-mat me, Ensign," Bajana ordered.

"Very well, Captain. Actualize." Caitlin pulled slowly down on the controls. The captain shimmered away with the box. At the same time, the other de-matter discs shimmered brightly and materialized into solidity with humanoids carrying pots of every description. A warm yeasty odor filled the room that made Caitlin salivate. It sure didn't smell like shipcook food.

She found herself looking into the friendly faces of five beings. Two were handsome young men with chocolate brown skin-tone and dark eyes, two were women with golden hair and silvery-iridescent rippling skin, and the last was a dignified blue-skinned woman, with a second set of arms, who carried two pots.

"Uh, welcome aboard," Caitlin said, at a momentary loss for words. "Would you please—"

Her instructions were interrupted by Captain Ki who shimmered back into solidity. Unlike her crew, the look on the captain's face was closer to rage than friendliness. "What is going on? Eireann, you tricked me!"

The de-matter doors whooshed open and Sukha came in, his stride like that of a man of much younger years, his eyes alive with energy.

"Oh, excellent!" he said. "You're all here. And Bajana, you have the injectable supply. Follow me, everyone."

"Sukha!"

Caitlin thought Bajana Ki might actually stamp her foot in frustration. Instead, she looked around her at the pleasant faces of her crew and the lifted expectant eyebrows of her mentor and Caitlin saw the captain's resolve to return to her ship with the vitamin supplies melt away in a defeated rush, like a stream in spring thaw.

Caitlin wondered what had motivated it. Shame at being unwilling to help when surrounding her was her own crew's evidence to the contrary? Or, more cynically, had she merely acknowledged she was out-numbered and was smart enough to capitulate? Caitlin figured she would never know. But she felt an immense sense of relief.

"Do you want me to carry the box, Bajana?" Sukha asked.

"No, I have it, Sukha. Lead on."

"Let's go then." Sukha turned to head out the door. Caitlin could have sworn he winked at her conspiratorially as he went by. She would have followed, if for no other reason than out of sheer curiosity about Bajana Ki's change of heart, but the first group of rice-bearing aliens was closely followed by the next. Caitlin steadied them as they stepped from the de-matter dias and gave them directions to the infirmary.

After Mouneera buzzed her and told her the last of the *Heaven's Bow* helpers was aboard, she gave into a desire to pat herself on the back. Everything was going to be okay after all. She closed down the de-matter console and made her way to the infirmary.

SHIM'ON GAZED AT the body of Ma'at, laying supine on sand made white by the moonlight. S/he had been abandoned when the miners recognized the presence of Ma'at for what it was—a distraction. Grouped into an unthinking mob, they had hauled off in the direction of the shuttlecraft.

Shim'on crouched down to feel for a pulse and breath. There was a tremulous thread of both. Shim'on carefully unwound the drying rags from Ma'at's feet and saw that the Nhavan's skin was flaky and black. Shim'on winced. Deimeons did not feel regret for cruelty or death but Ma'at...Ma'at had meant something to him once. The bonds that had hobbled Ma'at's feet had burned away. Shim'on unsheathed his knife and sliced apart those linking hir hands. Ma'at's arms fell away to hir sides.

Yes, Ma'at had betrayed him. Yet, as a much older man, he knew himself well enough to know he would have stifled under the rigidity of the military's command anyway. Those early pirate experiences of exhilaration and freedom and bonding that he and Ma'at had shared had left an indelible mark on him. He would have run afoul of the Deimeon hierarchy eventually and been faced with the same execution-or-suicide choice, with or without Ma'at.

Seeing Ma'at again after so many years made him reassess the events that led to his current life. In the end, he had chosen life over death, freedom over bondage. He had escaped from the confines of his autocratic, narrow-minded society. Did he owe Ma'at some part of that decision?

He didn't know. But he did know the fire trick, for which Ma'at had dearly paid, had bought him the time he needed to carry off this escapade and he did owe Ma'at that. He just didn't know yet if that time had been enough to result in success.

Shim'on heard a hard panting and a fast scuffle behind him. Before he could react, something thudded into him and sent him sprawling across Ma'at's body. There was no reaction from the unconscious Nhavan.

"Uuuhhg," Shim'on's assailant sputtered, the breath knocked out of him. He had rolled after the impact and was floundering in the sand on the other side of Ma'at.

Shim'on leaped to his feet and drew his syn-gun from his belt. He almost fired before he saw that his attacker was a child, a human boy of about ten or eleven years. The child's eyes were wide with fright. He scrabbled to his knees and raised his hands, palms up in supplication.

"I didn't see you. I was running," he cried. "Please don't kill me."

Shim'on's transcon beeped. "Don't move." He sheathed the syn-gun in his belt and lifted his transcon. It was Will Scarlet, his chief lieutenant.

"Complete success, M'Lord." Will said proudly.

"The treasure?"

"It was on the shuttlecraft contained in a single massive box. It is here at my coordinates. I am standing guard over it. You will swing by to de-mat it aboard the *Robin Hood*?"

"Yes."

"A few miners were killed but we have lost no men. The Sheriff was stunned. That's all."

"Excellent, Will. I'll be there in a few minutes. Out."

Shim'on called his pilot, Sir Much, whose sole responsibility had been to await Shim'on's orders to move quickly when the time came. Shim'on looked at the boy on his knees and the unconscious Ma'at. Their raid had been an unqualified success. He was in the mood to be magnanimous.

"Sir Much, three to de-mat up at these coordinates."

"Aye, M'Lord."

In the next moment, the three shimmered orangely in a de-mat of light and a whirl of turbulence that churned up sand. Then they were gone, leaving only the white moonlight behind.

"SO, I WAS wrong." Bajana Ki accepted six hypos and six stacked bowls of rice from Sukha Jabala.

"You had a different viewpoint," Sukha said diplomatically. "But you were open-minded enough to gracefully capitulate when the correctness of another way became apparent to you."

"We're not out of the woods yet, Sukha. I still don't know if it's correct."

"Actions speak louder than words."

"Which means I had better get to the bridge and get these into people."

Sukha said softly. "You are a far wiser commander than you give yourself credit, Daughter."

Bajana Ki tossed her long hair and turned to leave. "I was outnumbered." she said. Sukha laughed.

"As I said, wisdom."

LUKE HAD TO blast his way into the workbee. The operator had vanished and Luke could not afford to waste time. Still, he had done it efficiently and with a minimum of damage. The ramp door was secure enough for flight.

Even once outside the atmosphere of the planetoid, the shipboard computer did not notify him of any dangerous alterations in cabin pressure or oxygen supply. But the workbee's sensors were not sophisticated enough to tell him where he was in relation to *Boadicea*. So he manually plotted a course that would allow him to rendezvous with her in her routinized orbit around the planetoid.

Luke put the craft on autopilot and pulled the *Boadicea* transcons from his pocket. He laid them on the workbee's console. After studying them, he opened the one he knew belonged to First Officer Ma'at. The real First Officer Ma'at wouldn't need it. S/he wouldn't be calling the *Boadicea* any time soon.

Luke had checked on the prisoners in the afternoon. As far as he knew, no one else had bothered. They were gone, which had surprised him, because he doubted Ma'at's condition could have been too athletic. S/he should have been having serious trouble with hir jaw and hir temple and the stretched position should have made it nearly impossible for hir to free hirself. Still, Nhavans were notorious for sheer cussedness.

He had examined the scene. There was no indication that anyone else had sneaked by, like Rusty, and released them. For one thing, the stake at Ma'at's head had been yanked out of the ground. No external liberator would have done anything so tedious. He would have just untied the prisoners.

Luke had even followed Ma'at's footprints for a short distance. There was only one set, deeply imprinted in the sand. Ma'at must have been carrying the webbed-footed woman, which made Luke laugh. They wouldn't get far. They would die in the desert, Nhavan cussedness or not.

Luke had returned to camp and said nothing. Now he would be Ma'at. Or at least do a good enough verbal imitation of Ma'at to get aboard the *Boadicea*. Wouldn't Captain Forrest be delighted to have Ma'at home? Luke smiled to himself. He was so good at so many things.

SYLVESTRE ADAM JENKS was getting frustrated. "Dani, eat some of this stuff."

Captain Forrest's eyes were half-closed, like a child's, and Sly had to keep rousing her to take a bite of the yeasty brown rice Sukha's crew had provided. He had already injected her with 30 milligrams of thiamine. The thiamine would begin to reverse the polyneuropathic symptoms Dani suffered from but she also needed just good old-fashioned food. Sly knew the captain had not eaten an adequate meal in days. She needed carbohydrates to restore her energy.

"What is it?" Dani mumbled.

"It's brown rice gruel. Open up. C'mon. The disease was beriberi, Dani."

"Huckleberries, mmmmm," Dani murmured contentedly, "my favorite. Haven't had 'em in years. I remember once I took a girl up to the huckleberry patch behind our place." Dani's voice was dreamy with memory. "Her clothes got all stained eating berries and so she went to wash up in the stream. It was hot and we both got in the water and —"

Dani avidly chewed a mouthful of rice, her imagination replaying an adolescent event the ending of which Sly could easily picture — knowing Dani Forrest.

"Dani —"

"Sly," the captain swallowed and fully opened her eyes, "this doesn't taste like huckleberries. Tastes like rice." She stared down at the rich brown glop in the bowl Sly was holding.

Sly rolled his eyes heavenwards. "You don't say."

LIEUTENANT MOUNEERA HAD already received her thiamine injection and was nibbling away at the bowl of nutty-tasting rice that sat on her console. Eating was not normally countenanced on the bridge but this was an exceptional circumstance. There were no officers available to relieve those who were already on duty and besides, who ever quibbled when warm tasty food was brought to them?

The graceful and good-looking Captain Ki was moving among the bridge crew, raising smiles even while bearing loaded hypos. Despite the fact that it would take some time for the vitamin and the food to return people to normal, there was a sense of exultation on the bridge. People believed the worst of the crisis was over.

Mouneera had every confidence that Captain Forrest would be back in her command chair any minute. Then they could resolve the hostage situation with the miners, get Ma'at and the others back, and take a much-deserved shore leave.

As if in response to her thoughts, Mouneera's board lighted with an incoming hail. She had tried the miners dozens of times with no success. Could this be them? Her fingers crossed, Mouneera answered it.

"*U.C.S.S. Boadicea*, Lieutenant Mouneera."

"Lieutenant, this is First Officer Ma'at." The transmission was fuzzed and ragged but Mouneera's heart did a double-flip at the words.

"Ma'at!" She hadn't meant to shout, but even if she'd whispered it would not have prevented the bridge crew from tuning in to listen. Everyone seemed to have dropped their spoons back into their half-eaten bowls of rice and turned to watch her.

"Commander," Mouneera got hold of herself, "where are you?"

"I have escaped in a workbee, Lieutenant, and am approaching *Boadicea*. I require access to the landing bay."

"I'll order the doors opened immediately, sir. We're so glad to hear from you. We thought—"

"I'm not hurt, Lieutenant. You can expect me on the bridge presently."

Well, thought Mouneera, that was Ma'at alright. Always acting as if nothing had happened. "We have very little crew available, sir, but I will have an engineering team meet you in the landing bay."

"That will not be necessary, Lieutenant. I can soft-land the workbee without assistance."

"Very good, sir. I will let the captain know you are aboard. She'll be delighted."

"Please do, Lieutenant. Ma'at out."

Ma'at might be able to contain hir emotions, Mouneera thought, but she doubted Captain Forrest would bother to hide hers. She tripped the intercom for the infirmary to relay the good news.

Luke flipped closed the stolen transcon. Just as Lieutenant Mouneera had said, he had no doubt Forrest would be delighted to see him. She just didn't yet know Luke was the bearer of her death.

THE DISTINCTIVE RUMBLE of pirate fighters flying overhead was unmistakable. Luluai had heard three fighters take off from the camp and now she heard three land. So, they had decided to return. Luluai wasn't sure what to think but her body knew what to feel: her stomach was a hard knot of fear and sweat slimed her hands and forehead even though the air in the hut had grown cold with the cooling of the desert night.

A host of noises followed the hiss-slide sound of the crafts' landings in the sand: doors whooshing open and hearty laughter, the crunch of heavy boots as the men came toward the huts. There was a lighter quicker step among the heavy ones.

"In there," a voice said. Luluai felt her breathing constrict. The moment had come. Then someone, a rather small someone, was shoved through the hide covering of the door. It was a young boy. Surely, they wouldn't—

"I won't tie you if you behave," the voice continued from outside. "That means," the pirate poked his head in, almost jovial, "you sit against the back wall and don't move. And don't touch the woman." To Luluai's astonishment, the flap dropped.

Luluai took breath again. The boy scooted against the back wall as commanded and drew his knees protectively up to his chest. He stared openly at Luluai's gagged and tied form but didn't move a centimeter in her direction.

"Hi," she said into his mind, "I am Luluai. Can you untie me?"

The boy didn't seem in the least flabbergasted to be hearing her in his head. "Can't," he said out loud, "you heard him." His voice was high and thin, that of a pre-adolescent.

"Just the gag, then? It's hard to breathe. It's very uncomfortable."

"Can't," the boy repeated.

"Please. It would mean so much."

The boy turned to stare unblinking at the hide flap and Luluai assumed he would not help. Then she saw his body jerk toward her a few centimeters and stop. He turned his attention back to the hide flap and then, assured his move hadn't been detected, jerked toward her again.

A moment later he was struggling to pull the gag over her tangled dirty hair. A moment after that, almost as if it hadn't happened, he was back in his original place against the wall.

Luluai barely had time to telegraph 'thank you' to him before the flap was pushed aside. Had they seen him? It was disobedient, yes, but such a small act of mercy. She would plead on his behalf...

The two pirates who came in didn't pay the slightest attention to either of them. The first backed in, bent over the portion of a load he shared with the other man. When the second pirate was most of the way through the door, they dropped their burden and, without a backward look, went out again. Luluai gawked. It was Ma'at. Or rather, the body of Ma'at.

The flap flicked aside again and Shim'on came in, the features of his face shadowed in the half-light, giving him an evil menacing air. Luluai stiffened, expecting the worst. But the pirate leader ignored her, kneeling by Ma'at and feeling hir wrist.

"S/he's not dead?" Luluai had been so certain. Shim'on did not turn around and she didn't expect an answer. She had blurted out her question before she thought about it.

"S/he's badly burned. S/he's in shock." Shim'on shifted on his haunches to gaze at Luluai, his eyes stony. "I have no medical supplies. S/he won't live."

"You killed hir." She didn't know why she said it. She was hardly in a position to antagonize her captor. But she had known Shim'on would do it.

"Yes. I killed hir." His eyes blazed briefly with an emotion she didn't recognize. Then the blaze went out and he rose to his feet and looked coldly down at her. "But as much as you may think otherwise, I am a man of my word. I will honor my agreement with Ma'at. No one will touch you tonight. Sleep well, Lieutenant Luluai. We depart in the morning." He raised the flap and was gone.

No one would touch her? Depart for where? Her thoughts came

in a jumble. She looked across at the boy but he was already asleep, or at least doing a good imitation of it. He probably didn't know anything anyway.

She looked at Ma'at and felt her heart wrench. Hir borrowed pirate's tunic was singed along the bottom. Hir face was a blood-drained white but in the weak moonlight Luluai couldn't see where or how badly s/he was burned. S/he simply appeared to be sleeping.

There was very little she could do. She didn't even have anything to cover Ma'at with if she could have moved to place it over hir. Then she remembered the triumph of the previous night.

"Ma'at," she called softly into the Nhavan's mind. There was no response. "Ma'at," she called again more insistently. Nothing. She could not feel Ma'at's mind. There was a blankness as if s/he didn't exist. If s/he was alive, s/he had gone far away. Somewhere where no one could reach hir.

Luluai felt herself dragged emotionally downwards by the whirlpool of worry that had been swirling in her mind all evening. She cried briefly then surfaced again. So Ma'at was dead or soon to be dead. She must accept it and go on surviving. She didn't know what tomorrow held but at least Shim'on had assured her she would be left alone tonight. It was that promise that allowed her finally to sleep.

"INFIRMARY? IS CAPTAIN Forrest there?" Mouneera chimed the intercom.

"Here, Mouneera."

"Captain, what a relief!"

Dani lifted both eyebrows. She knew she'd been sick but her crew did not normally comment on her state of health, no matter how severe. Still, it was nice to know she was beginning to sound like her old self again.

"Captain," Mouneera repeated, "I didn't mean...I mean I've just heard from Commander Ma'at. S/he escaped the planetoid in a workbee and should be reaching the landing bay in a few minutes."

Dani raised her fist in victory even though Mouneera couldn't see it. "Good old Ma'at! I knew s/he could do it."

"S/he said s/he's alright and will meet you on the bridge. That is, sir, if you're able—"

"I'll be there, Lieutenant, with bells on. Was there any word on our security people or the other crew?"

"S/he didn't say, sir. The transmission was fuzzed."

"Alright. What otherwise is our status, Lieutenant?"

"We're maintaining the same orbit we have all along, Captain. Other than Lieutenant DeVargas and myself, there is a junior crew manning the bridge. Captain Ki is here as well. I understand that all of the *Heaven's Bow* crew — except those on the planetoid, of course — are aboard *Boadicea* helping with the mass feeding. Their helmsman, Mr. Deva, is the only one on their vessel. He's manning their bridge."

"I must say this has certainly muddied the diplomatic waters, Lieutenant, but as always we'll deal with it. By the way, how did Captain Ki and Sukha Jabala get out of the brig?"

"Uh —"

"I'm ordering you to answer, Patricia." Dani's voice went soft as velvet but Mouneera winced at the intimate use of her first name. The captain always got what she wanted.

"Ensign Eireann, sir."

Dani sighed. "I thought as much. I suppose we'll have to start framing arguments for her defense."

Mouneera could not suppress a giggle. "I'm pleased to hear it, sir." It was a pleasure to have the Forrest she knew back in action. The Forrest who would go to bat with the Explora Command hierarchy for a member of her crew if she believed what they'd done was right. Even if they had bent the rules.

"As soon as the good doctor releases me, I'll be on the bridge, Lieutenant. Oh, and by the way, cancel that distress call you made to Explora Command earlier. Tell them things are under control. Forrest out."

LULUAI WAS AWAKENED by the feathery sensation of a hand clasping her mouth. She struggled up, her eyes flashing open, just in time to see the hated gag slide over her face and cinch into place over her mouth.

"Don't know how you lost that," the Deimeon leaning over her said in mild bemusement.

Luluai screamed through the gag but all that came out was a muffled grunt. She pushed violently with her shoulder against the man's chest. Her hands were still tied behind her back and her ankles were strapped close together. None of her limbs were of much use.

The pirate fell back and grinned lopsidedly at her. Luluai felt disgust and fear. It was the small lanky Deimeon with the greasy hair who had tied and gagged her and told her about the pigs.

"Now, now. It's nothing to get upset about. Everybody likes a little fun. Especially a beautiful woman like yourself."

Luluai scrambled as far back from him as she could, her eyes wild. Shim'on had sworn she would not be attacked.

"Grrrhmmmbbbb!" she yelled. The gag, unfortunately, was a good one. She didn't think anyone outside the hut could hear her.

The boy, though, was awake. He hadn't moved but his eyes were locked on the pirate. She swung her head to him, her eyes begging him to do something.

The pirate followed her glance and grinned again. "So, we have an audience." He shrugged.

Luluai screamed again. The pirate leaned forward and grabbed at the neck of her tunic but the material was strong and didn't rip. Luluai scrabbled backwards again.

"Not a problem," the pirate murmured calmly and reached into a sheath at his belt and brought out a knife. Luluai's eyes went wide. But he didn't cut her. He brought it down to her ankles and, in one smooth movement, sliced through the bonds. He re-sheathed the knife.

"Now where were—" The last word never left his mouth as he went crashing into the heavy post at the center of the hut. Luluai heard a frightening snap, a grunted 'uh', and then silence. She thought for an instant the boy had done something, but the pirate had been impacted from the other direction.

The boy was still in his place, his body rigid, his back stiff against the wall. Was it Shim'on? A dark figure flew to her side and ripped the gag from her mouth. Luluai looked up into a handsome dark face and twinkling brown eyes.

"Nachi!"

"Shhh. Let's get out of here. Can you walk?"

"I think so. My hands are tied though." She twisted and lifted her shoulders to show him.

"Animals," he snarled. He went across to the stilled pirate and pulled the Deimeon's knife from his sheath. "I don't think he'll be needing this."

Expertly, Nachi sliced through the nylon strap binding Luluai's hands. He was getting pretty good at this rescue stuff he thought. Though he had not been a moment too soon with Luluai. He hadn't known if tracking the pirates would pay off or not. She could have been anywhere. She could have been dead. But the Preserver had smiled on him all day this day.

"Alright, done. Let's go."

"Ma'at," Luluai whispered, gesturing at the other recumbent body in the room, "and the boy."

"What about them?"

"We can't leave them."

"A dead person and a kid? Are you crazy?"

"S/he's not dead. Ma'at has saved my life several times."

"S/he was about to let you get raped."

"S/he's unconscious. S/he's dying."

"Well, then. My point, exactly." But just to make her happy, he crossed the room and took a look at this Ma'at person she was so concerned about. There was a very faint rise and fall to the person's chest.

"Okay, but you'll have to help me carry hir. S/he's going to be heavy."

"S/he's not heavy. S/he's Ma'at."

"Oh, very funny. You, kid," he lifted his chin at the boy, "do a recon. Come back and give us the all clear if it is all clear. My shuttlecraft is over a dune toward the right-hand moon. Got it?"

"Got it. Back in a flash." The boy was gone.

"I'll take hir head, Luluai. You'll have to get hir feet."

Luluai crawled stiffly across the hard packed floor and grasped Ma'at's ankles. It was then that she saw the damage to Ma'at's feet and lower legs. Flakes of charred skin came off in her hands. Her stomach turned over.

"Ugh."

"What now?"

"S/he's — " she swallowed painfully. "Hir feet — "

"Grab hir by the knees then. You're the one who wants to save hir."

She glared angrily at him.

"Sorry," Nachi said, "it's just that it doesn't look like there's much chance for hir, Lu. I'm not a doctor, but this is deep shock. I mean, be reasonable. We may not be doing hir a favor by moving hir."

"I don't care. I will not give up on Ma'at, Nachi. S/he never gave up on me."

"Okay, okay. I got the point. Do you think you can lift hir?"

Luluai grasped Ma'at's knees and pulled upwards.

"Gods. S/he is heavy."

The boy slithered back into the hut without a sound. "All clear," he whispered to Nachi. "I think everyone's drunk and gone to sleep. There was a big victory party."

"Good. You found the shuttlecraft?"

The boy nodded.

"Okay, you lead then and keep your eyes peeled for trouble. We'll follow."

Luluai strained to lift Ma'at and they started a slow staggering march to the shuttlecraft that might just as well have been a journey of a thousand kilometers. Towards the end, Nachi shifted Ma'at entirely to his shoulders out of sheer exasperation because Luluai could hardly crawl let alone give him much help with Ma'at's dead weight. Nachi gritted his teeth with the effort and persisted. The alien might be spare, he thought, but s/he had to be all muscle to weigh so damn much.

There was also the need for hurry. There was no guarantee one
of the pirates wouldn't wake up to take a piss and see them stealing
away in the moonlight. He didn't think it would be the one he'd left
behind, though. The man wasn't dead — Nachi heard his breathing
when he lifted his knife — but he wasn't going to feel well for awhile.

Doctor Torilli saw Nachi coming with the body and readied the
emergency bunk in the back of the craft. Nachi staggered up the *Lithe
Arrow's* ramp and, with a relieved grunt, dropped Ma'at's bulk on
the bunk. He gave the doctor a speculative look.

"All yours, Tor."

She frowned repressively at him and, without a word, started
examining her unexpected patient. Nachi went forward to power up
the motors. Doctor Tilorri had closed the ramp door the moment they
were all safely aboard. The boy had already latched himself into the
co-pilot's seat.

On seeing the doctors, Luluai had wanted to run to them and
hug the life out of them. Glimpsing their bright alive faces was like
exiting from the darkness of a dank cave into the caressing summer
sunshine. Instead she said to Doctor Tilorri, "S/he's in shock. S/he's
burned. S/he's dying." Her words came out in an agonized rush.

The shuttlecraft lifted into the air. Doctor Tilorri, seeing her
sister's already intense concentration on the patient, guided Luluai
by the shoulder to the bucketseat behind Nachi. She pushed her
gently down and snapped closed the safety harness. "We will do
everything we can."

"I want to help." Luluai reached for the clasp. "I have to."

"You have been through a lot, Luluai. You can do the most now
by releasing your thoughts about hir and your experience. Do you
remember that mental exercise?"

"Of course." She felt like a scolded child. Doctor Tilorri took
note of the reaction, grasped both of Luluai's hands in her own and
said: "I know it's difficult, Granddaughter. But we cannot erect an
effective healing field for hir with your thoughts of anxiety in the
background."

"I know," she grumbled. "I'll do the exercise. It's just that we are
bonded — at the level of the third eye — as Great Aunt Mayyaya would
say."

Doctor Tilorri smiled her reassurance. "S/he has been a mentor
for you, then. It is a powerful relationship. All the more reason for
you to release your thoughts."

"Yes."

"But you know how healing works. We will practice our art and
if hir consciousness wishes to return, s/he will heal. If not, s/he is
beyond our assistance."

"I remember."

"Do the exercise. It will help you to find peace. I must join my sister. She is beginning concentration for the chant." With a final reassuring pat for Luluai's shoulder, Doctor Tilorri walked away.

Chapter
Fourteen

IN A PURELY professional way, Ensign DeVargas, one of the ship's premier drag queens, was captivated by the statuesque, dusky-skinned Captain Ki. She was so foreign but so familiar, so strong yet so feminine, so lithe and elegant. He tried, between bites of rice, to engage her in conversation — he desperately wanted to know where she'd bought her belt — but she expertly put him off. Unfortunately, due to her distracting presence, he didn't notice the anomalous readings registering on his screen.

Junior officer Sue Mata, manning Ma'at's science station, brought them to his attention. New to the bridge and cautious by nature, she approached DeVargas in the manner of a deferential subordinate. She didn't want to make a frenzied announcement that might, without cause, wreck the fragile air of ebullience on the bridge.

But a cold fear gripped DeVargas when he saw the readings. He had seen the pattern before and he was 90 percent certain it indicated the presence of one of the only two powers in the quadrant that had cloaking device technology, Deimeons or Khrars. Both were equally unwelcome.

"Lieutenant Mouneera!" DeVargas swirled from his post with such force that he knocked his teetering rice bowl to the floor. DeVargas ignored the crash but there was a burst of guffaws from the bridge crew who thought DeVargas was horsing around.

"Yes, Ensign?" Mouneera didn't join in the hilarity but she enjoyed DeVargas's buffoonery as much as everyone else. It was music to her ears to hear the crew laughing again. But DeVargas wasn't grinning his mischievous grin.

"Can you run an exterior scan?"

"Of course," she answered easily, "why?"

"I think we have visitors."

As though his words had summoned them into being, six Khrar Predators uncloaked and wobbled into solidity. Their hovering shapes filled the *Boadicea's* viewscreen with menace.

"Red alert!" Mouneera shouted, ramming buttons, "Screens up!" The ship responded with the accustomed flash of light and sound and the raising of shields. The Khrar array held its position. DeVargas squinted and leaned across his console, his body taut with anticipation.

"They're not firing. Why uncloak if not to fire?"

"They're hailing us!" Mouneera cried.

"On screen." DeVargas raced from his console to take the captain's chair. Even as he did, Captain Forrest came onto the bridge. DeVargas leaped back to his station. When the alien commander shimmered into life on the viewscreen, Forrest stood erectly before her command chair as though she'd been in her place all along.

"This is Captain Forrest," she said crisply, "what is your business here, Khrar? You're in Coalition space."

"Ah, Forrest. Commander Korsaag here. Our sincerest apologies but we are investigating a heinous crime that has been committed against the Khrar Empire. I am happy to report we have tracked down the perpetrator."

Dani shot a sideways glance at Captain Ki, who, having completed her rounds, stood alertly off to the left. She was gazing intently at the Khrar.

"I take it, Commander, that the 'heinous crime' to which you refer is the destruction of a Predator, which we are investigating?"

"How, Forrest, can you investigate a crime you have committed? That isn't allowed in any system of justice." The commander smirked, happy with the point he felt he'd scored. Dani heard the satisfied grunts of the Khrar bridge officers in the background.

"Korsaag, are you accusing the Coalition, and specifically the *U.C.S.S. Boadicea,* of this action? Under the Rolt Treaty, such an act would constitute an act of war."

"Screw the Rolts and their interference, Forrest. I see two Coalition ships orbiting together. And that one," he gestured off to the side of the screen toward the serenely floating *Heaven's Bow,* "is the responsible ship. We have tracked and analyzed its ion traces, Forrest. And you, by your presence, are condoning its action."

This time Dani did not dare to look in Bajana Ki's direction. She prayed she would have enough sense to keep her mouth shut. The situation was delicate and, if Eireann was right, she knew nothing of the ways of Khrars. Dani didn't enjoy playing diplomat. If she had, she would have been one. But if bluffing would save the situation, bluff she would. Her ship and crew were too shaky to be going up against six Predators.

"Korsaag, I believe you're mistaken. Your Empire hasn't proved to the satisfaction of the Coalition that the *Star Spawn* even existed. Or that it was destroyed by an attacker."

"Proved to the satisfaction of the Coalition! What kind of garbage is that, Forrest?" Korsaag snorted and brought his mailed fist down on the arm of his command chair.

"It's not garbage, Korsaag. It's a valid question."

It dawned on Korsaag that Forrest was stalling. But why?

Forrest would only hesitate for a good reason. Korsaag's stomach tightened. It was time to bring the debate to a close. He didn't want to give Forrest time to plan an offensive strategy.

"But not one I'll answer. I have my proof, Forrest. Now, I'll have my revenge."

"If you fire on that ship, Korsaag, it will be an act of war initiated by the Empire."

Korsaag's eyes narrowed. What was Forrest up to?

"Wait! Commander Korsaag," Captain Ki stepped forward. "I am the Captain of the *Heaven's Bow*. We are not of the Coalition."

"Forrest," Korsaag roared, "who is this?"

Dani wanted to tackle Captain Ki. If she dropped her from sight, maybe Korsaag would think he'd imagined her. But there wasn't much hope of that. Her rare grace would stick out even in a Khrar's ponderous mind.

"This is Captain Ki of the...other ship. But she had nothing to do with your slimy little Predator, Korsaag."

Korsaag licked his lips. "Oh, really? Let's let her speak for herself, Forrest. Go ahead, Captain Ki." Korsaag thought whatever this woman screwed up and said, Forrest wasn't going to like it. He could tell by Forrest's tight expression.

"Commander, my helmsman...I mean I—"

"These are Khrars, Captain," Dani hissed *sotto voce*, "Lie."

Bajana Ki frowned in confusion. "Uh, we are not of the Coalition, Commander Korsaag. We are just passing through. Captain Forrest has been so kind as to help us with a technical problem. That is why we are here in a joint orbit with the *Boadicea*."

Dani had never heard anything so stiff in her life. She doubted Korsaag would buy it.

"And the *Star Spawn*?" Korsaag said sweetly.

"Never heard of it." Captain Ki produced a frightened smile.

"I don't believe you, Captain. Nor am I sure how you made captain with such lousy bluffing skills. And a woman, too. Did you sleep your way up?" He shook his head in mock dismay. Bajana sputtered angrily. Korsaag ignored her and turned his attention back to Forrest.

"I've enjoyed this little charade immensely, Forrest. But I'm afraid it's at an end. May the better man—or woman—win. Communications out." The screen went blank.

Dani stumbled back into her chair and slapped her hand to her forehead. "I thought you were such a good liar, Captain. What in the hell happened there?"

Bajana Ki clenched her fists and came at her. "I have been telling you the truth since we met. That's why I'm so convincing, you jackass! Not because I'm a good liar!"

Despite the red alert, there was a stillness on the bridge, all ears tuned to hear what Captain Forrest would say. No one could recall Forrest's ever having been called a jackass on her own bridge. Dani dropped her hand from her forehead and looked up at the wild-eyed woman ready to hit her. Then she broke into a grin.

"Well, I guess then, I have no choice but to believe you and your original story." She laughed her familiar infectious laugh. The bridge crew exhaled.

"Does this mean," Bajana said, "that you're willing to admit I'm not involved in a hare-brained scheme to steal gemstones?"

Dani put a hand to her chin. "I met with Sukha Jabala and Ensign Eireann just before I came onto the bridge. The evidence they presented was intriguing. You almost might say persuasive."

"And you left me to twist in the wind?"

"You have to admit, Captain, I have been rather busy since I arrived."

"True. I apologize." Bajana hung her head.

"Apology accepted. However, I can see I'm going to have to teach you a few tricks for dealing with Khrars. Your track record has been lousy so far. And it's about to get worse."

"Why? What happens now?"

"A lot of people die, Captain. Preferably theirs. Battlestations, everyone!"

NACHI THROTTLED THE shuttlecraft to the maximum speed it would tolerate without causing damage to the hull. He made haste because he didn't know the speed or weapons capacity of the pirate vessels. He hoped it would be dawn before they noticed the absence of their captives and engaged in pursuit. A good head start might mean the difference between life and death. He might even reach the *Heaven's Bow* before they caught up with him.

The shuttlecraft had no weapons systems, offensive or defensive. A tribute to the peace-loving nature of Nirvannini, he supposed, but damn inconvenient in real space. He did not have trigger-finger-itch the way Hasitam did but he thought a little built-in protection would have been nice. If he lived, he was going to agitate for its inclusion in the next design.

Although he rushed for the *Heaven's Bow*, he couldn't guess how he would be received. Rescuing the doctors would score him some brownie points. Stealing the workbee would not, even if the ends proved to justify the means. And on reconsideration, although Luluai had to bully him into doing it, the saving of this *Boadicea* crewperson might turn out to be advantageous.

It was hard to predict Ma'at's value to Captain Forrest, but s/he might provide just the negotiating edge needed with the *Boadicea*, a factor that could save his ass with Captain Ki. Ma'at wasn't in the best condition, but Nachi figured damaged goods would still fetch some kind of price. Surely a better one than dead cargo.

The big question was whether the doctors could keep Ma'at alive long enough to trade hir over. Nachi could hear the sing-song rise and fall of their voices in the back of the craft. The sounds, words, and rhythm meant nothing to him, but he had to admit it was soothing, much like waves slapping on the beach.

His other booty, the boy in the co-pilot's seat, was either unaware of the chant or too excited to be affected by it. He vigorously scanned the viewscreen, bouncing restlessly from side to side, straining against the seat's harness. When he first sat down, he had covetously run his fingers over the controls on the console but had ceased at a warning growl from Nachi.

It was hard not to see his hands clasping and unclasping in his lap, though, and he watched Nachi like a hawk, observing every control change Nachi made. Even though it took some time, the boy's attention was held transfixed as they passed from the planetoid's upper atmosphere and into the starlit blackness of space. Nachi finally had to say something.

"Didn't you come here on some kind of ship?"

"No. I've never seen this from a ship, this rising through atmospheres. Tam and I were de-matted down from a passing freighter. We had hitched a ride."

"De-matted down?" And who'e Tam?"

"He's the camp cook for the miners. And you know what de-matting is."

"No, I don't. Is Tam your dad?"

"Everybody knows what de-matting is. You're in one place one minute and then the next, you're in another. Tam and I've just been traveling together. He hid me from the slavers."

"Don't you have parents? And a home planet?"

"There was a planetary war. They were killed." The boy turned from his fascination with the viewscreen for a fleeting look at Nachi. "What's going to happen to me now?"

"Beats me. But whatever it is, it won't be the slave trade. My captain is kind." At least that's what Nachi preferred to think. At the moment, he was feeling dependent on her reputed kindness himself.

"That's good. Hey," the boy pointed, "look at that." They were nearing the area of the shuttlecraft's computed guess as to the location of the *Heaven's Bow*. Nachi looked. The *Heaven's Bow* was a small moving dot and the *Boadicea* a larger moving dot. But something looked odd to Nachi. There were a handful of other dots circling the two ships. Nachi slowed his engines and hailed the

Heaven's Bow.

"*Heaven's Bow* come in. This is *Lithe Arrow.*" He repeated it several times and had almost given up hope of a response when he heard Hasitam Deva's adrenaline-driven voice.

"Nachi, is that you?"

"Hasitam?" Why was Hasitam at the helm? He was supposed to be under cabin arrest.

"Nachi, get the hell out of here! I'm in a battle! Can't talk!"

"*Lithe Arrow* out." Nachi obeyed hurriedly. A battle? But with whom? As Nachi drew nearer, the shapes of the other ships became more distinct. They had draped wings and beetle-shaped heads and they looked exactly like the ship Hasitam had blown to particles a week before.

So, Nachi thought, retribution had arrived. And Captain Ki thought they had problems with the *Boadicea.* Nachi didn't see how Hasitam could hold out against so many ships, but he didn't see how he could help either. Without weapons, he would only be in the way.

And whose side was *Boadicea* on? Nachi watched for a few minutes. Predators swooped around the massive *Boadicea* like a horde of angry wasps stinging a dothora, the water buffalo of Nirvannini. The big ship reeled from one well-injected sting but righted itself easily enough.

It looked to Nachi like it was two against six instead of one against six, even though it didn't make sense. He had understood the *Heaven's Bow* was in just as much hot water with the *Boadicea* as with this other bunch. But how far would *Boadicea* go to intervene in a dispute that she must know was between the *Heaven's Bow* and these other beings? At the moment, she seemed to be drawing the fire of the Predators but not dishing any out.

Nachi knew it was a fluke that Hasitam had destroyed that other ship. And it never should have happened. There was no need for it to have happened. Just Hasitam's blood lust. Someone was going to have to pay. It was the nature of things, the way of karma.

As he watched, two Predators sheared away from *Boadicea* and dived toward the *Heaven's Bow*. The small delicate ship sat deadly still...until they got close. Then she raced toward them with kamikaze craziness. The unexpected move startled the Predators' pilots and threw off their aim. The *Heaven's Bow* suffered only a glancing hit from one of the two attackers.

Boadicea, more agile than Nachi thought possible, darted away from her goaders and fired on one of the Predators that was circling back to take another shot at the *Heaven's Bow*. A flash of light broiled across the vessel's shell like the feathery fingers of a hundred lighting bolts. The Predator turned white-blue with heat and exploded, chunks of it arcing in all directions.

"Whoa!" the boy exclaimed. Apparently, *Boadicea* would go pretty far. Nachi wondered why and could find no answer.

He turned the *Lithe Arrow* around and headed back to the planet. The shuttlecraft's fuel and life support systems were not drained to dangerous levels but he could not hang about in space for any length of time either. And if all that was left when the shooting was over were Predators, he didn't want to be in the neighborhood anyway.

All he could do now was ask the Preserver to protect the *Heaven's Bow*. If she exploded, twenty-four of his closest friends and the first off-world mission of his culture in ten thousand years would go with her.

He and Luluai and the doctors would be the only remaining representatives of that mission. And that, only if they could find a way to survive on this little planetoid they might very well now be calling home. The future did not look rosy to Nachi.

"SLY! I NEED every crewperson who can stand!"

"We're peddling as fast as we can down here, Dani. The criticals are taken care of but they can't help you yet. The *Heaven's Bow* crew is still feeding dozens of people. What in hell's going on up there anyway?"

"Khrars. Do what you can, Sly."

"Don't we always? Jenks out."

Dani would have to make do with the bridge and engineering crew who were already manning their posts. That little chat with Commander Korsaag might have allowed her to get a few more crew into position and even a single person could make the difference between life and death during a battle. But would it be enough?

"Ensign Hammerstein," she leaned forward in her command chair addressing the substitute helmsman.

"Sir?" Hammerstein was twitching, nervous as a man ordered to bust a bronco who'd never seen one before, which wasn't far different in challenge from the task Dani really did expect him to accomplish in the next few minutes.

Dani knew Hammerstein had never been in actual combat and she knew the man, despite being sick, had stayed loyally at his post on the bridge through several shifts. This combination of factors, inexperience and fatigue, was a dangerous one but Dani had no one with which to replace him.

"Relax, Ensign," she said lightly, "and think of this as the kind of simulation you've been through a hundred times as a cadet. The actions you have to take are no different. Just respond to my orders. You're one of the best in Minority Fleet or you wouldn't be here."

"Yes, sir. But it can't be the same as a simulation."

"Yes, it can," Dani interposed smoothly. "The consequences are different, but that's my concern as the captain. Not yours. Is that clear?"

"Yes, sir, it is. Thank you, sir. I can live with that."

The pep talk had been the right one. Hammerstein's tensions visibly dissolved, leaving only what alertness he could still muster after so many hours of duty.

"Good, Ensign. Our strategy is to get the enemy to waste as much firepower on us as we can safely tolerate, instead of using it against the *Heaven's Bow,* which isn't going to stand up to too much. In other words, Hammerstein, we're going to play chicken with them. We want to keep them distracted."

"Understood, sir. And if they go for the *Heaven's Bow?*"

"We'll have to fire on them."

The worst scenario would be if Korsaag split his attack fleet, which any intelligent commander would do, and used three ships to attack the *Heaven's Bow* and three to keep the *Boadicea* busy.

"Captain, de-materialize me over there." Captain Ki, who had been staring at the viewscreen as if hypnotized, came to life. "It's my ship. I'm responsible for it and for this mess."

"Absolutely not, Captain Ki. Your helmsman will have to make do. He's on his own."

"But what can I do here?"

"For the moment, watch and learn." She expected a howl of outrage from her but didn't get it. Ki's eyes were glued to the viewscreen and to the gleaming coppery vessel that was her lonely ship, now a target destined for destruction by one of the most ruthless of adversaries known to the Coalition.

Dani didn't need words to understand what she was feeling. She guessed that, just like herself, Ki would rather go down with her ship but Dani wasn't about to allow it.

Three of Korsaag's Predators sailed over the *Boadicea* and out of view. The other three made a dead run at her. Dani breathed a sigh of relief, if it could be called that. They hadn't split their attack.

"Let's lead them a merry chase, Mr. Hammerstein."

"Aye, sir."

Korsaag must have decided to disable *Boadicea* first. Dani could almost see Korsaag's Khrar mind working. *Boadicea* would be helpless to save the *Heaven's Bow* but would be forced to watch Korsaag take his revenge with her. It was a sadistic mindset but not an unlikely one for a Khrar in the mood for extracting vengeance.

Hammerstein did a good job of shrugging off the enemy. The *Boadicea* leaped and raced and rolled evading some, but not all, of the Predators' fire. Hammerstein wasn't Sabi, Dani thought, but he wasn't bad either. And the comparison was unfair under the circumstances.

When two Predators split away and went for the *Heaven's Bow*, Dani ordered Hammerstein to get aggressive. Dani didn't know if her guess about Korsaag's strategy had been wrong or if Korsaag had simply changed his mind.

After the first *Boadicea* torpedo took one of the vessel's crews to the Khrar afterlife, the *Boadicea* gunned for the second. Without much ado, it joined its sister ship. Their destruction seemed to make Korsaag decide to go after his main objective and get away without further loss. The four remaining Predators, including his flagship, ignored *Boadicea* and bore down on the *Heaven's Bow*.

On the whole, Dani was impressed with Hasitam. He gave the four Predators a run for their money by twisting and diving and stopping dead when they least expected it. Hasitam fired as often as he could, making the Predators miserable and wary, but not disabling them to any measurable extent. A natural Sabi, Dani thought.

The hits against the *Heaven's Bow* began to take their toll, though. After the first substantive one, which sent the vessel reeling, *Boadicea* blasted away another Predator, taking a hard hit herself from two of the other Khrar vessels, firing on her in tandem. The engineering room informed Dani auxiliary power was down.

After the second substantive hit on the *Heaven's Bow*, which reduced her running power, Dani hailed Korsaag.

"Have you had enough?"

"Hell, no, Captain. Vengeance is mine. That ship will be destroyed!"

"You've lost half your fleet, you thick-skulled Khrar!"

"This is to the death, Coalition! Korsaag out!"

"Cripes," muttered Dani. She hated that kind of Khrar.

"Hammerstein, move in on that one over there." Dani pointed to the left of the viewscreen.

"Aye, Captain."

"Fire!"

The Predator dodged, pulled out of range, and the torpedo missed. Korsaag's flagship *Qa'Hhogh* came in on the *Boadicea* and fired squarely on the primary hull. The *Boadicea* hurtled backward. Electronics crackled and sizzled on the bridge.

"Report!" Dani yelled.

"Weapons offline!" DeVargas shouted.

"Impulse engines down, sir!" Hammerstein echoed.

"Engineering, report!"

"Shouldn't be more than two minutes, sir, and she'll be back on." It was a confident voice in engineering, whoever it was.

"We can't wait two minutes! Give me auxiliary power."

"That's down, sir. From the first hit."

"Hell!" Dani remembered.

She sat and fidgeted. Her ship was a temporary sitting duck. Two minutes was a long time in a battle. What was worse, Hasitam might be a sitting duck. Dani had no way of knowing what worked and what didn't on the *Heaven's Bow*. She didn't dare call her to get an assessment either. Korsaag could easily listen in.

Qa'Hhogh pulled to a stop and hung in space. Dani knew Korsaag was gauging the situation, trying to decide whether *Boadicea* was damaged or merely faking. Korsaag's two remaining ships joined him. After a moment, the two moved off, almost casually for the *Heaven's Bow*. Dani knew it was for the kill.

"Damn," Dani cursed. "Engineering!"

"Almost ready, sir."

Dani was ready to chew down her nails. The beautiful *Heaven's Bow* hung in space without moving, the two Predators closing in on it. Hasitam powered up and moved away from them. Dani breathed again. And so did Captain Ki at her side. She had moved quite close to her command chair. The Predators increased their speed.

"Now, sir. Online." Engineering called.

"Thank Goddess! Go, Hammerstein."

The *Boadicea* raced forward. On the other hand, the *Heaven's Bow* came to a hard stop. The action sent a visible shudder through the ship's elegant frame. The Archer on her hull quivered in the soundless starlight. The gold-tipped arrow would never leave it's ornamented launch but, in her mind's eye, Dani saw it arc away through space as though shot toward some distant longed-for star.

Dani knew Hasitam had thrown the ship into reverse. And she knew why. The two Predators were so close on the *Heaven's Bow's* tail that they would never be able to stop or veer away.

The *Boadicea* viewscreen went blindingly white. It was a color Captain Ki had intended never to see again but there it was. She jammed her left fist against her mouth and clamped down hard to keep from crying out. The glowing aftermath lasted much longer than it had the first time. After all, it was three ships rather than just one contributing to that harrowing display of fire and light.

"Reverse engines," Dani ordered sharply.

"Reversing, sir."

"Mouneera," Dani tried to work saliva into her mouth, "hail the Khrar Commander. There's been enough killing."

"Aye, sir." When the image of Korsaag appeared on the viewscreen, Dani made no preamble.

"You got what you wanted, Korsaag. Now get out."

"I'm satisfied, Forrest. An eye for an eye."

"Making the whole world blind, yes. You Khrars will never

learn that."

"*Arrivederci*, Forrest." The image of the commander was gone and in an instant the Predator had vanished as well, leaving only a silvery streak of warp emissions where it had once been.

"I'm sorry," Dani said quietly, "truly sorry." She could feel Bajana Ki's grief without looking at her. It was like a wave that washed in all directions. The knuckles of her right hand were white where they gripped the arm of Dani's chair.

Ki looked down at Dani and her eyes were so dark with sorrow that Dani felt a radiating pain in her chest as though the other woman had bored a hole through her with her pain.

"I'm sorry," Dani repeated.

"You did everything you could." Ki didn't mean it as an accusation but Dani had never felt more like a failure.

"Bajana—" Dani stood to take the other woman's hand. She planned to get Ki off the bridge and get her some privacy, but Dani never got the opportunity.

The bridge doors hissed opened and a robed and hooded figure strode through them. The figure moved so fast no one was aware of it until it came to the front of the captain's chair and faced Dani and Bajana.

"Ma'at," Dani said in surprise. "Finally! I wondered where you were."

"Captain," said the muffled voice, not lifting the hood.

"Thank Goddess you're—"

The figure raised its right arm. As the sleeve of the robe fell back, Bajana saw that the extended hand held a weapon. There was a finger pulling back on its trigger.

"No!" Bajana screamed and slammed down hard on the figure's wrist. Dani sidestepped to the right and forward. The Khrar Discharger fired and Bajana screamed again and fell. Dani brought both of her fists up with a blow to the chin that knocked back the figure's hood and sent the man inside staggering against the rail. DeVargas raised his syn-gun and fired, and the man, clearly not Ma'at, slumped to the deck in a stun.

"Mouneera," Dani yelled, "get a medic team!"

A portion of Bajana's leggings had disintegrated and her right thigh was charred from the Discharger blast. Dani could smell burned flesh and she winced as she knelt by Bajana's side.

Blood spurting from Bajana's ruptured femoral artery splattered across Dani's uniform. A hundred smaller torn vessels leaked freely, soaking the deck. Dani straddled the other woman's leg, stanched what she could of the flow of blood with her hands and prayed for Sly's speedy arrival.

"Captain," Bajana whispered with effort, "he was trying to

kill you."

"Yes, I know. You stopped him, Bajana." Because of Ki's action, most of the blast had sliced between them and impacted on Dani's command chair. It smoked from the damage, releasing poisons into the bridge's air. The chair's lower panel was an ugly meltdown of plastics. Bajana had caught the edge of the blast but that little bit had mauled her thigh into a mass of ruptured tissue.

"Hurts," she whispered again with effort.

"Don't talk. The pain will be gone in a minute." Dani knew she was lying but it was a merciful lie. No Coalition painkiller could wholly numb the agony induced by a Khrar Discharger. The damage was too extensive.

But, in another moment, making good her promise, Bajana had a painkiller in her. Sly hypo-injected her with it and then spray-sealed the leaking blood vessels of her leg with plastigel. The *Heaven's Bow's* captain had gone unconscious.

Dani stood up and moved aside. Her sleeves were bright with blood to the elbows and the deck was slick with it. She wiped her soaked hands on her green leggings. They too were drenched with blood.

"Fortunately, it's human blood," Sly said grimly, watching Dani. "We can match it and replace it. Another minute and she would have lost enough to be in the morgue, replaceable or not."

The blood Bajana had lost, Dani thought, had been shed to keep her from dying. And she hardly knew Dani. Actually, Dani corrected, Bajana knew her well enough to have every good reason to hate her guts. Dani had treated her badly from the moment she'd met her. To top it off, she had not been able to prevent the destruction of Bajana's ship and the death of her helmsman.

"Let's go," Sly said to the medic team. Two crew hoisted the stretcher and started for the kinelift doors.

"Take good care of her, Sly."

"It's going to be a long surgery." Sly followed the stretcher.

"I know." Dani turned away. A different team, this one security, was carrying away her unconscious would-be assassin and she asked herself, why? She didn't know the man and his action had almost certainly not been personal. Dani was sufficiently notorious to have to live with the specter of assassination but still, when it was attempted, she wanted to know why someone had gone to the bother of hiring someone to kill her. And whoever had targeted her must have been promising big bucks to do the deed because the man being borne away on the stretcher had gone to a great deal of bother just to get aboard the *Boadicea*.

For one thing, he had managed to convince Mouneera he was Ma'at, which meant he had not only absconded with Ma'at's transcon but practiced imitating the first officer's speech patterns. That could mean anything. But the most obvious and grimmest of the possibilities that came to Dani's mind was that Ma'at was dead.

Dani had her work cut out for her; an assassin to interrogate, a raid to make on the planetoid with a heavily-armed security contingent and the still-missing *Boadicea* and *Heaven's Bow's* teams to find. Even if they were dead, she swore to herself she would not leave the planetoid until she found them.

She turned command over to Mouneera and walked heavily to the kinelift. She rode it to E Deck, exited, and made her way to her quarters. There she stripped off her blood-sodden body suit and stepped into the shower.

UNLIKE NACHI, LULUAI not only knew parts of the healing chant and some of the theory behind it, but she could sense the invisible, but very real, colors it produced. The colors changed in intensity and shade with the cadence and progress of the sounds.

Soon after she finished her meditation which, though it hadn't made her feel better, had distanced her from disturbing feelings, the soothing color of rose suffusing the shuttlecraft gave way to a settling lavender. That shade metamorphosed into a deep blue that encircled and protected like a maternal embrace. After a time, it was followed by a rich pulsating indigo. The sounds of the chant reverberated along the walls. Luluai knew the doctors were practicing 'stabilization', the first healing stage.

When the colors shifted to yellows and gentle oranges, she knew they had reached the stage called 'the dance'. The cheerful colors and upbeat rhythms of the chant were intended to awaken the patient's healing capacities. It was based on the principal that physical damage could not be repaired if the patient's mind resisted the process of repair.

After what seemed hours to her, the chant changed again and became a monotonic repetition, like the running of a summer brook. Hundreds of shades of greens wavered into existence then transmuted into other shades of green.

Luluai felt euphoric. Ma'at must have agreed to return to hir body. Cellular healing was underway. The healing process would move at a breakneck pace now, drawn forward by the intensifying rhythms of the chant. Strong lively reds replaced the greens.

It was no longer a question of life or death for Ma'at, but only of the length of recovery. Thus assured, Luluai at last dropped off into a heavy much-needed sleep.

Nachi did not wake her either. She slept through his decision to return to the planetoid and so was blissfully unaware of their, and the *Heaven's Bow's,* potential fate.

"ANY IDENTIFICATION?"

"None whatsoever, Captain." Security Chief Markett stood stolidly in the foyer of the brig. "All he had on him was the Khrar Discharger — black market version — Ma'at's transcon, Cindy and Eluthea's transcons, and this vidscreen short-range transmitter, also black market. He does have the burn tattoo of the LiShanNa on his shoulder blades."

"What does that mean?"

"That means he can kill quite effectively — and has killed — with just his hands. You don't get the tattoo until you've proved it quite a few times. I'm not sure how many. It's surprising he bothered with the Discharger."

"Wanted to be sure?"

"Possibly," Markett shrugged. "You're known in some circles, sir, as invincible."

"No one is invincible, Markett." And girl, didn't she know it. Anyone who thought she was invincible would be dead much sooner than otherwise. "Has he talked?"

"We haven't tried anything yet. He's just starting to come around. And, one more thing you should know, sir."

"Yes?"

"The LiShanNa are a society that are professionally engaged for this kind of activity. It probably isn't personal."

"At least not on his part, you mean."

"Not on his part, sir. He's a hired killer."

Well, that at least explained why Dani could draw no connection to the man. But who wanted to kill her badly enough to pay an expert?

"Let's have at it, Markett."

"Yes, sir."

The prisoner was sitting on the bunk staring at the wall, garbed now in a florescent yellow jumpsuit.

"We took the robe," Markett said in a low tone to Dani, "because we weren't sure there weren't weapons or something else sown into it. It's quite voluminous."

"Good idea. Find anything?"

Markett unfolded her hand. On her upturned palm lay a glittering array of soft round cabochon 'Star of India' blue sapphires, rose-cut amber sapphires, and rectangular blood-red rubies. Dani whistled softly.

"Double crossing the miners, eh?"

"Or payment for killing you."

"The plot thickens," Dani said. If it was blood money, the gems were evidence. But if the assassin was simply ripping off the miners, it wasn't Dani's concern. No theft had been reported. As for the illegal mining itself, unless it endangered the security of the Coalition, Dani had no jurisdiction. She doubted failing to file a mining claim was even a misdemeanor in this remote sector of space.

"Unless we can prove it's a payment, you'll have to give them back to him," Dani said.

"Of course, sir," Markett agreed stiffly. "I've already cataloged them and will put them in the *Boadicea* safe. When he's transferred to the holding pen at Spaceportal sixteen, I'll turn them over to Base Security."

It was easy to see why the prospect did not make Markett happy. Base Security would invariably 'lose' the gems, and despite an 'official investigation', they both knew the gems would never be recovered. Dani felt sorry for Markett and her dilemma but it was the proper procedure. She approached the prisoner's cell door.

"There's just one thing I want to know, Prisoner," Dani had no name with which to address the man, "and that is: who hired you?"

The man, lithe and dangerous-looking even in the hideous jumpsuit, walked over to the door and pressed his hands against the wall. If his head hurt from the syn-gun stun, he didn't let it show.

"I'll make a deal with you, Forrest. If I tell you, you give me back my gems and safe passage on the next passing freighter." Luke had missed his opportunity to be de-matted aboard Korsaag's flagship by a bare few minutes.

It had not been a miscalculation on his part. One of the hits *Boadicea* had sustained had caught him climbing down an access ladder in a vertical tube. He had lost his grip and fallen a good four meters to the floor. Nothing had broken but it had slowed him down.

"Why should I do that?"

"Don't you think the man who hired me is bigger quarry, Forrest? He's nearby and you want to catch him with his hand in the miners' cookie jar, don't you?"

Dani pursed her lips. "I could care less if he rips off the miners. But you, you seriously injured a guest on my ship."

The assassin laughed. "So what are you going to charge me with? Assault? How long is that going to keep me behind bars? Whereas," he cooed seductively, "hiring a killer. Now that's bad."

"Captain Ki could still die. Then it would be murder."

"Your real quarry, Forrest, is very high up in Explora Command. He needs to be stopped. I'm small fry in comparison."

Dani's eyes narrowed. "Who is he?"

"Safe passage and my gems?"

Dani stalked away from the cell, head down, and paced up and down the foyer. She worked her jaw and bit at her fingers. "Alright," she agreed at last, coming back. "Safe passage and your gems."

"How can I be sure you won't renege, Forrest?"

"You can't. But have you heard I don't keep my word?"

"No. Just the opposite, actually."

"Alright, then. Take it or leave it."

The man smiled thinly. "Admiral Jameson is your man. He should be arriving planetside in, oh, an hour or two. It should be just getting past dawn then at the miners' camp."

Gordon Jameson. The pieces were falling into place. "He hired the miners?"

"Yes. But he plans to leave them high and dry. When do I get out of here?"

"First passing freighter. Let's go, Markett. We've got a lot of work to do."

"Sir," Markett said, when they were in the corridor, "are you really going to give him safe passage?" She seemed shocked to her security chief's core by the very idea.

"It's not my fault he doesn't know me well enough to be able to tell when I'm bluffing, Markett."

"But sir, the pacing, the nail biting, the —"

"Big act. I had to make him believe it. You too, so you wouldn't give me away."

She strode off down the corridor, a woman in a hurry. The Security Chief shook her head and followed after her.

Chapter
Fifteen

GORDON JAMESON MATERIALIZED on the site of the coordinates provided by Luke, expecting to be met by him. But Luke wasn't anywhere in evidence. Luke had assured Jameson his arrival coordinates were outside the perimeter of the camp.

Instead Jameson found he had materialized mere centimeters from a well set amid a collection of huts. The nearness of the well frightened Jameson. He might have de-matted into its solidity and been killed. But Luke was not sloppy. Was Luke playing chicken with him? And where was he?

It was just after dawn but the campfire ring at Jameson's feet was cold and no cooking smells rose to greet his nose. Jameson eyed the ground. No detritus from an already consumed breakfast littered the area either. In a climate as hot as the one on this planetoid, men rose early to eat and work and slept in the heat of the afternoon.

But Jameson didn't think the men were at work. The camp had an air of desolation. Then he heard voices on the other side of an eye-shatteringly pink tent canopy. He walked around the corner of it, fastidiously ignoring the nauseating color.

A heavy-muscled redhead, whom Jameson assumed from Luke's description was Rusty, stood with two humans and one Mickite. The four were in the middle of an argument, their voices raised. The look on the face of the Mickite was murderous but Jameson didn't consider that an indication of much, since Mickites always looked baleful. Still, the whole set-up had begun to smell bad to him. He was just on the point of de-matting out when Rusty saw him. The man unsheathed his syn-gun.

"Who the hell are you?" Rusty bayed, his voice harsh with annoyance. "There's too goddamn many people de-mating in and out of here." Rusty advanced on him. Jameson estimated that, even at the distance closing rapidly between them, the syn-gun Rusty was cavalierly wagging had more than sufficient range to blow him to atoms.

"I'm here to see Luke." Jameson said, making an effort to sound authoritative and calming at the same time. "Where is he?"

"He's vanished too. Now, who the hell are you?"

Christ in Hell! Jameson silently expostulated, grinding his teeth. If he ever got his hands on that son of a bitch, Luke was going to regret it.

"You're Rusty, aren't you?" Jameson asked, stalling. With slow deliberation, and never taking his eyes from Rusty, he raised his transcon and flipped open the face cover.

"You're not going anywhere," Rusty said, coming close and pointing the syn-gun directly at Jameson's heart. "Porter," he called over his shoulder, "relieve this gent of his transmitter."

A huge black man meandered over and with the confident smile of the very large, held out his palm, easily the size of a salad plate. Jameson was willing to buy the argument that there was little point in physically tussling with a 350 pound miner. He dropped the transcon into the man's hand.

"Okay," Rusty said, "you know my name. Let's get back to my original question. What's yours?"

"I'm a friend of Luke's." Thank god he wasn't dressed in anything that could be associated with his rank in Explora Command. He was wearing unmarked civilian clothes, black from head to foot. "Name's...Dudley."

"Since you just de-matted in, Dudley, you may be able to help us. What kind of vessel do you have?"

"It's a small pleasure craft."

"Well, as you can see, there are only four of us. You just met Porter. This is Hans," he gestured with the syn-gun at a very ordinary-looking man of average build, "and this is Barrrk. The rest are dead or disappeared. Think we can fit?"

"You want transportation?"

"Just to the nearest Spaceportal. We seem to have lost contact with our employer."

"Employer?" Jameson stalled again. The last thing he wanted to do was give these petty criminals a ride to Spaceportal sixteen. How was he going to explain his association with them to Masterson?

"Yep. No men, no employer. Not even any goods. They were stolen."

"Stolen?" Jameson's mouth went dry. So Luke had not only made a fast getaway but taken the gems too.

"Deimeon pirates," Rusty said, waving the syn-gun again in agitation.

"Pirates? Not Luke?" Jameson saw he had made a mistake. Rusty's eyes narrowed. He stopped waving the syn-gun and brought its point to rest on Jameson's shirt.

"You're not someone named Dudley, are you?"

"Uh—"

"This wouldn't be a good time to lie to me."

"Yes, I can see that. I'm 'The Boss', Rusty. I think Luke has double-crossed us."

"No shit, Boss." The tip of the syn-gun jabbed Jameson hard.

"What exactly do you plan to do about it?"

"Look, Rusty. Everybody." Jameson spread his hands in a broad gesture. Barrrk and Hans had trailed over to join Porter and Rusty. They formed a tight ring around him of crossed arms and hard unbelieving faces.

"Don't panic. I'll guarantee you get paid for your labor and expenses. And I'll get you off this planet, no questions asked." Jameson had no idea what money he would use to pay them but figured he would cross that bridge when he came to it. Keeping alive was his first priority.

"But I need to know everything that happened, Rusty," he deftly changed the subject. "Maybe we can track down Luke. Maybe we can get some...military assistance...to track down the pirates. Deimeon pirates, you said?"

"Robin Hood and his band of Merry Men," Rusty said sarcastically.

"Robin Hood? Do you think Luke is working with him?"

"I don't know. Hard to tell with Luke."

"True. Still, we'll track them down and make them pay. All is not lost, people."

Even as he said it, he was proved wrong; more than a dozen beings, syn-guns drawn, shimmered into existence, encircling Jameson and the four miners. "Jeezus!" Jameson cursed. In all his life he had never had such bad timing. There could only be one reason: Luke had set him up. Jameson vowed he would not sleep until he caught up with Luke and crushed him into oblivion.

One of the new arrivals, a husky good-looking woman wearing the sleek green and gold bodysuit of an Explora Command captain, stepped forth from the anonymity of the circle.

"Admiral Jameson. Rusty." Dani nodded politely to each of them. "I just can't tell you what a pleasure it is to find the two of you here together."

NACHI HAD DECIDED the ideal place to land would be at any oasis midway between the miners' camp and the pirates' camp. That way he could keep an eye on both without either detecting him, if he was lucky.

There was enough water aboard the shuttlecraft to keep his crew healthy until tomorrow. After that, for water they would either need access to the well at the miners' camp or access to the spring-fed pool at the pirates' camp.

He remembered that during their pre-dawn escape they had flown over a small clump of trees due east of the pirates' camp. The trees would provide shade, some camouflage for the shuttlecraft, and potentially a separate source of water. He described the place to the boy and, once they'd re-entered the planetoid's atmosphere, they both strained their eyes watching for it.

It was two hours after dawn when Nachi landed. None too soon, he thought. He had been up all night for a second straight night. And what part of it he hadn't spent performing heart-stopping rescues, he had spent worrying over the fate of the *Heaven's Bow* and the future of his own small crew.

He turned off the engines and got out of his seat, his back stiff from the long ride. The boy had curled up, his eyelids fighting to stay open, his face drawn with exhaustion. Nachi gently unsnapped the boy's harness and tilted back the seat to a comfortable angle. "Give in," he whispered. The boy mumbled incoherently, already dropping off, and Nachi smiled.

Luluai was sound asleep in her seat, as was Doctor Tilorri. It was hard to tell with Tor. Her eyes were closed but her body was too erect for sleep. He thought she might be meditating.

None of them, except the boy, knew about the battle. As noiselessly as he could, Nachi swung down the shuttlecraft's ramp door and walked out to survey their location. The day was already heating up but he had taxied the shuttlecraft beneath a cluster of palm trees whose thin shade he judged would last another hour or two.

He put his hands on his hips and stretched backward to relieve muscle tightness. His eyes went upward, tracing the trunk of one of the palm trees. There were coconuts clustered near its leafy top. He guessed there were coconuts on the others as well. He walked around and counted.

About eighteen coconuts in all. That might keep them in liquid and food for a few additional days. He would have the boy shinny up the trees for them later. He proceeded with his reconnaissance. If there was a source of water, he didn't find it. But he knew there must be a source somewhere or the trees would have died out. He heard what sounded like a stumble and looked back toward the *Lithe Arrow*.

Luluai had come out of the craft. He watched her as she ambled sleepily down the ramp. Her cream tunic was filthy and torn, her face grimy, her hair a dark matted mess. Her ankles and wrists were swollen and her cheeks puffy.

But she had never looked more radiant to him, stretching her slender arms over her head and yawning. He grinned at her and to his surprise, she smiled back. A bit shyly, he thought, but definitely a smile.

"You look—"

"—an awful fright," she interrupted.

" —radiantly beautiful, I was going to say."

She giggled, which startled him far more than if she'd glared at him. He was used to her glaring at him, after all.

"We're alive, aren't we?"

"Yes. Amazing as it may seem." He wasn't going to ruin the moment by telling her of his fears, or of what he had seen taking place in the sky. "How's your pal, Ma'at?"

"S/he'll recover. Thanks to you, Nachi."

"The doctors deserve the credit, not me. But as long as you're happy, Lu," he said. "That's all I care about." Nachi didn't know what she and Ma'at had been through together but he could guess it had been ghastly. And quite likely something Luluai wasn't going to talk about for a long time. If she ever did.

Luluai gave Nachi a penetrating stare, remembering all at once Ma'at's mental commentary about disgust being a disguise for attraction. She had known intuitively s/he was right. That was why it made her so angry.

"Nachi?"

"Yeah?"

"I'm very happy Ma'at will get well but I'm not going to...marry hir or anything. S/he's a mentor, not a lover."

Nachi pursed his lips, a quizzical expression on his face. "Lover? I didn't think you were going to marry anyone, Luluai. Your views on the subject are understandably not very positive."

"And I may not, Nachi. But, with everything that's happened, I...I'm still confused, but I have learned a lot about myself."

"Meaning?"

"Meaning, maybe we have a chance."

"Wow. Really?" He walked toward her, his eyes alight with happiness.

"I don't know," she said, putting up a hand. "We'll have to go slow, okay? I need time to sort everything out."

"No problem." He clasped her by the shoulders and kissed her softly on the lips. "How's that for a start?" He looked down into her astounded eyes.

"That's—" She was stopped by the tightening of his grip on her shoulders. He was looking at the *Lithe Arrow* behind her. Doctor Tilorri was waving at them from the ramp door.

"Ma'at's awake," she called, "and wants to see you both." There was a curious glint in her eyes.

Nachi waved back. "We're coming."

"That's kissing?" Luluai said, touching her lips experimentally with her fingers. They seemed to burn, but in a curious, exciting way.

"It's a beginning." He grinned and took her by the hand and

they walked to the shuttlecraft ramp. His hand was warm in hers and she could feel his joy spilling around her.

Maybe it wasn't going to be so terrible after all, she thought to herself. She could grow fond of Nachi. There was already so much that she liked about him.

Ma'at half-sat, half-reclined in the bunk, hir body propped up by gear cushioned over with wadded clothing. S/he was sipping a fragrant amber-colored broth. S/he stopped drinking and rested the cup in hir lap when Luluai and Nachi came in. They and the doctors stood by hir bedside. S/he looked at each of them in turn.

"All of you," s/he finally said, tears edging the corners of hir eyes, "have saved my life."

"Shim'on, too," Luluai blurted out, although she didn't know why.

"Shim'on?"

"He brought you back from the raid, even though I was sure he would leave you for dead. If he hadn't, Nachi would never have been able to rescue you."

"Thank you for telling me, Luluai, or I would not have known. Shim'on is...an honorable man. But on to practical matters. Lieutenant Buono," —Doctor Torilli had informed hir of their pilot's name and rank— "where are we?"

"We're at an oasis between the two camps, sir," Nachi answered respectfully. With the fate of the *Heaven's Bow* and *Boadicea* unknown, Nachi saw no advantage in being high-handed and alienating this unknown being. Issues of 'who's in charge' would arise soon enough.

"We don't know if the pirates are still at their camp or if they've gone."

"And the miners?"

"Again, I don't know."

"Do we have enough fuel to get off the planet and to *Boadicea* or the *Heaven's Bow*?"

Nachi grimaced, his face uncertain. He opened his mouth to speak but hesitated.

"I take it the answer is no?" Ma'at asked, one eyebrow drawn quizzically upward.

"We might just make it, sir. It's just that I tried last night and the *Boadicea* and the *Heaven's Bow* were engaged in a battle."

"A battle?" All the Sirensi spoke together.

"Yes. There was no way to tell any of you earlier. Luluai, you were asleep, and the doctors were doing their healing thing. I was the captain of the shuttlecraft at the time and I made the unilateral decision to come back here. The *Lithe Arrow* has no defensive weapons system. I could not have done anything to help. We were going to run out of fuel if I hung around."

Ma'at waited. It was not for hir to judge Lieutenant Buono's actions, but it was easy to deduce from the exchange that Lieutenant Luluai outranked Lieutenant Buono. The young Sirensi bobbed her head back and forth as she considered what he had said.

"I'm sure I would have done the same thing, Nachi," she finally said. "Next time though, wake me up."

"Yes, Lieutenant," Nachi answered solemnly. But if he felt reprimanded, Ma'at didn't see it. In fact, Ma'at thought he looked rather pleased with himself for some reason. Ma'at wasn't finished though. S/he had more questions.

"Do you know who they were fighting or the outcome?"

"Six ships just like the one Hasitam destroyed."

"Khrar Predators?"

"I guess so. *Boadicea* seemed to be on the side of the *Heaven's Bow*, though I can't guess why. I left before the outcome but I did see the *Boadicea* decimate one Predator."

"So the status of the two ships is unknown to us."

"Right."

"And the status of the two camps."

"Right."

"What about food and water here?"

"We have a shipboard supply of water that, if we ration it, should last until tomorrow. I haven't found an external source of water yet. There are some coconuts on the palms trees here. I take it, by your question, that you feel we may be here for some time?"

"We must consider all possibilities, Lieutenant Buono. There is a sickness aboard the *Boadicea* that may have made her more vulnerable in battle. Under normal circumstances she should be able to handle six Predators without sustaining massive damage. As for the *Heaven's Bow*, I don't know her capacities."

"Couldn't we send out some kind of emergency signal to let the *Heaven's Bow* or *Boadicea* know we're here?" Luluai asked everyone in general.

"Yes, except a transmission might be intercepted by the pirates or miners or both and we don't want them to know where we are," Nachi answered. "Unless you know of some way to disguise our transmission, Ms. First Officer."

"Actually," Luluai said smartly, "I think I do, Mr. Navigator. If you will follow me to the control panel, you can assist." She turned crisply and went forward.

"Yes, sir," Nachi answered just as smartly, "Your wish is my command." He followed her.

Ma'at tilted hir head at the young people's exchange. Doctor Tilorri's face had an impish knowing look to it and Ma'at extrapolated from the few known facts.

"Is that acceptable?" s/he whispered to Doctor Tilorri.

"We can hope for the best," she whispered back. "That child has suffered so much."

"Indeed, she has," Ma'at agreed, "and she has grown."

"ADMIRAL GORDON JAMESON," Dani said, "I'm placing you under arrest."

"On what charge, Forrest?"

"Murder for hire, Admiral. Your little bird has sung. He's in my brig and, as you may have noticed, not all that successful at the task you assigned him. Although he did wound another starship captain."

"God in heaven! He's LiShanNa. He's not supposed to make mistakes."

"Your statement is duly noted, Admiral," Dani answered coldly. "In fact, I've no doubt the tribunal you face will consider it an admission of guilt."

"Forrest, you killer!" Jameson stepped forward, his hands raised and balled into fists. Dani casually lifted her chin. The four members of the *Boadicea* security team who were closest to Jameson formed a box and hemmed in the Admiral.

"As for you, Rusty," Dani turned her attention to the seething miner, "you and your remaining men are also under arrest."

"You have no jurisdiction, Captain," Rusty said. "This planet isn't claimed by anyone."

"Admittedly, illegal mining is a technicality and you can simply file your own claim. However, until I locate all of the *Boadicea's* and *Heaven's Bow's* missing crew people, I am holding you on suspicion of murder."

Rusty blanched, the natural high color of his face draining away. If the prisoners were dead behind the dune, Forrest was going to lock him up and throw away the key.

"Not to mention," Dani went on, "I have no doubt that eyeprint and fingerprint analysis will turn up some interesting information about all of your pasts."

There was more than one startled look from the men knotted at the center of the circle of syn-guns. Dani pulled out her transcon. "*Boadicea*, five prisoners and eight security people to de-mat at these coordinates."

"Doctor Jenks, Sukha Jabala, and yeomen Beethoven, Kinsey, and Alberts will remain with me on the planetoid for the time being while we conduct a ground search of the area."

"Aye, Captain," De-Matter Tech John Sibell responded. "We'll de-mat them to the landing bay."

"Request that Security Chief Markett and an extra security contingent be on hand to greet them there."

"Will do, Captain."

"Forrest out."

After the prisoners and their guards shimmered away, Dani was struck by a sense of desolation which was echoed by the silent emptiness around her. Where was her crew?

"Well, people," she said, "now we search." As a group, they started with the huts and found little but supplies, including case after case of food rations.

Under the bright shade of the pink florescent canopy were benches and tables holding the grinding wheels and specialized tools of the gem cutting trade. There were no gems, cut or uncut, in evidence.

"Alright," Dani said, when they had found little of interest, "let's move on." She was satisfied nothing of value was in the camp, so the team radiated out in a circle and into the surrounding dunes. Beethoven was the first one to locate the deserted stakeout area. He called out to the others.

"Jeezus, Dani," Sly said, sick to his stomach, "this is cruel."

"If Ma'at died that way, I'll have Rusty's head on a platter," Dani swore. They looked everywhere for footprints but found none.

"The sand shifts constantly here, sir," Alberts said, "footprints would have most likely disappeared by now."

"We don't know when this happened."

"No," Alberts agreed, "but no footprints probably means it was a while back."

"The first day," Dani muttered bitterly. She hadn't thought Ma'at was in this kind of trouble.

"Captain," Kinsey called, dropping to her knees on a nearby sand dune, "there's something half-buried here." A moment later, she had unearthed a gold tunic and a pair of black boots.

"The sand must have shifted," Alberts said. "Otherwise Ma'at would have seen hir gear and taken it with hir."

"If s/he was alive," Dani said.

"No one with a choice would leave hir boots behind in a desert." Sly choked on the words. Sukha reached out and touched the doctor on the arm.

"Sorry," Sly said, forcing control, "we're not finding any evidence at all of your crew."

"If it is meant to be," Sukha said, "we will find them."

"Keep looking," Dani said, her face a grim mask. "Dead or alive, we won't leave here until we find them all."

MA'AT WAS SITTING in the shade of a palm tree, hir blackened legs and feet propped up on storage boxes and seat cushions borrowed from the shuttlecraft. S/he cradled a large green coconut on hir lap and occasionally took a sip of its overly sweet milk.

It had taken all four of the adults, using a chair carry, to move hir to hir present location. S/he had pointed out it wasn't necessary but the doctors insisted s/he get fresh air and sunshine. The time was getting past midday.

The boy, who had finally given his name as William Henry Harrison, was high up in one of the trees, tossing coconuts to the ground, which Nachi was fetching and stacking into a pile. Luluai was watching them and giving the boy directions. Mostly, Ma'at thought, so that he wouldn't bean Nachi on the head in his enthusiasm.

The doctors were crouched around a flat rock, one holding a coconut while the other sliced at it, rather ineffectually, with the knife Nachi had stolen from the pirate. Ma'at's coconut was the first they had managed to open.

Ma'at's sensitive ears detected a sound that was not part of the activities being carried on by the small band of people around hir. It sounded like an annoyed grunting and it was coming from the other side of the dune in front of hir.

Feral pigs? s/he wondered. They were supposed to reside in the mountains behind hir, not in the direction of the miners' camp. Ma'at listened as the grumble, rising and falling in pitch, grew steadily louder. It was coming closer and its owner would top the dune at any moment.

"Goddammit, Dani. You can't just keep going."

Jenks, Ma'at thought, that could be no one but Doctor Jenks. When he did top the dune, Ma'at ensured hir expression was one of pleased serenity. Sly stopped in his tracks.

"Why, you lazy son of a gun! Here you are sitting in the shade, drinking coconut milk while we're combing the goddamn desert for you. It's hotter than friggin' Nhavan out here, Ma'at."

"I missed you as well, Doctor Jenks."

Sly would not take hir at hir word, s/he knew, but on this occasion Ma'at literally meant it.

Dani came over the dune. "Ma'at!"

"Dani," Ma'at tilted hir head in acknowledgement. "It is a great pleasure to see you."

Everyone in the little camp was suddenly aware of their visitors. The doctors stood up. "Sukha!" they cried in joint delight, when they saw him rise over the dune in step with Captain Forrest. Luluai stopped directing William Henry Harrison and ran. Nachi tossed the coconuts he was balancing in both hands onto the escalating pile on the ground and rushed to join the *Heaven's Bow* reunion.

"Ma'at," Dani said, "we thought you were dead. The stakes outside the miner's camp where we found your tunic and boots—" She didn't complete the sentence. She was staring at Ma'at's feet.

"I apologize for not rising, Dani."

"Ma'at—" Dani was open-mouthed.

Sly was already running his sensor array over hir body. "Third degree burns below the knees, second degree sunburn on the torso, ripped shoulder and arm ligaments, edema in the hands, hairline jaw fracture, mild concussion, fever, severe dehydration. Had fun out here did you, Ma'at?"

Ma'at blithely ignored him. "Without the help of a great many people, I would in fact be dead, Dani. Even apparently Shim'on."

"Shim'on? Deimeon Commander Shim'on? Wasn't he supposed to have committed ritual suicide?"

"He is now the pirate 'Robin Hood'."

"This is going to be some story, Ma'at."

"Yes, Dani, it is."

"Dani, s/he's in remarkable shape for anyone, even a Nhavan, with this much injury. Was it the Nhavan pain control technique, Ma'at? Is that why you're recovering so rapidly? You've only received these injuries over the last two days."

"Actually, Doctor Jenks, the Sirensi Healing Chant."

"I swear I'm going to have to have a chat with those lady doctors."

Ma'at looked from one to the other of hir friends and colleagues. "You both look well, or at least better. Am I to understand that the disease on board *Boadicea* is cured?"

"It was beriberi," Sly said. "My only excuse for not diagnosing it correctly is that I had it. Of course, if certain members of the crew," he glared at Dani, "had been more forthcoming about their symptoms, it might have helped. In the end, Sukha Jabala of the *Heaven's Bow* figured it out and used his ship's vitamin and food supplies to get us back on our feet."

"Sorry, Sly." Dani looked contrite. "I didn't know the 'hot foot' sensation was such a distinguishing symptom of beriberi. You were about ready to take my command away from me as it was."

"Next time, no holding back, command or no command," Sly said. "That's why the rule's there, Dani."

"That's extraordinary," Ma'at said, interrupting them, "I had just read an article last week in the *Journal of the Nhavan Academy* quoting two humanoid studies discounting the effectiveness of injectables as a long-lasting form of Vitamin B-complex supplementation."

"If I'd seen it, that would have helped," Sly said. "I wouldn't have been under the assumption that a mass-scale vitamin deficiency was impossible in our times." He was running the sensor array back and forth over Ma'at's feet.

"Even I," Ma'at said, "did not make the connection, Doctor Jenks." S/he turned hir attention to Dani. "But what was the cause?"

"Ion storm, Ma'at," Dani answered. "It damaged the shipcook."

"Speaking of damage, Dani, I want Ma'at in the infirmary, pronto. Hir feet are going to require surgery."

Dani pulled out her transcon. "De-Matter Room, lock on to Doctor Jenks and Commander Ma'at at these coordinates. Have a medical team ready to transport Commander Ma'at to the infirmary."

"Aye, Captain." Technician Sibell's answer was prompt.

Dani's two friends shimmered away and she went over to join the *Heaven's Bow* people. Sukha was relating the sad news of the fate of the *Heaven's Bow*.

Luluai was in tears. "But the *Heaven's Bow* was everything to you, Sukha. You've spent your whole life creating her and —"

"Do not grieve, Luluai. The *Heaven's Bow* was a means to an end, not the end itself. That end is the discovery of the Brahuinna homeworld."

"Well," Nachi harumphed, "fat chance of finding it now."

"I think you are going to find yourself surprised, Nachi. But more on that later. The real loss to us is not a marvel of engineering and metal, but a member of our crew. Hasitam died bravely and although it is not the practice of *amsa*, he took out two of the enemy ships in the process. They slammed into the *Heaven's Bow* and all three exploded together. The loss of those ships helped *Boadicea* bring the fight to an end."

"Maybe," Nachi took his opening, "*amsa* doesn't work out here, Sukha. I don't think we were prepared for space, for what we were going to encounter. I mean, we need weapons."

"It is true, Nachi, that most of the violence on our planet has been of an intellectual, rather than of a physical, variety in the last few centuries. Perhaps we were not prepared. I do not know yet how, or even whether, our philosophies should be modified."

"I think you'll find," Dani said, "that you're not so far removed from the views of many of the member states of the Coalition on this topic. Nhavan in particular, of which Ma'at is a representative, has a strong 'do no harm' belief similar to the one you possess."

"I have never met a more non-violent person than Commander Ma'at," Luluai said, "and I grew up in a non-violent culture."

"Killing is always to be abjured," Dani seconded.

"I watched you destroy a Predator, Captain." Nachi said. "I was there in my shuttlecraft."

"And I destroyed a few more after that one, too," Dani said, unperturbed. "But only in defense of the *Heaven's Bow* in a fight the Khrars started. The Khrars had sworn vengeance against your ship. They and the Deimeons are not members of the Coalition but we all hope for the day when they will lay down their arms and there will be peace in our galaxy."

"Hmm," snorted Nachi, only partly convinced.

"I never seek to kill, Nachi," Dani said. "Only in defense and, even then, only if there is no other choice."

"Without the *Boadicea*, Nachi, we would all be dead," Sukha pointed out.

"Actually," Dani said, "without the *Heaven's Bow*, we would all be dead." The two smiled at each other.

"Let's go home," Dani proclaimed.

THE LITHE ARROW'S liftoff was observed, not by the Deimeon pirates, who had left before dawn, but by Corky, Tam, and Snooker the Ectosian. They had managed to stay hidden by sidling from dune to dune, evading Forrest and her searchers.

"I guess the planet's all ours now," Corky said.

"I hope William Henry will be alright," Tam said.

"Explora Command will take good care of him," Corky assured," he has a chance of a normal life now, Tam."

"I know. This was not a life for a growing boy. Still, I'll miss him."

"Me, too. But it's one less mouth to feed."

Tam shrugged, not offended. "You're right there, Cork."

"Speaking of which," Snooker said, "is there anything to eat?"

Tam glared at him. "I'm not walking back to camp in this heat. You'll have to wait till evening."

"No, we won't," Corky said. "William Henry was throwing coconuts down like he was bombing cities. It's amazing he didn't see us. Let's go get some."

Together they trundled over one last hot dune and parked themselves under the cool shade of the trees in Nachi's abandoned camp.

"Cheers," toasted Corky, when they'd finally managed to open three coconuts.

"To the quiet life," Tam said.

"Won't we get bored?" asked Snooker.

"Shut up!" the other two said in unison. Then all together, they clinked coconuts and drank.

CROW WAS NOT Dani's favorite food but when she was obligated to dine on it, she didn't flinch from the task. Still she hoped to evade Sly when she passed through the infirmary; she didn't want to answer any questions. It turned out to be easy because the doctor was still in surgery with Ma'at.

Captain Ki's eyes were closed when Dani reached her room and Dani backed out on tip-toes, almost making it to the door before the other woman opened her eyes.

"Captain?" Bajana whispered, her voice weak.

"I'll come back when you're feeling better," Dani said, glad for the reprieve. But Captain Ki dragged herself up against the pillows, grimacing in pain.

"That's okay," Bajana said. "What is it?"

"Captain Ki," Dani came over and stood near the head of the bed, "I owe you more than one apology and more than one thanks."

She figured getting it all out in a few brief sentences was the quickest and most painless method. Bajana didn't smile but Dani saw a flash of amusement in her eyes. If Bajana laughed at her, it was going to make the whole situation far more mortifying than it already was. But once Dani decided to do a thing, she did it. She struggled on.

"Your crew saved my crew, Captain. And you, personally, saved my life at great cost to yourself."

"Sounds like a karmic tangle to me, Forrest."

"Huh?"

"Without your crew being sick, my crew would have been on the *Heaven's Bow* and would all be dead. And, if you hadn't thrown me and Sukha in your brig, we would be dead too. I did try to get back to my ship, you know."

"You did?"

"Yes. I threatened Ensign Eireann into transporting me to the *Heaven's Bow* but she double-crossed me somehow and I ended up back here. That was when I surrendered to destiny...and it's a good thing I did. You owe me no apology, Danielle Artemis Forrest." Bajana's eyes softened.

Dani pulled up a nearby chair and took Captain Ki's hand in both of her own. "Accept my gratitude and my thanks then, Bajana."

"I was hoping," she said mischievously, "to accept a whole lot more than that."

"Excuse me?" Dani's mouth quirked into a grin. "Did I hear you right?"

"We'll have to wait until I'm better," Bajana said, her eyes teasing.

Dani's heart raced. She had considered the alien captain as unattainable as the Far Zone. Her eyes lit with happiness and she laughed. "I think I can manage that, Captain."

Bajana grinned. "Glad to hear it, Captain. I look forward to getting to know you—"

Dani stood, leaned across the bed, and brought her lips down on the other woman's. When they separated, several long seconds later, she whispered, "Don't forget me, Bajana."

"Not likely, Dani." Bajana's eyes glowed like dark inviting stars. Her revenge was indeed going to be of the sweetest possible kind. She would make Dani Forrest fall in love with her in a way Dani had never fallen before.

Dani left the room, her head spinning. With the exception of her relationship with Castle, she had always been the conqueror, not the conquered. But hell, she thought, maybe it was time to surrender herself, to let go of the past, try a few new tricks. As Ma'at had said, there was a first time for everything.

Epilogue

IT WAS THREE solar days later. The rec room had been cleared of the ship's entertainments and was jammed to capacity with rows of chairs that were filling with *Boadicea* and *Heaven's Bow* crewpersons. Captain Ki and Commander Ma'at, both in platform wheelchairs, held pride of place in the first row.

Captain Forrest sat between them. Doctor Jenks lounged to one side of Ma'at. Nachi and Luluai were further down the row with the Sirensi doctors. Luluai's hair had proved impossible to repair so Doctor Tilorri had cut it into a stylish page boy that made her look downright spunky.

Next to Nachi, William Henry Harrison swung his legs to and fro against his chair. The boy hadn't let Nachi out of his sight since coming aboard *Boadicea*. Unknown to William Henry, Nachi had already approached Captain Forrest about the Coalition protocol involved in adopting the boy.

Sukha Jabala perched on a chair on the stage with calm assurance while Ensign Eireann nervously paced, fiddling with the button of her multimedia presenter. At precisely 0900, Caitlin cleared her throat and introduced herself and Sukha to the assembled crews.

"I learned from Sukha Jabala," she began, "that the *Heaven's Bow* was in space on a mission to locate a specific planet. The reasons for this mission were not idle interest on Mr. Jabala's or his peoples' part." In a few succinct paragraphs, Caitlin detailed the history and politics of Nirvannini germane to her topic. The information was ingrained in the minds of the *Heaven's Bow* crew but new to the *Boadicea* people.

Caitlin went on to relate the process of discovery she and Sukha had embarked upon, concluding with, "The hypothesis Sukha and I reached is that the Planet of Many Splendors described in *The Glorious Interstellar Journeys* is Earth."

There was a sharp intake of breath from the *Heaven's Bow* crew and murmurs of interest from the remainder of the crowd.

"Interesting," remarked Ma'at.

Caitlin ordered the room's lights to dim and the gigantic screen behind her lit with a space shot of Earth, then zeroed in on the Indus Valley of the Indian subcontinent.

"A little over 10,000 Shivani years ago or what would have been around 2760 B.C.E. by Earth's calendar, Indrashtra crash landed on Earth near a small settlement named Chak Purbane Syal, here." She laser-pointed at a tiny dot beside a thin line representing a river.

"While Indrashtra struggled to repair his ship, he met with high priests, architects and engineers of the already-advanced civilization of the Indus River Valley. Indrashtra invited a group of these learned people, as well as some horsemen from nomadic tribes in the Russian Steppes, to travel back with him to Nirvannini. These people are the ancestors of today's Brahuinna. In other words, the Brahuinna are Earth humans."

A rustle of astonishment traveled through the room. Nachi raised his hand. "What makes you so sure the Brahuinna came from Earth?"

"Thanks for asking, Lieutenant Buono. That leads me to my next point. My first inkling that the Brahuinna might be from Earth was the inordinate number of loan words between your language, Atravayasana, and two very ancient Earth languages, Indo-European and Indo-Brahui. The clincher though, was a source document Sukha provided of an archaic religious text. It had been translated into Atravayasana from a different language. That text, written in a unique script, shows an 83 percent match to the Indus Valley script. The Indus Valley script has never previously been deciphered."

Caitlin's voice was steady but the gleam of triumph in her eyes was plainly visible to those in the first row. She punched her hand-held remote and the map of the Indian Subcontinent was replaced by columns of script.

Sly whispered in Ma'at's ear. "She's certainly acquired some poise, hasn't she?"

"Quite a bit of it, Doctor Jenks. And she has made an important discovery that will have a far-reaching impact on a number of fields. She has every right to bask in the glory of it."

"I didn't know the phrase 'bask in the glory of it' was in your vocabulary, Ma'at."

"It is a perfectly valid —"

"Shhh," Dani hissed at them. Caitlin had moved on to the question and answer segment of her presentation and the lights came up in the room. When it had wound down, Dani bounded on to the stage.

"Thank you, Ensign Eireann. Thank you, Mr. Jabala. I would like to make a few announcements. The first is that we have been granted shore leave —" a cheer went up from the crowd," —and because of these rather special circumstances, we have been granted shore leave on Earth." A second even louder cheer drowned out Dani.

"And, to top it off, the *Heaven's Bow* crew has been especially invited by the government of Earth to take a V.I.P. tour of the planet." This remark was met with open-mouthed astonishment on the part of the *Heaven's Bow* people and a roar of approval from the rest of the assembly.

"Further, Mr. Jabala informs me that, as part of his mission, he is authorized by the governments of Nirvannini and Elysiansus to act as the Inter-Solar Alliance's First Ambassador should any circumstances requiring that role arise. As they have indeed arisen, he has decided to undertake initial talks with the Coalition regarding Coalition membership."

There was no longer cheering, there was wild applause. Sukha stood, placed the palms of both sets of his hands together in what looked to the *Boadicea* crew like the Hindu *namaste* greeting and inclined his head. "Thank you all," he said simply, "I am deeply honored."

"As are we," Dani said. She turned forward again and smiled at her crew. Crews, she amended, in her mind. Even if just temporarily, the *Heaven's Bow* crew was under her authority as captain of the *Boadicea*.

"Dismissed," she said. She jumped down from the stage. *Boadicea* crew people crowded around the *Heaven's Bow* contingent, shaking hands with them and slapping them on the back in congratulations.

"Well," Dani said to her two closest friends, "that about wraps it up."

"Dani," Sly commented, "the oddest thing about this whole affair has been all these weird coincidences. For instance, the similar construction of our ship to *Heaven's Bow*, our crew being sick with beriberi, their crew offering the solution—"

Ma'at spoke up. "Perhaps 'synchronicity' is the word you're looking for, Doctor Jenks."

"Synchronicity?" Dani cocked an eyebrow, remembering what Bajana had said. "You mean like the *Heaven's Bow* crew being safely aboard *Boadicea* when that ship was destroyed?"

Heads nodded thoughtfully. Sukha joined them. "Our destroying the *Star Spawn*, which led inadvertently to discovery of the Brahuinna homeworld—"

"—which turns out to be Earth which is our homeworld too." Sly finished. "That's all a bit strange, isn't it?"

"Is that synchronicity, Ma'at?" Dani asked.

"Technically, synchronicity means meaningful coincidence, Dani. This is a tangle of fascinating coincidences but what criteria do we apply to decide if it's 'meaningful'?

"You don't think being alive is meaningful, Ma'at?"

"Of course, Doctor Jenks. But it's the chain of events and their influence upon one another that constitutes meaningful coincidence. Is it meaningful coincidence that Luluai saved my life that first freezing night? If she hadn't, I couldn't have saved hers. But she couldn't have known that at the time, either, because my saving her life followed in time. We are, after all, linear creatures, bound in time."

"But," Dani said, "what gave her the impulse to save your life?"

"That—"

"Has it occurred to any of you that you're not talking about synchronicity?" It was Captain Ki wheeling into the fray.

"What are we talking about then?" Dani asked her, a smile in full evidence.

"We're talking about mutual trust enhancing the likelihood of survival for all."

Ma'at tilted hir head in agreement. "Succinctly stated, not to mention true, Captain Ki."

Sly nodded. "Can't argue with that, Dani."

Dani said, "Bajana, you've just defined the Coalition. It's what we're all about."

MORE CLEO DARE TITLES TO LOOK FOR

Hanging Offense

Mandy Barnes, her trust betrayed by her husband Jay, needs a summer away to think about her marriage. She opts for a seasonal job at Bryce Canyon National Park in remote southern Utah and there meets Jo Reynolds, a lesbian park ranger from California. Mandy is attracted to Jo, but uncertain of her own sexuality.

On a hike into the wilderness, Mandy chances upon some vintage coins in a rusted can and is then plagued by violent dreams of a murder from the past. Are the coins connected to the dreams? Will deciphering the mystery of the past help her unravel the tangled knot of the present? Can she overcome her fears to find renewed trust and true love in Jo's arms?

ISBN 978-1-935053-11-8

Faultless

How can enforced R&R turn so quickly into disaster? No sooner does Captain Dani Forrest try to relax at a desert resort that a murder takes place and reports are received that an entire village has been wiped out. Buxom, blond and alluring mythologist Lindie Davis tries to keep matters in perspective for Dani through the telling of ancient hero tales but Dani's guilt over the recent suicide of her friend and fellow Minority Fleet Captain Sherri Wilmstead only escalates. Meanwhile, an entire rift valley is shaken by more than a natural earthquake and Dani must find out, before it is too late, who is at fault.

Available July 2010

OTHER QUEST TITLES YOU MIGHT ENJOY

The Ties That Bind
by Andi Marquette

When the Albuquerque paper reports that an unidentified white man was found dead along a remote stretch of road on the Navajo Reservation in northwestern New Mexico, UNM sociology professor K.C. Fontero thinks she might be able to use the case as an example of culture and jurisdiction in one of her classes. But it's soon apparent that this dead man might have something to do with a mysterious letter that River Crandall, brother of K.C.'s partner Sage, recently received from the siblings' estranged father, Bill. What does the letter and Bill's link to a natural gas drilling company have to do with the dead man? And why would Bill try to contact his son and daughter now, after a decade of silence?

From the streets of Albuquerque to the vast expanse of the Navajo Reservation, K.C. and Sage try to unravel the secrets of a dead man while Sage confronts a past she thought she'd left behind. But someone or something wants to keep those secrets buried, and as K.C. soon discovers, sometimes beliefs of one culture jump the boundaries of another, threatening to drive a wedge into the relationship she's building with Sage.

ISBN 978-1-935053-23-1

Tunnel Vision
by Brenda Adcock

Royce Brodie, a 50-year-old homicide detective in the quiet town of Cedar Springs, a bedroom community 30 miles from Austin, Texas, has spent the last seven years coming to grips with the incident that took the life of her partner and narrowly missed taking her own. The peace and quiet she had been enjoying is shattered by two seemingly unrelated murders in the same week: the first, a John Doe, and the second, a janitor at the local university.

While Brodie and her partner, Curtis Nicholls, begin their investigation, the assignment of a new trainee disrupts Brodie's life. Not only is Maggie Weston Brodie's former lover, but her father had been Brodie's commander at the Austin Police Department and nearly destroyed her career.

As the three detectives try to piece together the scattered evidence to solve the two murders, they become convinced the two murders are related. The discovery of a similar murder committed five years earlier at a small university in upstate New York creates a sense of urgency as they realize they are possibly chasing a serial killer.

The already difficult case becomes even more so when a third victim is found. But the case becomes personal for Brodie when Maggie becomes the killer's next target. Unless Brodie finds a way to save Maggie, she could face losing everything a second time.

ISBN 978-1-935053-19-4

OTHER QUEST PUBLICATIONS

Brenda Adcock	Pipeline	978-1-932300-64-2
Brenda Adcock	Redress of Grievances	978-1-932300-86-4
Brenda Adcock	Tunnel Vision	978-1-935530-19-4
Victor J. Banis	Angel Land	978-1-935053-05-7
Blayne Cooper	Cobb Island	978-1-932300-67-3
Blayne Cooper	Echoes From The Mist	978-1-932300-68-0
Cleo Dare	Cognate	978-1-935053-25-5
Cleo Dare	Hanging Offense	978-1-935053-11-8
Gabrielle Goldsby	Never Wake	978-1-932300-61-1
Nancy Griffis	Mind Games	1-932300-53-8
Lori L. Lake	Gun Shy	978-1-932300-56-7
Lori L. Lake	Have Gun We'll Travel	1-932300-33-3
Lori L. Lake	Under the Gun	978-1-932300-57-4
Helen M. Macpherson	Colder Than Ice	1-932300-29-5
Andi Marquette	Land of Entrapment	978-1-935053-02-6
Andi Marquette	State of Denial	978-1-935053-09-5
Andi Marquette	The Ties That Bind	978-1-935053-23-1
Meghan O'Brien	The Three	978-1-932300-51-2
C. Paradee	Deep Cover	1-932300-23-6
John F. Parker	Come Clean	978-1-932300-43-7
Keith Pyeatt	Struck	978-1-935053-17-0
Rick R. Reed	Deadly Vision	978-1-932300-96-3
Rick R. Reed	IM	978-1-932300-79-6
Rick R. Reed	In the Blood	978-1-932300-90-1

About the Author

Cleo Dare is the author of the romantic suspense novels *Brushstrokes*, *Melting Point* and *Hanging Offense.* Her erotic short stories have appeared in anthologies published by Bella Books, Pretty Things Press and Alyson.

VISIT US ONLINE AT
www.regalcrest.biz

At the Regal Crest Website You'll Find

- The latest news about forthcoming titles and new releases

- Our complete backlist of romance, mystery, thriller and adventure titles

- Information about your favorite authors

- Current bestsellers

- Media tearsheets to print and take with you when you shop

Regal Crest titles are available directly from our web store, Allied Crest Editions at www.rcedirect.com, and from all progressive booksellers including numerous sources online. Our distributors are Bella Distribution and Ingram.

LaVergne, TN USA
10 May 2010

182198LV00003B/19/P